INERTIA

MARK EVERGLADE

ISBN: Hardcover 978-1-945286-71-1

Softcover 978-1-945286-70-4

eBook 978-1-945286-69-8

Thanks to Athina Paris, Editor for your dedication and tireless effort.

Published By

RockHill Publishing LLC

PO Box 62523

Virginia Beach, VA 23466-2523

www.rockhillpublishing.com

ACKNOWLEDGEMENTS

Special thanks to my wife, Angelique, for her awesome support, assistance with editing, and providing the basic concept for the series. Thanks to my son, Hans, for designing the book cover of the first novel and offering continual humorous relief during the writing process.

Science fiction author Frasier Armitage was instrumental in helping me move the plot points when I got stuck and suggesting that the Old Guard would make a great antagonist. Cyberpunk author and critic Dr. Joseph Hurtgen provided support throughout the process, including his insistence that *Ash* was a stronger nickname than *Pasha*.

Others who encouraged and supported me are too numerous to mention, but I would be remiss to not call out Matthew Goodwin, Tanweer Dar, and Jim Keen, all great cyberpunk authors in their own rights.

And of course, I thank the RockHill Publishing team, owner James Hill, and editor Athina Paris, for giving me the opportunity to share this story with the world.

INERTIA

By

Mark Everglade

CONTENTS

PART I

TERROIR

1

ASH STEPPED OUT OF THE SLOUMSTONE APARTMENTS AND trudged through knee-high water to work with the rest of the wage slaves. The floods were getting worse each day, and the whole place stank like a gym locker in dirty dishwater. She pushed the floating debris aside and left the lower quarters for dry land, swiping away some rotten ground meat from her blouse. Her soaked skirt clung to her legs, having caught within its weave everything from pencil shavings to the broken tips of used needles. So much for dressing business professional.

She squeezed downtown through the sludge of the morning crowd, belt buckles brushing the back of her hand. Everyone rushed to forge their identities in a copycat world. They strode hand-in-hand, merchant and consumer, manager and employee, brandisher and lover, master and slave. They stood tall and proud until they knew you weren't looking. By day's end, they would be saying their goodbyes from the edges of catwalks, their fallen bodies finally still, lit by the hushed glow of the red-light district. And Ash among them; foggy-headed, with only sewage for perfume, shuffling her feet to work at Geosturm, where there was no room for a shade of grey.

The pale morning light expanded its beam to reveal Blutengel, the largest city on the hemisphere formerly known as Evig Natt. The hemisphere had been previously named for the constant darkness that had once enveloped it. That all changed when a revolutionary group, O.A.K., increased Gliese 581g's rotation to bring daylight cycles to all, breaking the planet's tidal lock. The red dwarf star still shone a ray for each person who had been sacrificed to make the sunrise possible. Its light reflected off the steel monstrosities scraping the skyline, and burrowed into closed fists on each rooftop where the Invisible Hand broadcasted corporate propaganda. But even the sunrise wasn't dependable.

In just hours, the sun would rise again, the planet spinning out of control.

Ash's virtual Head's Up Display, or vHUD, flashed a message. The words appeared superimposed over the street: *You're late to work and we have an emergency!*

No time to dry off; she could barely afford her rent as it was, and she'd been late ten times this month already.

Hovercraft traveled above like electrons through a conductor, bound to aerial lanes marked by contrails. Skywalks interlaced between Geosturm's corporate buildings. Ash yanked the doors open and entered the lobby, which was ten times the size of her apartment, dripping on the golden floor panels.

"Get an umbrella already," the receptionist scoffed, holding her nose.

Ash couldn't say she lived in the flooded quarters, so she nodded and pounded the elevator button. She went up hundreds of floors, got off, and raced down the skywalk to her workstation. It was too early for this, and the last emergency at Geosturm had more to do with profits falling than monitoring the planet's rotation. What a waste. Becoming a geophysicist was supposed to have made her one with nature, yet most mornings, she was forced to falsify research and sell out the planet for whatever dead currency they were paying her with this week. All majors had become business majors.

"Out of the way, we have a crisis here, people!" An executive ran past her and slammed his hand on an alarm.

Sirens screeched and the glass corridor bathed in bloody light.

Ash cupped her palms over her ears until all she could hear was her blood thumping and the faint voices of the managers arguing. This wasn't a drill; maybe her life was worth a damn.

"The data's not reliable," her regional manager, Malik Aldweg, argued with the well-dressed man.

The executive placed his hands on his hips. "How can you say that? The planet's rotation is off the charts!"

"Because there's no guarantee that subsequent measurements will produce the same result."

"If the rotation keeps increasing, there'll *be* no subsequent measurements!" The executive shuffled through a handful of files but a line of employees ran by and knocked them out of his hands in their frenzy. "Whose side are you on, anyway?"

"The data's."

"Yesterday, the sun rose three times. Three times! What more proof do you need? Have one of your girls fetch me a summary of what we know."

Rows of glass teardrop-shaped workstations hung from below the skywalks to maximize workspace, suspended mid-air by taut cables. They swung in the crosswinds that raged between the buildings and knocked the offices into one another. From a distance, they appeared like a string of upside-down lightbulbs, dangling the employees over the city, out of reach and out of touch.

Ash opened hatch twenty-two from the floor of the skywalk, the corroded metal handle cold against her hand, and slid down the ladder into her coffin-tight office. She closed the hatch and softly lowered her feet to a clear, curved floor, the glass too thin

3

to put sudden weight on it. Working twelve hours a day, she hardly cared if it broke and she plummeted to her death, having been passed up for promotion for the third time despite being the only nineteen-year old to have earned a geophysics degree. She had bound her youth together with textbooks and was ready for the payoff, but was stuck in this hellhole instead, swaying in an office above a careless city.

The office window framed her, reflecting a lush wave of purple bangs on one side of her face, and a tightly shaved head on the other. Buildings aligned in the distance like a bar chart, but her age group had been left out of the equation that had produced it. Aldweg stomped across the glass ceiling of the skywalk above, rubbing his crotch. Glass was smooth to the touch, but dangerous once broken. She'd show his entire generation just how sharp it was, their façades crumbling before her awakening.

She sat in a chair upholstered with Aphorid hide that bolstered two thick armrests. She placed her arms in their grooves as they folded down. A needle emerged from each support, baring their sharp points and forcing their way into her arms with burning stings. They fed her an intravenous drug designed to keep her focused during the workday, though she usually left at the day's end too tired to even make dinner because of it. A gyroscope connected with a pin to her shirt, measuring how much of her movement was not work related. A feeding tube connected to a circlet above her waist, one of Geosturm's ways of not having to provide lunchbreaks. A thick cable extended over her shoulders. The hair on the back of her neck rose as it connected to her head with a *whoosh*.

Though her cognigraf implants could access cyberspace from anywhere, they were laggy and easily compromised, so Aldweg, the asshole who had been promoted over her head despite being a complete failure, refused to let her telecommute. He argued he needed to keep an eye on her work, but his gaze was only on her.

Gone were the days when she admired someone simply for being called her *superior;* the only people worthy of titles were those who let go of them. Most people stole their titles and paraded them about, wearing them like poorly-tailored clothing that dragged on the ground behind them. Ash would earn hers the right way, even if her boss only recognized her from the neck down.

Aldweg yanked the hatch open, his bald head, large ears, and thick-rimmed glasses bearing down. He wrinkled his nose, crinkled his forehead, and yelled, "Get to work. I need you to write a geological history of what happened to the planet over the past thirty-five years since the Great Rotation began."

"That's your idea of an emergency?" she shot back. "Sounds like another justification for unpaid overtime."

"That's all a stupid kid like you needs to know," he replied, dropping the hatch door with a clang that could shatter the glass that suspended her above the city.

How dare he? That was a task for a new hire, not a trained geophysicist. She belonged on the frontlines, measuring soil levels. After all, her parents were master terraformers, having been instrumental in increasing the planet's rotation to bring daylight cycles, though their calculations must have been off because no one anticipated this crisis. She had followed in their footsteps, only to be assigned a simple historical report while less experienced workers were sabotaging critical research with their incompetence.

Ash logged into a virtual interface that fed into her occipital lobe. It displayed the network as a series of rivers. Data fed into her brain from tributaries, each channel a tension headache as information compressed and emptied into a digital sea. Most people would have seizures under such a flood of stimulation, but between her intelligence and implants she could process files ten times faster than anyone else.

She swiped her hands across the interface and flickered her

coffee eyes. Search queries sprang from her stream of consciousness, the keywords following every tangent of her thoughts.
Thousands of files splashed upon the shore of her awareness, a
few glowing bright red – classified. She fired up some background processes in vHUD and decrypted them. The data
seemed innocuous, and must have been labeled *classified* by
error, though it did suggest that her parents' calculations hadn't
been at fault, and that Aldweg was purposefully withholding a
stockpile of intel to make it hit the media all at once when the
timing was right. She summarized her findings:

*Gliese 581g is the last remaining colony of the human race,
located twenty light years from Earth. The planet was once tidal
locked to its sun, with one side forever swallowed by darkness
and the other half sizzling in perpetual sunlight. Oppression was
rampant, especially in Blutengel. The city earned its name
during a violent dispute regarding whether religion would be
outlawed.*

*A lot changed after a radical group called O.A.K. increased
the planet's rotation to bring daylight cycles to all in the name of
equality. All was not well, however, when decades passed and
new generations dealt with continual floods as the newfound
sunlight melted the icecaps. The Coriolis effect confounded
matters by aiding the heat transmission across the planet. Rising
sea levels brought new rivers to snake across the landscape,
flooding residential districts.*

*Days shortened as the planet's rotation increased beyond
projections, increasing heat distribution further. More glaciers
melted; more towns sank. The breaking point was reached this
year, 3,120, when hurricanes crossed the planet at records
speeds. In came Geosturm to monitor the events, quantifying,
constraining, controlling. Modern societies are not known by
temples or prophecy, they are known by databases and evidence-
based predictions.*

She reviewed her progress. The major events of history, from the bio-terrorist acts that had caused humans to leave Earth, to their colonization of Gliese 581g, to the present crisis had all been reduced to points on a line graph, its sharp edge extending off the page into a future they might not reach. She refused to let her generation's legacy be just another datapoint, another refinement to the model of creation and destruction lying at the core of everything, so she added references to the classified data:

The abruptness of these changes and their unpredictable nature suggest someone is intentionally manipulating the energy belts and atmospheric emissions that regulate angular momentum.

In other words, someone was messing with over three decades of so-called progress, increasing the rotation far beyond what her parents and the original O.A.K. activists had planned. But whom? Could she find a way to reverse the rotational effects and rid the world of its floods, and if so, was it better for entire towns to drown or to throw half the world back into complete darkness? At her paygrade it didn't matter what she thought, since she had been hired to run analytics, not to solve the fate of the world. She sent the report to Aldweg.

Ten minutes later, the hatch above yanked open again. Aldweg penetrated her office with his scream, "Ash, you're fired."

"What? I'm your best worker, Mr. Aldweg. Please, no, I need this job. I can barely afford to live at Sloumstone as it is," she pleaded. "What reason do you have?"

"Reason? I don't owe you a justification."

"My evaluations were perfect, Sir."

"Then they were evaluating the wrong criteria," he retorted.

"*You* evaluated me."

"That report you sent is reason enough. This crisis is a natural phenomenon and not something caused by... how did you put it, intentional manipulation."

"But the data—"

"Fuck the data," he yelled.

Her co-workers remained oblivious, suspended in their own teardrop offices.

"You wanna talk about data? Some of it was beyond your clearance level. How did you get access to it? Who else did you send it to?"

"No one, I swear. And the data was relevant."

"You better hope no one saw it. Security will see you out," Aldweg replied, stomping off.

Two bulky men dropped into the cramped space and yanked her from the chair, the needles ripping from her veins and spurting hot blood.

"Ouch," she cried.

They weren't security guards, that was sure; maybe mercs or Enforcers. They restrained her by each arm, fingers digging in her wounds, and drew her back as if to give them room to... To throw her out the window!

Fear shot spikes through her head. She struggled, pulling her arms back, wrapping her feet around theirs, but it was no use. A sticky flood of hot sweat poured from her armpits. Her pupils dilated, expanded, took it all in. Every sound was deafening. The computer fans whirled like helicopter blades. The wind churned and beat against the window as if all nature had come to witness her demise, but when she cried out, the world lent no ear.

A loud crash stopped them right before they sent her flying, their hands sliding off her arms. The ceiling shook. Her office swayed. One by one, the row of teardrop-shaped offices dropped from the skywalk where they had hung, each tethered cable snapping. Coworkers and furniture plummeted four-hundred stories, bouncing off aerial traffic and shattering on the streets.

Her office disconnected from the skywalk at the hatch with a loud snap.

Ash kicked off the chair just high enough to grab the handle of the open hatch before her office plummeted beneath her. The guards' ragdoll bodies fell through the air, their screams fading.

Come on, pull! Her small arms strained to haul her up to the skywalk, which was shaking but intact. She raised her foot to the ledge and nudged her right shoulder onto the platform, crawling up. It was all gone. Each office that had hung from the bottom of the skywalk had fallen. The hatches lining the corridor opened to only a four-hundred foot drop. The alarms were silent, despite the disaster.

She ran down the corridor into the corporate building and slammed open the door. Voices on the stairwell echoed, either coming to save her or finish her off—that is, if they knew she was still alive. Was she counted among the dead? The timing of the attack was too coincidental to have not been related to her report. Those mercs must have been sent to ensure she didn't flee before the fall. She descended ten flights and took the next exit to a second skywalk that led to the adjacent building, weaving back and forth between the edifices until she was back at ground level ten minutes later. She expected to find office chairs strewn across the street, crashed vehicles, broken glass from the shattered offices, and bodies, bodies everywhere.

There was nothing. Furniture, missing. Walls, missing. Bodies, missing. Business as usual at street level. A few onlookers were shunned by Geosturm security. Automated vehicles took flight in ascension columns; people carried shopping bags out of malls; couples argued over neuralmod addiction. Geosturm had removed all traces of the incident, as if the planet had just swallowed the catastrophe, the blood not even washed away, just gone.

A swarm of Geosturm maintenance bots gathered a few remaining glass shards and polished faint blood stains. So there was evidence, though it had been cleared away before she could document it. The bots danced upon metal spheres as they sliced, diced, and incinerated street trash, the diabolical ballerinas

9

dressed in that stupid corporate logo – a black planet gripped by an iron hand. A drone flew overhead and stopped to scan her. Beeps blurted. The droids turned her way with a collective creak, the buzz of their engines simmering on standby. One by one they reactivated and channeled towards her. The spheres spun with a grinding noise, chipping up concrete. Manipulators reached out, their ends snapping like crab claws. Compartments opened in their torsos to arm them with blowtorches in one hand, and long blades in the other.

Ash bolted down the street, the droids buzzing behind her, for she was the last remaining piece of evidence of Geosturm's attempt to cover their tracks. Their blades nicked into her back, their blowtorches warm behind her neck. She leapt upon a hover-craft as it began to ascend, the driver waving her away from behind the windshield. She was airborne, clutching the hood as the raging wind streaked across her face.

Why, why?

To get to the bottom of this she needed help from the man who had shoved the planet thirty-five years ago, the man she had avoided her entire life, the guy her mother would disown her for communicating with.

Severum Rivenshear.

2

Men shouted everywhere, "The floods will take our very souls." Holding protest signs like swords, they smashed them against Severum's face. He pinballed side to side through the crowd. Half the population worshipped him as the man who had brought the collapse of the firefly currency that had been the basis for inequality, back when all other sources of light had been outlawed. The other half vilified him as being responsible for the hurricanes, tidal waves, floods, and sinkholes brought by the Great Rotation of the planet thirty-five years prior. He was neither hero, nor villain, just a man trying to make it in an unforgiving world, and so far he'd been successful for almost seventy years, though the results of his sacrifices seemed random at best.

Advancements in autophagy meant he was barely middle-aged; but quantity and quality of life were different. His smock of hair had turned salt and pepper gray, falling just below his ears to frame his deep-set eyes, gun-barrel nose, and full lips. Gone were the military camos and cybernetically-enhanced war suits – he had retired, living off a pension from a government that had barely withstood the assassination of Governor Borges that ended the reign of terror wrought by the Old Guard. Served them right. He had betrayed them after learning their leaders didn't play by the rules they imposed upon the masses. They had betrayed him in turn, hiring him as a mercenary before putting him on a hitlist to cover their tracks.

The New Order was a step forward, however small. They kept his pension intact – they had to, as it was a payoff in return for preventing his admirers from overthrowing the new regime. At least it was paid in credits and not insect parts or some other dead currency.

His vHUD lit with an incoming call. A young woman's face was superimposed over reality, someone familiar yet unknown. "Yeah, what is it?"

"Is this Severum Rivenshear?" a shaky voice asked.

"Who wants to know?" After a long pause he pressed, "Who is this?"

"I'm Ash. Used to work for Geosturm. The government outsourced us to provide analytics on the terraforming disaster your generation brought upon ours."

"Not my problem anymore. Maybe it's just time the human race returned to Earth," he shrugged. "Been long enough since we colonized Gliese 581g that the viruses and radioactive waste from the bioterrorist attacks should no longer make it unin-habitable."

"The only bioterrorist I know of is you, Mr. Rivenshear."

"Another protestor, great," he scoffed. "So why the hell you calling me?"

"I'd like to meet you," she stated, so affectless it sounded forced.

"With a Pulser behind your back no doubt. Stand in line with the rest of humanity and wait your glitchin' turn."

"To work with you on solving this crisis. My history texts state you were a terraforming prodigy before being contracted by Governor Borges to hunt down O.A.K., the organization who initially increased the planet's rotation to bring daylight cycles.

But you went rogue and turned on those who hired you. Now, I want you to help me clean up the mess you left behind. Something is happening with the rotation. Days are getting shorter, and the Aporia Asylum is talking about the end times coming. Maybe they are just fundamentalist ramblings, but there was an incident this morning."

"Is that the way they're telling my story? Listen, kid, this wasn't a history book to me, this was my glitchin' life, enveloped in darkness each day. Now you wanna drag me outta retirement for what, so I can reverse the progress my friends and I sacrificed our lives for, or just to investigate what a shitty job we did?"

"Progress! Progress?" she yelled. "Half the cities on Evig Natt are underwater, international relations have been a joke without an A.I. to regulate them, currency values are all over the place with no standard, and sinkholes are swallowing homes. I get soaked every time I even walk in my apartment—"

"Yeah, my flat's dry and the economy will work itself out," he said.

"We're talking about the lives of a whole generation here. How can you be so callous?"

"No matter what I do it ends up wrong. I'm hated by half the world, so what's the difference?"

"You know, some people revere you as a hero, Mr. Rivenshear."

"Yeah, I've heard that."

"Well, they're wrong," she replied.

"What'd you say your name was?"

"Ash."

"What's with you kids and your names today? What kinda name is that?"

"It's a nickname for Vispáshanah, meaning insight," she whispered.

"Wait a minute; that's what my ex-wife, Akasha, and I were going to name our—"

"Yeah, I'm your daughter, asshole."

Severum dropped the call. It had been about two decades since he'd last seen Akasha'Shirod, former Head Priestess of the Aporia Asylum and love of his life. She had run away years before after they had a falling out back in college, then got back together after the Great Rotation, only for her to leave him again years later after a lifetime of being apathied by what she called emotional neglect. Times had been rough, and he never dreamed when she ran away the second time she was carrying more than just his heart, but his child, too. Could she really have been pregnant and not told him? Was he that bad of an influence that it was better for him not to know his daughter existed? No, this woman on the phone had referenced history texts, no doubt learned about him, and was just playing with his head. But that name, so uncommon...

He started to call back, hesitated, then flicked his eyes across a virtual keyboard to complete the call, emotions dammed behind a well of curiosity.

"Took you long enough," she answered.

"Where you wanna meet?"

———

RAINDROPS SLID down the slick glass of the uptown bistro. Ash pressed her face against the cold windowpane at the table, then cocooned it in the collar of her grey wool sweater. She tugged on the sleeves of her black, military camo jacket.

The war-chipped tenements downtown were sketches on the horizon, the haze obscuring the outlines of their imperfect angles, each patchwork building having been added to over the years with tarps often replacing the uneven roofs. Uptown though, every angle was perfect, clear, unobscured. She unfolded a triangular napkin on her lap. Middle-aged customers clanked martini glasses, the impaled olives swaying in a sea of temporary absolution. A gentleman took the long toothpick from his glass and slurped the olive off, dropping bits of it on his narrow tie, then crumbled a cannoli into his mouth. Perfect straight lines.

But she had never walked them anyway.

Fog swelled in the streets outside. Ash had been told it was a low-lying cloud, but she knew better. It was the misty wings of her guardian angel, too laden with the ashes of past battles to tread upon the heavens any longer. Without his guidance, her voice had been lost amidst the whispering winds of change. Hush, and you can still hear their quiet roar. Now, her guardian —her father—was materializing from her fantasies, and yeah, that came with expectations.

The fog of war that blanketed the planet would suffocate them all if they didn't uncover who was behind the attack. She brought a heavy mug of white-capped beer to her mouth, wiped the foam on her sleeve, ignored the stares, and waited for glitch-face to arrive.

———

SEVERUM HAD ALWAYS IMAGINED what his child would look like, but here in every strand of purple hair, every movement of her lithe fingers, every twinge of her tapered face, the hypothetical future became real, alive, breathing. It was almost too much to bear even without trying to fill in all those missing years. Facing Aphorids on the battlefield, ripping their lungs out through their skin flaps, dodging their massive bodies and thrashing teeth, that was nothing compared to this.

He turned from the window and entered the bistro, walking past the host and plopping on the chair across from Ash. She had her mother's dark deep-set eyes, bathed in pale green eyeshadow, downcast, pretending not to notice him. Her scent was more like self than other; on some biological level he knew she was his daughter, but could he even call her that without having played the role? Could he ever have been the kind of father who took his kid to the playground, one hand on the swing, one on his Pulser, one eye trained on her smile and the other on the shadows? Despite the way he dragged destruction at his heels, Akasha had no right to deny him this part of his life, hiding her away as if he were a deadly plague.

The threat of tidal waves was the least thing that would crush him today.

"Nice jacket," he said. "Old-style camo. Your boyfriend in the military or something?"

"Listen," she replied, looking up, "I'm not here to play catch-up on family history or dig up old secrets. I just want to solve this geological crisis."

"You may be just telling yourself that," he replied, hopeful. "There's dozens of people with my credentials you could have called."

"You increased Gliese 581g's rotational speed to begin with; this is your fault. What were you thinking joining O.A.K., a group half the planet considers eco-terrorists to this day, a group you were supposed to stop? I'm only here because no one knows terraforming like you, 'cept maybe Mom, who barely talks to me."

"Just say outright what you blame me for," he snapped, wringing the napkin in his hand.

"Not saying I blame you for anything, but the whole rotation thing was as short-sighted as the moment you conceived me," she said, her breath accelerating.

"I didn't choose that. I didn't choose any of this." he yelled, the other tables looking over.

The waiter rushed over as if to distract attention. "May I offer to refill your water?"

Severum slapped the pitcher out of his hands, the glass shattering on the tiled floor. "Can't you see I've something to say here?"

"You'll do it outside, Sir," he replied.

Ash stood up, raised her chin, and spoke loud enough for everyone to hear, "I already have my answers from two minutes of speaking with you. I get why mom *left* you and I understand where I get all my worse traits from."

"Ash, stop," he insisted, putting his arm on her shoulder, but she twisted away.

"You're right. You didn't choose this, you didn't choose me," she spurted, storming out. "Meaning, I was a mistake. Thanks a lot, glitch-face."

Severum grabbed her beer mug and headed outside. The neon-bathed street offered nothing but a torrential downpour for solace. His soaked clothes clung to his skin. He stopped in front of her and said, "I want to help."

"You want to help? My boss, Mr. Aldweg, just tried to kill me. Apparently, I got into some sensitive files and next thing I know my whole office complex is plummeting four-hundred stories to the ground. Now, I know why the workstations were suspended over the city to begin with – it was easier to cut us loose if we started asking the wrong questions."

"What are you talking about?" he asked.

Ash slowed down and continued explaining.

"I'm glad you're okay."

"Mom won't even return my messages."

"She does that, withdraws. She vanished from my life about a couple decades ago, around the time you must have been born. She showed no signs of being pregnant. How is she?" he asked, swaying Ash's beer mug.

"Fuck if you care. I just need to know what's going on and I need your help."

"I'll do it, but only because it's you and you're in some kind of trouble. Where do we start?"

"You can start by paying my university loans, deadbeat. You're not getting off just 'cause you didn't know I existed."

Rain slapped the cobblestone path, splattering on their ankles.

"I'm on a fixed income, but I'll see what I can do. I need to understand what's happening though."

Ash ducked under a store awning and projected a hologram of the planet from her palm showing it orbiting around its red dwarf sun. "O.A.K.'s plan to increase the planet's rotation by installing conveyor belts around it and using space fountain technology to continually channel momentum was successful at first."

"You forget the atmospheric gas ejections at precisely the right angle," he added. "That angular momentum was the true key; the rest was just designed to amplify the effect."

"The question is, why is the spin increasing beyond calculations? The days keep getting shorter. I uncovered a document that suggested someone is intentionally manipulating it by adding energy to the system, but it makes no sense why they would do that?"

"Who would benefit the most?" he asked.

"I don't know. Even if someone wanted to eliminate life on the planet for some nefarious reason, there are quicker ways to extinguish it. The system was finally obtaining an equilibrium, and given the changes in the UV light, the planet's magnetic field, the wind currents, the heat distribution, the melting of the icecaps, and even the subtle impacts on effective gravity, it was a good start. But the rotational speed continues to increase at a far faster rate than you planned."

"Well, it should be easy enough to head to the Twilight band and find out," he said. "Someone can check the devices, make sure they're all in place and operational. Who knows, could just be a maintenance issue."

"There's no maintenance issue. Geosturm monitors the

devices. And they don't call it the Twilight anymore. It receives nearly the same light as the rest of the planet. Has for decades."

"The Prime Meridian. You know where I mean. And after what you said, all their data is suspect. Run all the observations again. Monitor the energy being sent to the belts and scan for additional volume in the atmospheric ejections"

"That is the problem. No one can get anywhere near the place now. Enforcers sealed the whole area off so that any measurements have to be obtained at a distance instead of on-site. Even the airbus route stops right before it reaches the rotational mechanisms."

"And you're sure this is tied to the attack on you?"

"It has to be. Can you scope the place out?" she asked.

"I'm too old for this stuff, Ash. You missed my better years, sorry."

"What do you want in return for helping me?" she pleaded.

"Nothing. This is ridiculous. If the gov' sealed the area off, then that's good enough for me. They pay my way in life because I've already given enough. Call the Enforcers if people are attacking you, I'm retired." He gulped the beer.

"They may have been the ones who restrained me during the attack." She took a deep breath, squinted her eyes, and said, "What if I bring Mom to see you?"

"You're using my ex-wife as leverage? Who the hell you think you are?"

"I'm your daughter, *Dad,*" she slighted, raising the side of her mouth.

The first time he had heard the word *Dad* and it was said with contempt. He hadn't even been given the chance. She wasn't his. He couldn't control her, couldn't predict her behavior. But looking back at the years with her mother, any woman he tried to control became less predictable for it. People weren't objects to possess, he had learned that the hard way, but it frustrated the hell out of him to admit it. "Keep away from your home. Come stay with me a while if you feel the need."

"Never."

Years in the military had taught him to objectify people, because your best friend might get ripped to pieces by Aphorids the next day. He rubbed his fingers along a fallen friend's holotag which he still carried around his neck, the metal edges indenting his flesh. He wouldn't fail again. He wanted to help, but the thought of Akasha scheming against him all these years, the lies told in silence, assaulted him harder than any bullet, and Ash looked too damn much like her. "You're worse than she is," he spouted.

Ash folded her arms and plastered her long gaze down the barren street. For the first time she was more than some carica-ture of himself. She pushed past him, spilling the beer on her jacket.

"I'm sorry," he made out, hand covering his face.

"Save it," she shot back, avoiding his eyes and walking away.

"I can at least buy you a new jacket. That one's old and stained."

"It's not mine anyway. It's the only thing Mom let me keep."

When will life just leave me alone? Enough was enough after sixty-nine years. Then he noticed the initials embroidered into the lower corner of the jacket: SR. It was the one he had worn when he enlisted in the service when he was about her age. Every torn thread carried its story, each scuff his history. He sighed and caught up to her. "Okay, I'll help. Where do we begin?"

3

END OF THE DAY AND THE SUN WAS ALREADY RISING FOR THE third time, blood-stained light seeping through the white gauze of clouds to reflect off the grimy street puddles. Managed to lose both her job and any hope her father wouldn't be an asshole in the same day.

You're worse than she is, he had said.

Was that true? Why did he hate her mother so much? At times Ash hated her too, and mostly, avoided her. She had concealed his existence for years before finally providing his contact information, but she had never called. Better to have the hope of decency than to confirm he was as bad as her mother had painted him to be. Despite this, she felt abandoned by someone who hadn't even known she existed.

She sloshed through the knee-high water back to Sloumstone Apartments. Debris bobbed on the surface and gathered at intake valves. The urban drainage basin had been overflowing for months. Engines hummed as they pumped millions of gallons of water through a pipeline into the next town, where it would eventually flow back downhill, since Blutengel was closer to sea level. Everyone was banking on enough water evaporating in the process, or being absorbed by the limited greenery, to make it worthwhile, but like any quick fix it was bound to come apart.

Three men with makeshift weapons banged on the pipes, trying to bust them. Enforcers arrived, shoving them against the wall and placing their hands behind their backs. The thugs had likely been hired by a neighboring town to sabotage the pipeline in the continual water war that was as much a political statement as a public safety issue. Geosturm workers in bright orange uniforms repaired the damage and redirected one of the pipes away from her building where the water would flow to high-end commercial buildings instead. That work wasn't normally contracted out, and it was unusual for the poorest residences to be spared the flooding at the expense of the fortunate. Something had changed; there must be an anomaly in the building – perhaps a new resident with a ton of political influence, or connections to Geosturm, but not enough funding to afford anywhere else to live. That meant the person would be young and just about to come to power.

Ash kept her eyes peeled. A woman in a Kiburi brand dress kissed a man before getting into a taxi on the elevated street above. Ash's vHUD picked up on the interaction and spouted advertisements in the corner of her vision: *Love is Kiburi*. She'd never be able to find her pride in an expensive dress, but such haughtiness had no value anyway.

A father walked by with a toddler in his arms and said to the boy, "Looks like you need a diapey change."

Diaper ads plotted across Ash's vision until she thought, *I don't even have kids and I'm being marketed this crap?* Between her reaction and her implants accessing her profile, the ad changed to, *Meet the guy of your dreams who will become the father you never had at iMeet&Match.* The ad captured her attention and a dozen variations soon spawned, flying across her vision.

So much stimulation, and it was hitting closer to home. Ash

shuddered deep in her bones, her throat tight, her hands clammy. Doc had said her shakes weren't panic attacks, just normal glitches from her implants adjusting to her becoming an adult. She knew better. Indeed, she had become a young adult, somewhere between the onset of the climate crisis and the empty promise that every generation would live better than the previous one, but it had been a nail-biting experience. Sure, she had enough implants in her head to run a powerplant, but being able to read five news articles at a time didn't change the fact that the news was mostly bad. Likewise, being able to reply to three social media posts at once was convenient, but she still wouldn't recognize most of her friends' faces in reality.

Ash turtled her face and opened the apartment complex's double doors. Water surged in. Elevator had short-circuited, so she trekked up dozens of flights of stairs to her place, soggy socks squishing in her boots. Rotationists... what the hell had her father and them been thinking?

The conversation had gone horrible. *What if I bring Mom to see you?* Of course Severum had been upset at her manipulation, but a part of her had *meant* it, just to see them together for once in her life. If he had that little empathy then no wonder Mom had left him. He didn't even know her. *Father* used to be an abstract, foreign word, a placeholder without a face to pin it on, but now it had a visage, an image to haunt her, as if blaming him for her past would somehow justify her future. The nickname her mother had given her was bad enough, *Ash*, the remnant of a once fiery love affair gone stale. Now she was risking his life by asking him to investigate the planetary crisis, but he knew the former Twilight region inside out and would know where to look for interference.

Ash dragged her index finger across her apartment's door code on the keypad, and caught her breath before entering. Low place like home. She unlaced her boots, peeled off her socks, and hit the switch to activate the nanobots that ate the mold growing on the damp walls. She tugged her sweater sleeves over her fingers to keep them warm and the heating bill down. After losing her job, eviction was right around the corner. She hadn't even been a threat, though they had probably known about her connection to Severum. If Geosturm assumed she was dead, she was safe for the moment, though the cleaner bots had targeted her after the attack and their video feed could be accessed.

Airbuses shot through pressurized tubes outside; nanobots hummed as they ate the moss inside, but otherwise the world was silent. The incident wasn't being covered by the media, despite dozens of employees who never returned home. Even her mother hadn't returned her messages. She fired off another one labeled *high importance*.

No reply.

Ikshana perched over her bed, but it was too still. The metallic falcon's long, shiny torso was indented with a feathered pattern. She plugged it in to charge. Its auburn eyes opened and it fluttered its wings.

"Who's been a good bird today?" she asked.

It cawed in reply. Having been connected to her implants, it knew how exhausted she was and nodded towards the bed.

Spinning a dial, Ash adjusted her hover-bed's field to soften it and lay down, dragging the frilly, pink blankie up to her neck that she had kept since childhood. She had always tucked herself in alone, before burrowing in the shadows. Her muscles still ached from pulling herself up to the skywalk when the world had come crashing down beneath her, her body tense as if it was still happening. She soothed the wounds on her arms and readjusted the dial to make the bed harder – needed that assurance of solid ground.

A group of loud teens pounded their feet down the stairwell, the thin, crumbling walls vibrating. She thought nothing of it until they came to a halt and quickly turned direction as if some-

24

thing spooked them. More footsteps, ascending this time, at least three people, but these steps were too quiet.

They stopped at her door.

The message to her mother! Had her comms been intercepted?

They didn't even knock, just kicked the door in.

She leapt out of bed and parted the bedroom door to see a guy's leg still sticking through her front door across the kitchen. His black pants were stamped with a red emblem – Enforcers, but it was their old logo. *Oh shit shit shit,* she fretted, pulling on the bedroom window hinges to unlock them and access the fire escape, but the hinges were rusted and wouldn't budge. She kicked the window and the glass shattered, crinkling on the floor, but the frame held its wooden grid together. She stepped back to get a running start, but they were already in the living room and on their way in, all three of them, their trapezoidal hats pulled halfway down their foreheads, eyes intent, unalarmed, in control.

Ikshana screeched, the shrillness raking across her eardrums. She was unarmed, and the metallic falcon sported no weaponry. She yanked open her nightstand drawer, but had misplaced her pocketknife, and all that was in it was a loaf of moldy bread from a midnight snack a few days old. The humming of the nanobots increased in the other room as they searched it out to consume it.

"Hold it right there!" the first guy screamed, Herald by the name on his badge, a green-eyed Veteran judging by his stars. "You're under our custody now!" They weren't drawing weapons yet, didn't feel threatened by the moldy loaf of bread in her hands.

Big mistake.

The humming of the nanobots grew louder and louder until a cloud of them, thousands-strong, showed at her bedroom door in a thick smog to consume the mold.

"Hungry?" she asked, throwing slices of the moldy bread at the Enforcers' faces.

Before the bread even hit the floor, the nanobots swarmed to each of the men and pressed their tiny bodies against the slices, pinning them to their faces and consuming the mold off them. In the mass confusion the swarm had a hard time telling where the soft mold ended and their eyes began. Blood dripped down the gooey recesses of the Enforcers, their occipital circuitry hanging from each socket.

They cried out in pain.

Ash grabbed the nearest one's Pulser, but it emitted a weak shock causing her to drop it. Gun must be linked to his cognigraf signature. She grabbed his shock baton instead and slammed it against the rusty window locks; they gave way. Sliding the window up, she slipped out to the fire escape, gripping the cold, wrought iron rails, and sliding down the wavering staircase ten steps at a time. Enforcers yelled above, but these were women's voices, meaning a second group had been planted on the roof. She reached the final landing at ground level, but they drew their Pulsers just three stories above her.

Ash gripped the rubber handle of the shock baton and bashed the buttons to activate it. Azure sparks shot from the device as she slammed it against the iron railing, her own feet planted in the soil. The whole rail lit up like a lightning bolt, Pulsers flying from the Enforcers' hands as their bodies shook and they collapsed onto the nearest landing.

Sirens in the distance.

Ash called Ikshana and it came flying out her window. She overrode its autonomy, sending it commands via vHUD, and tapped into its vision to surveil the city block. The street appeared in the corner of her vision from the bird's eye view. Two dark vehicles soared in, emitting exhaust to hover over the streets before touching down. They headed to the front entrance, she to the back.

Ash ran, for her life. Her footsteps pounded the pavement, arms moving like pistons. When you have nothing, anything can take it all away. Turning the corner at an old coffeeshop, she slammed into an invisible barrier at the intersection, knocking her wind out. Her chest heaved atop a cold platform. The cloaked Enforcer sedan materialized, the hood now visible beneath her, and the windshield inches away from her face where a burly man sat behind the wheel, fire in his eyes. He reached out the window and lobbed a grenade as he backed out of the blast radius. The two other vehicles screeched around the front of the tenement, speeding her way. There was nowhere to run. She covered her eyes, not wanting her terrified reflection in the windshield to be her last sight. The flash grenade exploded with a blinding light. The car door slammed. The engines of two other vehicles grew louder.

But they didn't count on Ikshana.

Tapping into the falcon's vision, she could still see the scene from its viewpoint. The Enforcer approached with handcuffs. The cold metal touched her wrists and was about to lock. She flickered her eyes to send a command for Ikshana to divebomb from the sky and it soared right through the approaching vehicle's windshield, then returned to the clouds. The dark car swerved, running the one beside it up the pavement to crash through the coffeeshop. The Enforcer dropped the handcuffs and ran, avoiding the rogue vehicle that was still heading towards his car.

Ash bolted, watching the streets from the sky since her vision was still whitewashed from the blast. After weaving through a few alleys, she lost them in the confusion, but at this rate, she wouldn't make it another day. Layers of questions channeled through her mind: Why had the Enforcers worn uniforms with the old red emblem? Was it funding issues, or something else? How was Geosturm so well-connected? Would Severum figure it out? Would she make it through the night? The thoughts combined, recombined, bred, split apart, and inserted themselves into every perception. They tunneled and excavated even the most secluded corners of consciousness until no other thought stood a chance against their tenacity. This was her new life, however short.

Ikshana scoured the city blocks one last time. The first groups of Enforcers were still passed out on the fire escape. The ones at the intersection had split up, but were heading by foot in the wrong directions. An ambulance arrived to treat the first group's eye injuries.

Vision returned, and she called Ikshana to her shoulder to avoid her location being given away. Its sharp talons dug into her skin. They'd live; they'd all live.

It was her life at stake.

4

Severum spent the day in his apartment in Phalanstère 625. Neuralmod addicts scurried like roaches out in the hall, but at least his feet were dry. He reviewed how O.A.K., the radical group he had once been ordered to shut down before he defected, had brought the planet daylight cycles by increasing its rotation speed. After thirty-five years, the coordinates were still drilled into his head for the belt system installed along the Prime Meridian, the angular atmospheric ejectors, and the energy transfer mechanisms installed on the hemisphere previously known as Dayburn, since it used to receive only daylight. The floods were never supposed to get this bad. Had O.A.K.'s calculations been off? Impossible. Although their founder, Gestalt, had been playing both sides, this went deeper than her betrayal or some failed physics calculations.

He packed a supply pack and readied for ASCOPE reconnaissance to examine the Area, Structures, Capabilities, Organizations, People, and Events of the region. He would start at the Prime Meridian. From there he would head to the K.O.A. Commune, the offshoot of O.A.K. that its leaders, Thalassa and Arcturus, had created to maintain the rotational technology.

Before he left, he poured a shot of special reserve bourbon and raised it to no one. "Here's to my final mission." Shot it back and headed out to the hall.

His neighbor's door, Randi Thompson, said #pacifist and #lover on the profile glowing above his security panel, but his screams penetrated the door as he roughed up his girlfriend again. Severum pounded on it, the door shaking in its frame. "Everything alright?"

Randi parted the door, a long, dark goatee tapering from his chin like dripping oil. "Mind your own business, old man."

Old man? It was the first time anyone had referred to him with that term. He slammed his fist into the door, knocking it back and Randi stumbled, but instead of following it up with a punch he cupped one hand over his fist, rubbing it to soothe the ache, flexing to see if he broke anything.

"Gone soft, eh?" Randi taunted.

"Just leave the girl alone," he replied, his heart an elastic band that snapped back harder each time it beat. His vHUD issued a warning that his heartrate was critical. The rattling of his ribcage was once exhilarating, but now it threatened his life.

Violent people come to violent ends.

"Make me, pal."

Catching his breath, Severum walked away from the scene and made an anonymous report. The screams died down, but no thanks to his efforts. He was useless, had no place or purpose, but that would change because he had someone to fight for now. He descended the staircase with aching legs, his back weak from carrying the supply pack. The double entry doors reflected the wrinkles on his forehead. He had once been strong enough to take down a horde of Aphorids in armed combat, or the time he had assaulted The Towers of the Crystal Palace in an attempt to take out Governor Borges, but physical strength faded. And what had it all meant in the end? Those memories didn't include pretend play with his unbeknownst daughter, nor the patience to listen to Akasha's feelings beyond what had been necessary for her to put out that night. The planet had increased its rotation because of him, bringing light to Evig Natt despite the ecological cost, but planets were easier to change than a woman's heart.

He took the nearest airbus to the Prime Meridian, rubbed his back, and fell asleep, taking advantage of the darkness afforded by the day's first of many sunsets.

————

A WARNING FLICKERED across his dreams, *Everyone Off! Next stops on this route are off limits to civilians!* Severum awoke and disembarked the airbus on the edge of what had once been the Twilight City, and he would always know it by that name. If the next stop was off limits, that's where he needed to be.

The sky was blotted with jade clouds that were outpaced by the red dwarf sun. Daylight cycles had changed the landscape, melting glaciers into rivers that eroded the terrain and allowed life to flourish. He displayed the route in vHUD – about a three-hour walk. It would be nightfall again before he arrived, but vehicles were too easily detected to risk not going on foot.

He walked for an hour along a river lined with purple anemones, their ochre-tipped tentacles swaying in the current. The winds beat against him, flaring his collar and flapping his jacket. Storm clouds gathered and darkened into hunter-green tones. The sky churned, getting angrier by the minute. There was little shelter on the horizon save for a forty-foot tower with an obsidian façade. It was too isolated to be a watchtower, yet too well maintained to be unused.

The tower was riddled with giant phosphophyllite crystals that jutted skyward in groups of three like swords. Their oceanic hues contrasted against the dark stone that bound them. Each crystal's face was stippled with corrosion from acid rain that was made worse by the Great Rotation.

The door was barred by a barrier of light that wrapped around the tower, a beam that shot through a clear cylinder between metal posts. The light didn't illuminate the landscape; it was self-contained. Maybe he could just duck under it, but when his fingers combed the air in front of the beam, the heat was too intense. If he broke the cylinder containing it, it might explode.

The rains came suddenly and the river gushed and swelled over the bank. Water flowed around a dirt mound that had been raised around the tower as if a dust-mole had been burrowing. Severum kicked the dirt pile, revealing a buried electrical cord. He followed the raised ground to a small building downhill where a wooden wheel creaked, spun by the river. He opened the splintered door, turned the generator off inside, and its humming died down. The barrier fizzled out around the tower, leaving a golden vapor that illuminated the rain as it vanished.

He climbed four marble steps up to the tower door and was about to open it when the ground threw him from his feet – no, not the ground, the tower shook. The phosphophyllite crystals detached from the stony base. Brittle shards curled like fingers, gem facets forming and reforming, somehow fluid enough not to break. The minerals traveled along the tower's edges before flaring into two giant legs. Crystals emerged from the top of the tower as if seeping through the darker stone. Almost fluid, they consolidated to form a head, torso, and arms. The structure ripped itself free of the tower that had held it, and a spiked golem stepped forth, shadowing Severum in its wake. Its turquoise brilliance captured every celestial beam within its bulwark, the light infinitely reflecting within its gemmed faces. Two trapezoidal jewels in its head turned towards him, but the light inside them was different. It was the light of…

Awareness.

Life was about as much phosphorus-based as carbon-based, but nothing proved the theoretical possibility of sentient stone like the stomping of those giant, crystalline feet, the land caving in around each step. Severum stumbled back. The light barrier hadn't been there to prevent people from accessing the tower – it had been there to trap this creature. How light could manipulate stone was a mystery he saved for later.

He ran for the river. If it was as acidic as the rain, he might have a chance based on the stippling he had observed in the rocks. Phosphophyllite was sensitive to acid and quite brittle.

Loud stomps crashed into the landscape behind him, kicking up rubble. Pebbles picked at the back of his neck. He leaned forward to push against the wall of wind as the storm increased. Making it to the wooden shed, he grabbed a bucket and held it under the waterwheel so the current filled it. The crystal golem came on full charge, with a raised, giant, glittering fist. Severum threw the water from the bucket at its foot. Smoke emitted and it melted, dissolving with a gush of heat. The golem stumbled to one knee and fell, creating a sinkhole, and the river flowed into that crater to fill it with acid. The creature dissolved with a gassy hiss.

Severum caught his breath as he reached the tower again, then opened the door. The sky was whirling now, and a tornado was imminent. Inside, the tower was similar to a lighthouse. He took shelter beneath the base of the stairs and drew his canteen as the winds raged against the swaying tower walls. Words were etched into the stones. He recognized the script and the ink dye from his former companion's accounts of the Florinik, a sentient species who resided not far past the Twilight. Opal Fitzgerald's research had brought the Florinik to the world stage, modernizing the small, pacifistic tribe in the process. He ran his fingers across the indented words and read: *Beware what lies below.*

———

WHEN THE STORM CLEARED, Severum parted the door to continue his journey. Sunset blared upon the landscape, the ruby light gleaming off the sparkling stones and bursting against the tower. The swollen river bled upon the shore. Terrestrial stingrays, flying fish, and aquatic blobs littered the landscape, their carcasses having been tossed by the winds. The sun soon plunged beneath the horizon, still dusting the navy sky with streaks of pink.

Night fell but offered no clemency. Scavengers swooped from the air and rushed across the Albino Marshes to finish off what the wind had wrought. Fireflies reflected off the water. Having previously been used for currency, they were making a comeback in the wild. Severum grabbed a handful of pale, glowing cattails to boost the light his implants could amplify. He trekked forth, the cool, night air filling his lungs, expanding within as if he had swallowed ice cubes down the wrong pipe.

Soon, the Twilight City emerged, its walls stretching like a horizon in each direction. Holes had been blown into various sections, steel blossoming from the blasts. Buildings had been reduced to leaning, scalene structures. He passed through an entrance, monitoring for drones. Looters had taken anything of value, leaving chip-trip casings and graffiti that read, *Go Hack Yourself!* Inactive droids reached for disconnected limbs in the mechanical graveyard.

Whole place was a data dump.

The region had once been ruled by an artificial intelligence in hopes that the A.I. Core could regulate economic relations between the hemispheres better than humans could. It had designed the city to hold its machinery with little regard for human aesthetics. The technocracy had been short-lived when the A.I. became destructive, resulting in Severum and O.A.K. striking out to dismantle the region. His former neighbor and friend, Aurthur Fitzgerald, and he had disabled the master communications tower, making the rebellion a success. Hadn't heard from the guy but a few times since he had married Opal.

The street was more circuit-board than pavement. He strode

across the substrate, breaking various components as devices crackled beneath his boots, trying not to get electrocuted. Hover-lights were splayed across the ground, having fallen from the sky. The electric chandeliers were shaped like giant jellyfish, tentacles strobing and spitting sparks with a sulfurous smell. After a few miles of trekking through flaccid wires, fallen drones, and sharp-edged machinery piled like retaining walls, he dropped to his knees and brought his hand to his head.

Neuralmods surged through his mind a few commands later, chiseling at the granite exhaustion that locked him in place and breathing springtime through the winter of his achy bones. He had been against neural enhancers his whole life, took reality straight-up with a hard afterburn, yet he fell prey to their embrace when times were hard. He tightened his jacket, jumped to his feet, and continued through the abandoned industrial tech buildings until vHUD outlined four groups of armed men patrolling in the distance. He discarded the cattails to avoid giving away his presence, kicking them beneath a broken concrete slab. Would they shoot on sight? He was useless anyway, not able to even walk a few hours without running enhancers. His past injuries wore heavily on his body. He should give up, go back, let a younger man carry the burden, but no. His value wasn't based on labor; that's how an economist viewed the world, not how the humanitarian he wanted to become would view it. For a moment he almost called K.O.A. for assistance, or an old comrade, but this was too personal. This was a trial Ash was putting him through and he needed to go it alone, as if to redeem himself in her eyes, a test of the father he might have been, or might be.

If he survived.

Severum approached, keeping within the armed men's blind spot and slipping behind some crumbled panels and cargo crates. He should have scoped the scene from afar as planned, stayed in the shadows, kept to the fringes, but prolonging the reconnaissance carried its own risk, as did the winds, the chill, and the threat that more crystalline creatures would rise from the ground. A guard raised his Pulser to the sky and fired until it expended its charge amidst the cheering crowd. These weren't trained soldiers, perhaps mercs like he used to be. He turned up his aural implants and activated Chameleon to blur his image. The pricy neuralmod drained his mental processing power, and he needed every bit, but it would give him the edge he needed to get closer between the service buildings to pick up what they were saying. Unless they were on full alert, they'd see him only as a shimmering air current.

A hover-light splayed over the cracked concrete road, illuminating the area. A few grizzly men passed a two-story building. He zoomed in on the group until he could count the greying strands in the leader's long hair, falling around his tanned, wrinkled face.

The leader addressed a group of six, "Did Aldweg take care of things on Geosturm's side?"

"Tied up the loose ends real nice, Mr. Culptos," a young man replied, smirking.

"Good. You've done well for the Old Guard. Where the hell's the scientist at?" He scanned the area.

Chameleon counted down, the effect wearing off. Severum backed away, looking for concealment. A woman exited a building with a guard, faces out of sight.

Culptos approached her, grabbed her by the arm, and asked, "How many months 'til the floods wash away what remains of this pathetic new world?"

He slapped her when she wouldn't respond, pushed her down, and motioned for a guard to lead her around the corner. She struggled in vain to free herself. In his younger age, he would have taken the risk, freed the captive, but if he couldn't face what was going on in his own apartment complex, how could he face a group of armed men in the heart of their compound? He would gather intel and report back to Ash. Then he'd hit up K.O.A. for equipment and return to free the scientist after things had calmed. She would know what was going on inside the lab. No use calling the Enforcers; these mercs carried government-issued weapons so they had connections. Plus, they had mentioned the Old Guard, a once derogatory term for the previous regime that had ruled the Western Hemisphere when it had been called Evig Natt.

Sharply-defined shadows cut into the landscape behind the building. He slipped into that negative space, then slipped again as his legs flew out from under him, the hard impact of his back on the concrete knocking his air out with a *whoosh*.

Damn, that hurt. Oil leaked from a fallen droid, the culprit of his fall. He grabbed a rusty metal pipe and used it as a cane to pull himself up, leaning against the building for support, but he put too much pressure on it and it flew from his grip, clanging to the pavement just as Chameleon fizzled out and revealed his presence.

"I heard something! Go check it out!" one of the guys yelled from the other side of the building two-hundred feet away.

Shit. Maybe they'd blame it on the wind if he could disappear. He ran down the side of the building, ducking under the windows. The fallen hover-light was just ahead. Its frayed cords draped across the pavement and tossed purple sparks into the night. Disabling it would cloak him in darkness, and even with night-vision upgrades the mercs would have a hard time hunting him. He peeked around the corner; they were nowhere to be seen, but their footsteps gave them away until the steps stopped. A hiss of air spurt forth, then another, a sound Severum knew all too well.

Air propulsion.

Two mercs soared over the building and landed behind him, emitting blue flames from the bottom of their boots as they touched down. He drew his Pulser, aimed at the fuel canisters on their backs, but the closest guy immediately swiped the gun from his hand.

"I got lost," he feigned, noting the sparking cords on the ground again.

"You are lost, lost to history, pal," the first guy remarked, drawing his gun.

Severum dove to the ground, grabbed one of the rubber hover-light cords in each hand, and shoved them into the gaps between the men's boots and their armored pants. A brilliant, white light bolted up their juddering bodies, the electricity short-circuiting their cyber-rigs. But suits like that carried enough electrical shielding that they wouldn't be stunned for long. He refused to finish them off, having lived that same life long ago, but he needed another way out, fast. The rest would be on his tail soon, taking flight to scope what had become of their comrades. He couldn't return the way he had come, and the surrounding buildings would only offer temporary respite, that is, if they didn't house reinforcements.

He crossed into the next block where intact hover-lights lit the area with their swaying neon tentacles. Dead end – the city was walled off. Even if he could get over it, he couldn't step foot on the road to do so. The substrate carried live current into whatever machinery was still maintaining the place.

A third assailant soared in and spotted him.

Severum tugged the dangling cord from the hover-light as if it were a vine. It held. The hover-lights were positioned just right that it might work. He got a running start and leapt to the nearest light, grabbing the cord and swinging back and forth to gain momentum before leaping to the next. On he went, swinging from light to light over the live current running across the road below, the cold wind burning the edge of his nose and ears, his stomach tumbling with every leap.

The hovering mercenary pursued, descending to intercept him mid-swing, and raised his Pulser.

Severum twisted as he swung. The shot went wide, buzzing past his ear. He kicked at the assailant, but his target thrusted aside. Severum let his momentum fall backward until he flipped over the hover-light. He was inverted for a moment, held within that throng of gravity and centrifugal force, suspended above the world. The merc hovered closer, but Severum jumped off the light to land on his shoulders. The weight was too much for the guy's hover-boots to handle, and he touched down on the electrified substrate. Severum jumped off him right before he hit, grabbing the nearest dangling light and retracting his feet up to keep them off the circuit-riddled road. The mercenary was shocked and thrown against the wall of a mechanics shop.

One more pump of his legs and Severum swung over the wall at the opposite end of the compound from where he had entered, not far from the next airbus station. Crossing the fringe of shadows, he kept watch on the city gate. Any second the entire armed force might go airborne.

5

METROPOLIS CLOSED ITS EYES AS MERCHANTS' SIGNS FLICKERED off, for it saw only in terms of wealth. Homeless, Ash took refuge in a coffeeshop wedged between two skyrises, but it was just as cold inside. Transportation workers brought steaming cups to their chapped lips. Everyone was a ghost of their daytime self at this hour. A bot served her at a table in the corner. She buried her face in a mug of chai masala, the steam misting her face, and concealed any expression of need that would be interpreted as an excuse for every guy in the place to strike up conversation. Letting her fingers warm on the mug, she placed them delicately on her eyelids, the warmth soaking through the thin skin. She needed help, but anyone she contacted would be put at risk, including co-workers, the few friends she maintained, and her mother, who hadn't returned her calls. She didn't dare return to her mother's place either – they would definitely search there.

As for Severum, he owed her a couple decades of investment, but she had already sent him halfway across the planet into the throng of the enemy. Her old friend guilt clung like a forsaken lover, tugging at her chin. She dug her fingernails beneath their nailbeds until they burned, and journaled on a virtual keyboard. Her mind was a construction site where workers scurried to build a foundation in a sunken quarry, if only the jackhammering inside would allow a moment's respite. One day, she'd auction off her diary and the buyer could have her heart, if they didn't just tear it in two from the absurdity.

For ages, she had stepped into the same river twice each morning, thriving on routine, but those times had passed. She scanned headlines for mentions of her name, expecting to find her picture in every newspaper, the world hunting her, but there was nothing. Somehow, that absence was even more terrifying – whoever was after her didn't just want her dead, they wanted to erase her very existence.

VHUD flashed. "Severum here. I'm on an airbus traveling away from the Twilight City in case you hear hissing. Look, we're onto something big here, Ash."

"No shit."

"Still putting up the tough girl act with me, huh?"

"Go hack yourself."

"If I'm as bad a person as half the world thinks I am, then I wouldn't be out here risking my life to investigate the possibility that the Great Rotation was a mistake, or at the least, to fix what went wrong, so listen to me."

"I *am* listening," she scoffed.

"Good, then keep it up, because there's another reason I'm doing this. I want to support you," he said, choking on the word *support*. Maybe it tore him up inside to realize he hadn't been there her whole life, or maybe he realized how much of a burden she was.

"Let's stick to the intel. What you got?"

"A series of new buildings have been erected in the former Twilight region. They're guarded by at least twenty cybernetically-enhanced mercs centralized in one area. They don't guard the gates, though, since I don't think they care about people looting the place if they stay away from this one sector. A scientist was kidnapped and is being held at a lab there. I also overheard them alluding to the incident with Geosturm, and I confirmed they're working with the Old Guard. What do you know about them?"

"Not much," she replied, sipping her chai, the foam popping on her upper lip. "The old government was very conservative, and after it fell there was a movement to return the planet to what they called the golden age, back before it had daylight cycles, back when half the planet lived in darkness and traded in fireflies."

"Yes, it seems they're trying to take back the power they once held by messing with the planet's rotation, but they're not just reversing the work that O.A.K. did decades ago when we sped it up."

"Right," she agreed. "They're speeding the planet even faster. Now why would they want to increase the rotation beyond what's needed to produce normal daylight cycles?"

"Days are getting shorter, causing the negative ecological impacts to become worse and less predictable."

"Exactly. And get this, I think they're trying to prove how dangerous the rotational technology is by exaggerating those negative effects," she said.

"Begging the question again as to why not just reverse the effect, since they occupy the region controlling the rotation?"

"That's easy. They don't want to reverse the effect, they want people to buy *into* it, to *want* the Old Guard and its oppression to return, guaranteeing them stability. Then they can say, *See, we tried your idealistic vision of daylight cycles and it failed. The greater equality that it brought was too dangerous and the planet resisted it. Now, join us as we return to the old ways. We can save you from the floods.*"

"If your theory is true, then they should be rallying support soon."

"No, they'll wait until the crisis point is reached. People need to witness the dangers first. They'll terrorize the planet, beat the people down until they beg for order. As for me, I was too smart, and those who abuse power always fear intelligent women, which is part of the reason we're so rarely voted into office. Where do we go from here?"

"I'm heading to the former Dayburn area. Haven't seen it since it was a desert. I'll convene with K.O.A. and then return to rescue that scientist. She should know what's going on, and we can't allow the enemy an asset like that. Plus, the guilt of leaving her there is killing me."

"Probably just a young, sexy girl," Ash shrugged, recalling the stories her mother told about his philandering.

"Didn't see her face."

She hesitated, leaned forward in the booth, tapped her aural implant in her ear where Severum's voice fed through, and finally said, "How do... how do you deal with your guilt?" The words hung in the air, perforated with the fear of intimacy, and ready to tear down that line.

"What?" he asked, almost laughing. Almost fucking laughing at her. "Your life's at risk and we need to strategize our next move. There's no time for—"

"Forget it!" She ended the call and gulped the remaining chai before storming out into the cold.

If she was being hunted, she could either wallow in fear, or become the hunter herself, taking charge of her life and running her own investigation. She grabbed a large, empty box from the back of the coffeeshop and a rock and went down the street to a mechanics shop. A fountain-lift running on a stream of circling energy pellets sat outside it to allow mechanics to reach the skylanes. She opened the gate and took the lift a few hundred feet up to a long platform above the city designed for emergency vehicular maintenance.

Ash entered an empty tollbooth on the platform, the operator having been replaced with a scanning device years ago. She brought the box over her head and used the rock to prop it up enough to allow airflow. It was the safest place she could think of. The box slats provided a narrow view of the aerial traffic. She jacked into cyberspace, the datalag sluggish from not being directly connected. Ran iNconspic to mask her travels.

Now she was a ghost on the datastreams, a bloodhound catching the stink of the money trail.

But blood was all she would find.

6

SEVERUM HAD MESSED THAT UP, SO SURPRISED BY THE SUDDEN glimpse of intimacy his daughter had displayed that he couldn't bear it, the collision of an imagined role with the failure of reality. He sighed and disembarked the airbus on the hemisphere formerly known as Dayburn. He rented a horseshoe-shaped hovercraft; its beige camouflage no longer useful now that the desert had turned to lush, moist greenery in many areas, given the rivers the melting icecaps had created. The ultraviolet rays that had once threatened life on the hemisphere were no longer an issue due to the increased rotation, since its impact on the magnetic field shielded them. Perhaps he had brought some positive changes to Gliese 581g, that is, if the indigenous cultures had learned to cope.

The K.O.A. Commune was to the south, past the Florinik village of Amorpha. Their leader, Arcturus, had accepted him into K.O.A. decades ago after he had helped O.A.K. bring daylight cycles to the planet. After the ashes settled, though, he had done little to develop their utopia.

Most hovercraft only flew a few feet above the ground, enabling them to fly over floods and unpredictable terrain, with the exception of the aerial models used in Blutengel. The rackety rental barely made it that high. Its hover-fans whirred as he boarded the dual-seat craft and took off across the grassy plains.

The morning sun scraped across the sky, the light exaggerating the shadows between his wrinkles reflected in the steel steering wheel. Leaving that scientist behind played hell on his guilt. Had he backed down because it was the right thing to do strategically when outnumbered by a superior foe, or out of fear? He always thought he'd be more of a risktaker as he aged, for there was less life left to wager, but he had grown more cautious instead.

The Florinik village of Amorpha appeared on the horizon, its size rivalling even the trading posts of Nathril-Xoynsia to the north. What was once a series of huts had become a bustling hive of activity across dozens of two-story buildings. The civilization that had once shunned technology now embraced it. A sliver of turquoise crystal made a path that led into town, but neither wagons nor travelers stepped upon it.

Trouble ahead. Aphorids emerged from the tall grasses and rushed him on all fours, crossing the plains in seconds. They leapt at his hovercraft with gnashing rows of blood-stained teeth that gleamed in the sunlight. He swerved left, slamming the craft into its jaw to knock it aside, but another jumped at him with its strong hind legs to board the craft's platform, swiping at him with diamond-edged claws that ripped right through the steering controls. The craft spun in long circles, creating a dust storm as its edge dragged in the sand. With one foot planted in the seat, Severum kicked it in its drooling mouth, but the creature lunged again, its dark layers of skin flapping as it breathed. Balancing on the edge of the craft, he grabbed the broken steering column and struck upward deep into its belly at the height of its leap, impaling it on the jagged metal. He threw it aside, the Aphorid bouncing along the ground before coming to a dead stop.

The craft spun quicker until he was dizzy. Nausea billowed in his stomach. A hollow square sat where the steering column had been connected. He dug his hands inside it, ripping a few nails from their cuticles, and pressed hard enough to straighten the craft as he sped away.

Too close. Those things had scraped the faces off many good soldiers he had once known.

The damaged craft came to a halt outside the village with the Aphorids still at his heel. Florinik rushed to meet them head-on, pulling metal helmets over their rugged, hairless scalps. They grimaced as they entered battle, their faces resembling wood carvings. Burly arms as thick as tree trunks raised to shoot Pulsers in one hand, while launching spears with the other. The points dug deep into the Aphorids' flesh as they galloped to the gate, while the shots burned through their bodies, setting their fur aflame with a sulfuric odor. They fell one by one, their momentum tumbling them into the wooden gate, which though it splintered and creaked, held strong.

The raid on the village was of no concern to Severum, though the Florinik had helped him in the past, but with his craft busted and the Aphorids afoot, his safest bet was to secure one of the giant camel-like creatures known as Dijyorkvoken stationed at a nearby stable. With two Aphorids at his back, he ran for the gate and ducked behind the Florinik's cover-fire just in time.

One of them clamped its razor-sharp teeth into the young male guarding the gate, who shrieked and squeezed his egg-shaped golden eyes shut; but what would have been a fatal blow to a human was only a surface wound to the thick-barked Florinik. He recovered and knocked it aside with his long limbs, then headed off to nurse his wound shouting, "That's the last of them!"

"Bring the seedlings, saplings, and blossoms from hiding then," the tallest Florinik ordered, and though there were few differences betn sexes, Severum recognized this one to be male, for he had met the chief before. His amber eyes lit up at seeing

Severum and he chuckled, "I should have known 'twas you at my gate, Nightwalker."

"Why's that, old friend?" Severum asked.

"You always bring trouble in tow, like clouds bring rain," the chief replied, placing long arms on Severum's shoulders that felt like sanded wood, and rocking them up and down. He smiled, his face like a wooden frog's.

"Without the Great Rotation I pulled off, there would be no rain here. It's been a long time indeed," Severum acknowledged.

"Even longer when you can see sun crossing sky. All days used to be one day, and this was all sand. Now, you can see we have done much over the years, our tiny village becoming major trading hub, but with great wealth comes great envy, hence, Aphorids at doorstep," the chief replied. "You might say cup is easier to hold when not overflowing."

"So true. Have you built schools?" Severum asked, cocking a brow.

"Oh yes, many. We've mastered your language, many languages in fact. It's necessary to avoid being taken for fool in trading negotiations. The Aphorids, on the other hand, speak simply but refuse to negotiate," he replied, surveying their broken bodies.

"Indeed."

"So, have you come to mine my land again, take my metals to make fancy devices?"

"No," Severum replied. "I need to rent a Dijyorkvok, that is, unless you have hovercraft available."

"The few vehicles we have are checked out. You're free to secure a Dijyorkvok, but you must stop and take rest with us first."

"I'm fine."

"No, older trees when they reach a certain height stop growing. They know when to rest. You have been wounded much, Nightwalker, and each injury will take longer to heal."

"Only a few scrapes and cuts," he shrugged.

"Your mind needs healing, it needs rest."

"Fair enough," he replied, heart still thumping from the encounter.

Two short seedlings looked up at him with great, golden eyes that filled half their wide faces, then scurried off, their bodies vibrating with laughter. "The tiny faced one has come," one said in a high voice to her mother.

The mother scolded the seedlings, "Keep your distance from that Dimdweller. It's his fault the sun is out of control."

"Can the sun be grafted?"

"No," the mother replied. "Only Orbis can save us now."

The chief led him to a large home with stucco walls, his orange wrapping fluttering as he walked. Sunlight fell through a domed ceiling to be filtered by dust particles dislodged from the dirt floor. Manufactured ornaments showed both his status, and how much the Florinik had changed, for they had once preferred practicality over embellishment. A few broken shelves were slanted diagonally, their pottery shattered.

Two females, noted only by the fuchsia scarves they wore like belts and the woven vines that passed as shirts, rolled out a rug between two long sofas. Years ago, most had gone naked without shame, but the modern world had forced change. One brought him a cool beverage that smelled like honey and cinnamon but was slow as sap to hit his tongue, while the other cleaned the mess.

"As you can tell, many changes brought upon us," the chief began, sitting. His cavernous mouth softly roared, "When Gliese's rotation increased and darkness cloaked our hemisphere for the first time, when shadows lengthened and moved across landscape, we were at first terrified. On your side of the planet, you were used to night, but many of us believed nightfall meant Orbis was weakening, since our deity maintains reality by observing it, which is the source of its power. Some attributed it

49

to lack of faith, others to contact with Nightwalkers like yourself."

"Reasonable enough," Severum nodded, entranced by the grandeur of the chief's presence. "We had to make major adjustments in the Western Hemisphere as well. When the sun rose for the first time, crowds flooded the street, smashing jars of fireflies that we used to use as both currency, and light to see by."

"This is why I called your people the Nightwalkers, the Shadowbringers, the Sundimmers. Seems I need new derogatory terms now," he laughed, shaking the floor with his giant feet. "I received word that our counterparts in the Lost Shores believe their deity has also weakened, for they worship the ice that envelopes consciousness. Of course, our tribes split long ago, but when the ice melts, they fear their destruction. Given the flooding, which has impacted your hemisphere more than ours, their reasoning may be incorrect, but conclusion is same."

"Naturally."

"But then we saw the stars!" the chief exclaimed. "Having never seen them before the Great Rotation, they inspired a wealth of questions which our religious cosmology couldn't answer. Ever since first nightfall, my people have been fascinated by those celestial bodies. Now, some among us wish to travel to those stars, believing that our vines of consciousness will wrap around every planet we observe, increasing Orbis' power through collective omnipresence."

"What about the rest of you? Where do you stand, Chief?"

"As a documenter of what is progress for my kind, and what may be regress. We've lost some of our culture, our mannerisms, even our speech patterns. Yet, we maintain certain wonder at universe. One of our groups is researching wind patterns across dunes, not with instruments, but by opening their minds to nature's will for change. Those wanderers are becoming less common, however."

"So there's a pressure to modernize then?"

"Oh yes. The weather patterns have made travel easier between hemispheres, distributing heat that we may colonize new regions with technology we once shunned. But now, we discovered the greatest truth."

"You learned about evolution?" Severum suggested.

"No, it's about Orbis. It's nothing but a computer server. Think about it, fleshy one. Cyberspace views all, knows every thought, every activity, every social interaction, every piece of research, every blueprint, every idea documented across history. It observes all, every song that has been sung, every poem that has been written. It is not merely like a deity, it *is* deity, fully omnipresent. If anything has evolved, it's Orbis, our savior."

Severum put his palm to his face and replied, "Many, like Opal, our anthropologist friend, find beauty in your religion though. I never meant for my actions to fast-forward your culture."

The chief nodded. "Though it did create conflict, you did us favor, friend. We are still evolving, channeling old ways into new. We used to stare at the flickering of our communal cooking fires at end of day; now we stare at the flickering of a screen that provides different insights. Not better, but more complex. We analyze predictive analytics instead of tea leaves. We revised our cosmology to include all our new discoveries, and to try to reconcile the growing conflict between science and religion."

"Your cosmology? You mean your origin story?"

"The universe's birth! See, the universe began with the condensation of data in the void, the less dense data rising to form the heavens, the heavier data land. When data transfers we call it Yang, when it is received we call it Yin. Our bodies are data that has taken shape, a continual balance of this Tai Chi. We now understand this. Just look at the young seedlings doing their daily meditation."

Out the window, a dozen seedlings sat in a circle outlined in wires in front of various rusted technological devices. They bowed to the electronics and chanted incantations in unison,

"Form me, form me,
download me in your grace,
and when I'm recycled,
upload me to better place.

WHEN I AM in awesome wonder,
consider all the data you have transmitted.
I see the stars,
I hear the rolling thunder,
thy power through cyberspace emitted."

"WE HAVE SEEN THE FUTURE, and it is grand," the chief continued. "By merging our consciousness into cyberspace by taking part in online interaction, we spread our influence through the world, empowering Orbis. But I ask you this. Recently, I had dream, and in it I was an avatar. Am I a Florinik who had a dream I was an avatar? Or am I an avatar dreaming I am Florinik? Some have told me the real predates the virtual, but who can tell anymore?"

"The real and the virtual are two sides of the same coin, perhaps like life and death," Severum replied. He used to find such statements nonsensical, but after living with Akasha for many years, the former head priestess of the Aporia Asylum, he realized the spiritual significance such musings would hold if they were true. His faith came in moments, and left just as suddenly, but when it did it left a vestigial of openmindedness.

"Indeed!" the chief exclaimed.

"Can you tell me about the golem I saw?"

"Golem?"

"A rock-like creature based on phosphorus that was imprisoned in a tower. I sort of, let it out and killed it."

"Oh no," he replied, his wide face diving into a frown like a bullfrog. "Ardhieneo will not be pleased."

"Who?"

"More like a what than a who. You must have seen the turquoise path leading to our village. It is but part of a wider network here, a landmass that once existed deep under the sand. When climate changed and rivers ran again, the sands were washed away, exposing the land beneath."

"And am I correct that it is phosphophyllite?"

"It changes form, and whether it is ultimately crystalline or light I know not. Now and again, we are forced to imprison one of its scions when it becomes agitated. We dare not walk across the tinted land."

"So it is conscious, then? It can be reasoned with? Or is this whole thing like reading wind patterns on the dunes of time or whatever you said?"

"We do not know. But the rumbling worsens daily, just as the days shorten. Before you came there was mild quake. It shook my home. Maybe you could try communicating with it?"

"This goes beyond my terraforming studies, and I must soon be on my way."

"Favor demands favor in turn. You not enough time to even speak to stone path?"

"You're asking me to speak *to* it?"

"Yes, indeed, oh fleshy one."

"I'll give it a try," Severum replied, heading out of the hut and through the front gate.

The turquoise path glittered in the mid-day sun. Although small grasses grew along it, no weed dared penetrate its unbroken expanse. What language would stone even speak? If Akasha were here, she'd say the planet speaks the language of one's heart. While such sentiments sounded pretty, they did nothing to help him communicate with a network of crystals. Severum lowered his head, raised his voice, and called, "Hello? Ardhieneo, are you there? I am Severum. I seek the audience of the stone." He tapped his foot on the path.

Nothing. Then, some mild tremors came as a reply strong enough to jiggle his toes. Severum knew the rumbling heard during a quake was mostly produced on the surface from objects shaking. Actual rumbling within the planet occurred too deep to be audible. Not this time though, as this sound was being produced near ground level, meaning it must be a more shallow quake than the planet normally experienced.

It's just a coincidence. But he brought up a seismograph program in vHUD that displayed in the corner of his vision to be sure. Although it didn't measure the quake directly, it accessed a network of sensors and user reports that provided enough data to estimate the tremor's strength based on his location. He had seen many readouts over his career, but had never encountered the unusual pattern this tremor emulated. The magnitude was too capricious, modulating almost like human speech, but much lower. He zoomed in on the graph of the tremor's sine wave and raised the pitch, compressing the tones, but the result was gibberish. Anything approaching human speech would be difficult for any animal to produce, let alone rocks. Then he recalled that the Florinik were obsessed with data. If they were the audience of these communications, then perhaps the stone was using the simplest means of communication possible – binary code.

Severum converted the modulations to a binary state, parsing them out so that when the frequency was above the median average, he assigned it a *one*, and when it was below, he assigned it a *zero*. The spikes of greater and lesser intensity were easily modeled in binary, like most things. Unlike most things, translating this code revealed a single phrase:

You will do our bidding.

"Or what?" he yelled, stomping on the crystal path. Stronger tremors knocked him down to one knee. He translated,

Or be swallowed.

"Fair enough," he shrugged. "What do you want?"

Weaker tremors: *Divert the river and the quakes shall stop.*

"That makes sense, given that the tributaries have brought large amounts of acid rain to the region which would threaten you. I understand your need for protection," Severum stated.

A few Florinik traders looked at him like he had lost his mind as they passed, carrying their wares.

"But if I divert the river, this place will eventually return to desert, and will no longer be a successful trading post."

The largest tremor yet found Severum at its epicenter. The ground rippled away from him, dislodging bushes and tumbling rocks.

Our demand has been made.

Severum stepped away from the path and returned through the gates to the Florinik chief, who was sitting inside his hut. "There's a problem," he said. "The tremors will only stop if we divert the river away from here. The acid rain that gathers in it threatens the land, but without the river your economy will suffer."

"Severum, my people have always placed the land first, but we cannot go back to the way things were even if we wanted to. Trees do not ungrow or willingly trim their own canopies."

"There are a few solutions here, Chief. You could set up a network of irrigation pipes, diverting the river away but keeping its water, but the runoff will still find its way into the land."

"Can we get rid of the acid in the rain?"

"Impossible, it's from our factories in Blutengel."

"Then humans should pay to remove poison from our water," he replied, standing on tall legs.

"Yes, but no one will agree to that. Without the A.I. Core in the Twilight regulating the relationships between the hemispheres anymore, our political negotiations divulge into constant conflict. I'm afraid humans have nothing to gain by helping you, though, do not count me among their insolence. Perhaps we can install a filter to cleanse the acid from the river before it reaches your village."

"That would work," the chief agreed, "but again, who would pay for this, since your factories brought this poison? It was never issue before Great Rotation."

"I will bring this up as an item with K.O.A. when I meet with them. They are the offshoot group from O.A.K. You remember Thalassa, Opal, and Aurthur, right?"

"I think fondly upon them, except the one with the tiny swords carry. She, I not sure about."

"Daggers, yes, and that makes two of us regarding Thalassa. As you know, they're an environmental activist group that runs a nonprofit. Perhaps I can secure funding from their leader, Arcturus, but I need transportation first and will need to make way soon."

"Come, I grab you Dijyorkvok for your trip, then," the chief said, leading him outside to the stable where a huge, hairy beast kicked up dirt.

Soon, Severum was on his way to the K.O.A. Commune. Having brought the Eastern Hemisphere its first nightfall so many years ago, had he freed the Florinik from their ignorance of the modern world, or merely replaced it with a greater form?

7

THE GLIMMERING MATRIX WAVERED LIKE A SNAKE THROUGH cyberspace. Ash had rendered it in many ways over the years, interfaced with it through the finest skins, but the virtual forest was the ultimate escape. It displayed the entire network, bypassing her eyes to feed the visuals right into her mind as data flooded her implants.

Geosturm's corporate intranet was indicated by a clump of dead trees at the copse between the public and private domains. The trees grew as they rendered, forming a circuitry canopy. She soared to their nodes, bypassed credentials, crashed subroutines. She created a flurry of new user accounts in a batch upload of false demographics, then used each to create a super-admin account with full permissions. She coded a quick program to bounce between accounts to ghost herself, as each one was set to be traced to a different location. Then, she changed the actual administrators' passwords to lock them out of the system and buy her time after verifying they weren't in use, which would have tipped them off. Finally, she typed a single name: Aldweg. Time to uncover this guy's financial statements.

A door opened, leading deeper into the digital forest. Orange sparks fired through glass tree trunks of twisted wires, each tree a directory branching to folders, each leaf a glowing file. But how could she locate a single incriminating document in a cyberforest of a billion leaves?

Birds carried data packets from node to node beneath pixelated clouds. Hot-pink mushrooms spit spores that clung to her avatar, slowing her connection and blurring her vision as they accumulated. She activated cleaner tools to swipe the spores away, and followed a river of light coursing through the woods with the blare of white noise. Soon, she stumbled upon a trail of intranet traffic worn into the dirt, kicking up dust bytes with each step.

She stopped. No cold winds blew against her avatar's green tunic, no drones hummed overhead, and the intranet traffic was almost at a standstill. Emulated god-rays fell upon her face and the surrounding trees. It was beautiful, but it wasn't real and could never last. She snapped to awareness and eased herself out of cyberspace by touching a portal.

In the real world, she was huddled inside a box within a tollbooth on a maintenance platform overlooking the city. Cars sped by, dipping and raising their noses to change aerial lanes. Everything was clear, so she tapped her temples to dip back into the warm bath of cyberspace.

Ash pulled a low branch and cupped a leaf in her hand, the data seeping into her as the file downloaded. The leaf changed color to ochre, then burnt orange due to a passive algorithm that indicated the file was moderately sensitive. She ran her hand along the entire branch. It turned color, but closer inspection revealed nothing but tax documents. Low-lying data like this was easy to acquire, but she was gung-ho on reaching the canopy where the corporation stored the best secrets. Up there, the leaves were re-rendering constantly, their edges serrated, meaning someone was accessing and changing the files while she searched for them.

Weeds spread pirated software from one side of the forest to the other like wildfire, kept in check by leafcutter ants. Leaves fell, not in a gentle spiral, but in a hard plop, embedding themselves into the soft substrate where mushrooms recycled them. The 'shrooms would then list the altered intel on an auction site. Ash was too experienced to purchase the altered data, and the minute she did, the corp would trace her account anyway. Even script kiddies avoided such traps.

She climbed the tallest tree, avoiding the hypnotic glow as its wires pulsated, and dodged a swarm of trollbot spiders weaving spyware webs. A string of malicious code snaked its way through the underbrush, caught her trail with a hiss, and shed its datashell. It lurched up the tree, barely missing her feet as she raised them tight around the trunk. The code string's mouth opened to reveal rows of fangs like sharks' teeth. It bit deep into her calf, stinging her in the real world through haptic feedback. She jerked her leg back and kicked it off the tree. The burning poison coursed through her veins.

That wasn't supposed to happen. Haptic feedback should be a slight sting, a vibration, but this was different; this was real.

The snake's code must have increased the sensitivity of my haptic responder mod, she reasoned. *Looks like it also locked the setting. Have to be more cautious. While I don't have any actual wounds, the pain's disorienting and could accumulate into shock.*

The woods caught fire behind her, burning with a scent that tinged the nose. Someone was destroying a server, dumping datafiles, erasing temporary caches, covering their tracks. The flames shed ember sparks and the poison coursing through her veins meant she'd feel every one of them. She scurried up the tree, touching every leaf on the way up until she found a series of leaves that turned red. Classified intel – massive find!

She grabbed the leaves and slid down, severing stems along the way and dislodging a cocoon tucked between two branches. It fell, splitting open across the soil to reveal a segmented metallic carapace from which transparent wings unfolded. Circuity was embedded along each vein. Its antennae extended, the ends illuminating on rhythm with the data flow. It took flight with three sharp flaps of its wings, circling overhead to vocalize an alarm that resounded like a banshee cry.

Forest green became blood red, the sky turning burgundy, the plants becoming outlines, the canopy now threadbare and offering no concealment. Four more code strings raised their heads and surged forth, but these weren't snakes, they were eels floating in the cyber-ether, jaculating their bodies, sniffing her orifices, feeling for an entry point into her brain.

She shook them off and ran. The portal behind her vanished, but another was dead ahead. That swirling nebula offered the safest way to disconnect, since hard crashing a VR this immersive would leave her with a mindfuck hangover, but it was too late. The code eels swerved and encased the portal, blocking the exit.

Ash jacked out the hard way, by crashing virtual reality, the pressure building at her temples until she cried out in pain in the tollbooth. The poison in her leg still burned; the effects were supposed to end once one left cyberspace. Not this time. Her cognigraf replayed the bite, sending the pain repeatedly up her leg, though no wound was present. She risked a hard reboot, taking her implants offline to reset. For a moment she was a raw and primitive human without any augmentations, the lack of stimulation creating an emptiness inside only a datafeed could cure. Implants restarted with a faint hum inside her ears. Back online.

Four files. All she could grab was four sensitive files. Time to see what she recovered.

Yet the hard crash of exiting VR so suddenly left her dizzier than expected, and she shook her head to regain composure. A few seconds later, the box was yanked over her head and a man grabbed her, pushing her up against the tollbooth and telling his superior, "I investigated the alarms, Sir. It's her, she's alive, I don't know how but she's alive." A pause, then, "Yeah, she was snooping around your files. You really want me to drag her all the way out there, or just throw her off the platform nice and clean, let gravity do the work for us?" Another pause.

Ash kicked and screamed but she was too dazed to make an impact.

Then he ended the call by saying, "Research? Whatever you say. I'll transport her immediately." The blurry face looked Ash dead in the eye. "Night night, little glitch."

And the rest was darkness.

8

THE K.O.A. COMMUNE WAS A SERIES OF FLAT, METALLIC DISCS stacked upon one another at odd angles to form five-story buildings. Smaller, archaic dwellings sat around their bases. A canopy of solar panels ran across the geodesics of a central dome draped with ivy and the setting sun reflected off it like fireworks. Hovercrafts swarmed the perimeter with buzzing engines and flew over rooftops where trees grew. Florinik and other species moved goods to-and-fro in giant cargo trucks, or in quaint hand-pulled wagons. Old men hauled dormant cyborgs in rickshaws, but their bellies were much fuller for their position than they would have been in Nathril-Xoynsia or other areas, and the openness with which children ran through the streets made Severum relax. The guards seemed more a formality than a necessity, not on alert for raids as they had been in Amorpha.

The community must have had twenty to thirty-thousand inhabitants, but despite the bustle their expressions were calm. It was far from the refugee camp it used to be when Arcturus Vegas and O.A.K. had implemented the Great Rotation under military assault, though he doubted the entire encampment was as dedicated to ending inequality as she was.

Severum dismounted the Dijyorkvok—the tall, tan creature kicking up a dust storm on the worn trading route—and tied it to the nearest post. Plainly-clad women leaned over glass balconies to note his arrival, neither waving nor arming themselves. His vHUD augmented the city with neon labels showing popular destinations, prices of goods, populations of residencies, and areas to avoid.

A wooden bridge arched across a large pond in the center of the community leading to the palace. Although it was situated within all that polished metal and greenery, the palace was an unadorned stucco building, atavistic and unapologizing for its homeliness. The door didn't so much as open as crumble in his hands, the splintered wood jabbing his finger.

A male receptionist with a welcome video running across his shirt greeted him, "Welcome to K.O.A. What may I help you with?"

"I'm here to see Arcturus Vegas," he replied.

"Do you have an appointment?"

Severum slammed his hands down on the guy's desk, papers bouncing. "Do I look like I need a glitchin' appointment?"

"Yes," the receptionist replied, calmly shuffling his papers back into well-organized stacks. "Now, do you have one or not?"

The stance he had once carried no longer had the same impact. Hated to say it, but he had to be...nice. "I apologize," he mumbled, the phrase foreign on his tongue. "My back's aching and the pain mods haven't kicked in yet. I need to see her as soon as possible."

"We have secure channels for that."

"I can't rely on them. Still too risky, and something strange is afoot. I'm the Architect, by the way."

"The Architect?"

He sighed. "Yes, I replaced Gestalt, your founder when you used to be called O.A.K." The guy still looked puzzled, so he added, "History's important, you know. I'm what the A stands for in K.O.A."

"Oh, wow, I thought the word was just an extinct tree. She's on the ground floor down the hall. She refuses to sit in the penthouse suite, takes the lowly quarters and gives the suites to her custodians. Says their work is harder than hers. She's the real thing, you know."

"Damn straight." He headed down the hall and knocked on the secure door. Knocked again. Nothing. Then it opened. "Took you long enough," he said.

"I placed the door at the end of my task queue," Arcturus replied, avoiding eye contact and turning to sit at her desk.

Arcturus was a childhood prodigy, having specialized in the sociological impacts of human life extension, understanding society from its superstructure to its base, while understanding the body right down to its telomeres. In her late teens, her focus had given her the maturity to soar through the organization's ranks. Now, she was about his age. Her eyes flickered as if running calculations, but his presence wasn't among them. Her skin was creased with small mountains that smoothed into rolling hills as her expressions changed, her lips moving silently as if enraptured by an inner monologue. Her frizzy, white hair curled about her unadorned face and fell over a simple dark sweater that had replaced the elaborate leather jackets she had once worn. She lowered the opacity of the windows in the small office.

People retreated into their towers and traders took flight as night fell.

"The sun will rise again in two hours forty-six minutes," she said.

"That's why I'm here."

"Obviously. You neglected the duties of your position for years, leaving a gap in our leadership. You abandoned us once the so-called excitement ended, just like Thalassa. Seems it takes a global catastrophe to get either of your attention."

"Nothing less," he smirked, but Arc wasn't impressed. "Okay, it takes a paycheck."

"As you can tell, we have solidified our position on this hemisphere, and while we can afford to pay you, we will not do so."

"Because you expect your leaders to live as simply as you do," he replied.

"Wrong as usual. We promoted you due to necessity, not because we liked you. Your early attacks on us—"

"You had a traitor in your ranks before I ever joined. Gestalt was going to take you all down, and you're the one who shot her in cold blood, not me," Severum retorted, words outpacing his better judgment.

"Drink?" she asked, expressionless, ignoring his outburst and pouring a cup of white liquid at the desk.

He took the glass and leaned on the windowsill, the fumes rising to burn his nose as he downed it with a puckered mouth. "What the hell is this crap?"

"Palm toddy, made from fermented coconut sap. Very expensive. I do allow some pleasures."

"I appreciate what you've done here, and yes, I could have done better to support you after the Great Rotation. But I'm here now, and we need to discuss the increasing rotation cycles in addition to a strange anomaly I discovered in the terrain nearby. Here's what I know," he said, laying out his findings over the next ten minutes.

Arcturus finally rose. "We can provide you resources to divert the river's flow outside of Amorpha. Filtration is an option. As for these allegations regarding the Old Guard, you will find a cybernetics dealer downtown. Get what you need to investigate their labs properly and put it on our tab. I have seen enough death, however, and I refuse to provide you personnel to use like pawns in your slaughter. We lost enough in the Rotation War, mostly due to your poor leadership."

"They're calling it a war now, huh? I fought wars when I was young, and they were more than just a battle or two like you engaged in. At what point does a war become a war?"

"When loved ones die, Severum. When you watch Ciara, Ozone, and others fight against a standing military with no training because they believe that strongly in what they are fighting for. You lost an entire legion of troops during the insurrection, yet you call yourself a leader."

"Half of them left before we even got started. The other half couldn't even fire their Pulsers without overcharging them until they exploded in their hands."

"Maybe you should reconsider your role in life. Now, leave."

He slammed the glass down and it cut into his palm.

"Just leave."

9

ASH WAS HUNGOVER FROM HARD-JACKING OUT OF VR AND whatever had knocked her unconscious. VHUD flickered nonsense – GPS showed her halfway across the world. She scanned for injuries but nothing showed. Tried to communicate, but any incoming or outgoing signals had been blocked.

Where the hell am I? she fretted, rising from a cot on a concrete floor in a small room. *They must be holding me, same people who tried to kill me before. I got too close. I was ghosted though, and few people could have detected my actions in the network in such a short time. But why even keep me alive?*

Seamless white walls encased the room, which lacked any features save for a digital keypad, a fluorescent light, and a chemical smell as if the room had been recently cleaned. The door was locked and the keypad didn't accept a numerical code; must be cog-linked to her captors. Whatever was happening, she had to escape.

She removed the paper-thin sheet covering the cot and tore into the cheap fabric, using her weight to bend back two metallic springs. They popped loose. She lifted the bed and took the rubber caps off the bottom of their posts that prevented them from scratching the floor.

Returning to the keypad, she straightened the springs and inserted the ends into each side of a large screw holding the panel together. The panel came loose and fell, but she caught it to avoid the clank. A few wires connected to a small screen. Magnets in her forearm alerted her through vHUD that a live electrical current was present, highlighting the wires it was flowing through. The rest might be there to transmit audio and video, so she had to work fast. She placed the rubber caps over her fingers to prepare to cut the wires with a swipe of the springs, but there was still a risk of electrocution. Then she had a better idea.

She returned to the cot, stood it on end vertically, and poked the springs into it so they jutted out from the center of its height. Heaving the cot to the keypad, she aligned it, leaned it forward, and let it go. The cot fell and the protruding springs hit the keypad just right to stab the wires. Blue sparks jumped. The door clicked. A momentary relief. She cracked it.

The curved hallway was a series of smooth, white panels installed over an older structure. The gutted building showed through in areas, revealing rusted doorframes, worn paint, and a moldy smell. The lack of construction equipment or materials meant the remodel had been completed, despite the haphazard unfinished job, but why remodel an area designed to keep people illegally under lock and key? The building must have another primary purpose.

Lights flickered. Crooked employee safety signs hung over locked doors and she moved with measured steps, scanning the name placards on each door. No one she recognized, and if anyone was here they were silent. She leaned closer to a tinted office window. Scientific equipment had been piled inside. No one put employee offices near a prison cell. Either the cell had been quickly improvised, or the employees were also being held captive in nearby enclosures.

The building might have been originally intended to attract employees, but at some point whoever ran it gave up finishing the remodel and decided to just capture the right people instead. Hadn't Severum said a scientist had been kidnapped? She had been spiteful at the coffeeshop, her first night homeless, and had hardly listened. Whatever projects were being worked on here had to be illicit. What had she gotten herself into? There she was blaming herself again when she was the victim. She rubbed her hands through her purple bangs, one foot sprinting ahead and the other locked in place.

Rounding the corner revealed a lab with four armed guards surrounding a scientist in a long, white jacket with her back turned, focused on monitoring holographic readouts of the planet's rotation. That explained why Ash had been captured and not killed on sight; at some point they realized they needed her skills. Few people knew terraforming like she did, except her parents and their eldest professors. She sighed. Where would she be if they had stayed together, if Mom hadn't ditched her education to run the Aporia Asylum, always running from her problems, and if glitch-face hadn't fucked up the planet? Somehow, that thought was more powerful, more threatening, than the armed guards.

Curiosity drove her more than self-preservation. She slipped past the lab entrance. A barred gate sectioned off the next area. She turned back, but voices and footsteps resounded down the hall. The curved walls blocked her line of sight, but a few more steps and she'd be seen. Nothing to hide behind but a vending machine. She could enter the lab and pretend she was sent for duty, but when they discovered she had escaped they might lose patience and just kill her right there.

She pulled the vending machine from the wall with a scraping sound and scrunched her body behind it, her shoulder blades tense against her throbbing neck. The machine was protruding too far from the wall to conceal her, but she was in luck, as it had hid a small square-shaped hole above the floor, probably a large vent at one point. She lowered to her knees, legs jammed against the heat flushing from the back of the machine, and squeezed inside it. The hole was a dead end, but it let her wiggle the bottom of the machine back closer to the wall to be less conspicuous.

Blackness, her body a tight cube, chin on knees. Footsteps. The gate opened with a creak. She risked the scraping sound giving her position away and pushed the machine forward just enough to squeeze out, running through the gate before it shut. More people ahead. She opened a custodian closet where two dormant droids sat on spherical balls, and hid inside, closing the door inch by inch.

She stood in the dark, back to the wall in the tight closet, overhearing fragments of conversation for the rest of the day until she snapped to attention when a young man said,

"She escaped!"

"Their daughter. You mean the one with the weird name?" an older-sounding man asked.

"Yes. I understand she's one of the keys to this. We thought we could handle it, Sir, that the science wasn't above us to understand, but we're playing with fire here."

"Find her. We will bring back the glory of the Old Guard, or die trying," the older man replied. "Severum and his family are responsible for this and they're going to be the ones to fix it. We're going to speed the rotation up so fast that everyone will be forced to see how dangerous this technology is. Once they give up this absurd dream of playing god, they'll beg us to bring back order and rid the world of these daylight cycles, which have brought only destruction to my loved ones."

"But, Sir, that would plunge half the world back into darkness," the younger man argued.

"So be it. The Eastern Hemisphere will still be light, and accessible to anyone who can afford a vacation. I lost my children in the floods that Severum brought. The winds, the rains, the sinkholes, it's all broken beyond repair, and all this done out of some long-dead idealism. Equality doesn't build us up, it cuts us all down equally."

"Don't forget K.O.A.'s role in this. Should we, shall I say... *convince* some of them to join our efforts?"

"They know nothing. History says only their founder, Gestalt, truly understood terraforming the way Severum did, and she was shot by her own people. The one calling herself the Orchestrator, Arcturus, is protected by her commune, and Thalassa, the Kontractor hasn't been heard of in years, went off the grid."

"We'll recover the girl, Mr. Culptos, force her to cooperate, otherwise the whole planet's going to be crushed by your little exercise. It seems your dead children proved the technology was destructive enough without all this. But this isn't right; it's dangerous and it's going to fail."

"You ever think you should be more sensitive with the way you discuss my kids?" the older man, Culptos, growled. "You know, my father once said compassion is what drives us. It's our greatest quality."

"Agreed, that's what I'm saying."

"And also our greatest weakness."

A Pulser discharged and a plop hit the ground outside the custodian closet door, blood spilling beneath the doorframe. The older man cleared his throat just as the droids beside Ash activated, filling the closet with auriferous light. She tried to hold the door shut, but their metallic arms were far stronger and wedged it open.

The older man looked half back, Pulser still smoking in his hand, and smirked at the droids. "Now that's efficiency," he said, walking away.

Ash stepped out and cringed at the sight: brain goo on the walls, a young man's body on the floor, and a droid already cutting it open to remove its organs, no doubt to sell on the underground market. The droid took the organs down the hall, the gates opening for it, until it reached the vending machine. Its segmented fingers opened it and placed the organs inside the refrigerated compartment for preservation before closing the fridge casually as if it had just grabbed a soda. She was about to be sick, but with Culptos out of sight and one guard down, she had an idea.

She traveled further down the hallway to a barred gate and vomited so that it spewed through the bars. The cleaner droid left the vending machine, went through the first gate, and approached her next to the barred gate, issuing a command to make the bars rise to vacuum the mess. Ash bolted beneath them and down the hall, pulling a side door open as more men approached.

The brisk night air hit her. The few hover-lights that weren't broken illuminated the compound, their long tentacles dragging almost to the concrete. She recognized the area from terraforming class; it had formerly been referred to as the Twilight, the same place she had asked Severum to investigate due to its proximity to the rotational components.

Delivery trucks came and went in military convoys. She licked her chapped lips, the taste of bile still in her mouth. She could hitch a ride out in one of the trucks, but she'd never make it amidst the commotion. She hid behind a garbage incinerator instead, the stink of rotten food and discarded chemicals filling her nose. She counted the stars as she waited for the motion to calm, because if she was going to die, the stars were as good a last sight as any.

10

THE CYBERNETICS SHOP WAS A HOLE IN THE WALL, NOT EVEN A proper wall, but one that had collapsed in on itself because it was too lazy to stand. Body augmentations hung from heavy racks. Arms in all sizes dangled from hooks. Leg fittings were splayed upon rusted countertops beside sets of occipts floating in jars... But it was all crap. Severum grabbed a dingy suit of armor, but the metal was so heavy it would reduce mobility to nothing without the corresponding power generators, and he wasn't going to risk running out of fuel on a one-man mission. It was suicide anyway, but he had to prove himself, had to prove that age was just in his head, that the Great Rotation hadn't been in vain, and that his life meant a damn to that little girl with her mother's eyes who clung to his old jacket like it was a precious artifact.

The rest of the wares were no better, rugged, used. You don't attach a torso mod that's being held together with duct tape.

"What you here for, old man?" the young clerk asked, rubbing his goatee, and pulling at his dark soul patch. "Cock augs are in the back, please your woman as you age."

Severum had fought legions of Aphorids in his youth, didn't need to defend his masculinity against the likes of him. "Something to make me fly, and put it on Arc's tab."

"Oh, so you're the one she mentioned. But flying, that's some top gov' shit right there, man."

"You got it or not?"

"Nah, can't getta holda it."

"This stuff's trash. You're not installing any of this in my body."

"Too bad, it's toppa the line."

"No, it's not. Arcturus wouldn't be happy to know that you're hiding the good shit while making her pay full price for junk. Now, 'fess up."

The floor was dirty except in one spot where the thick dust had been scraped across it in an arc as if a door had swung open. He knocked on the wall in various spots, noting how hollow it sounded. It had been reinforced with too many studs for such a simple structure. The clerk cleared his throat. Severum turned and said, "I want whatever's back there."

"Then lemme show yous the back, for *special* customers. Name's Gus by the way, Gus Poteamorrow."

Gus used the back of a hammer to pry open a wooden panel, reaching behind it to hit a button. A hidden door eased open and they entered the backroom.

Severum shielded his eyes from the glare of the polished titanium pieces under the shop light. "Now that's more like it," he said, grabbing a few lightweight items and testing their flexibility. Yet, there was little in the way of weaponry; K.O.A. was more interested in building their damn utopia than protecting it. He grabbed a sniper rifle, the latest hover-boots, and a new Pulser, but it wasn't enough. "Got a grafter on call?"

"Always, my man," Gus nodded. "Clinic's right next store. When you schedulin'?"

"No time like the present. Who's the doc?"

"I am," he replied, rolling up dirty, blood-stained sleeves. "What we installin'?"

Moments later, Severum was knocked out with anesthesia by the best med-school dropout an unemployed revolutionist could afford. The recovery lasted a few hours, the painkillers doing their job, but he stayed another sunrise for monitoring in case his body rejected the augmentations.

A hovercraft waited for him when he left the clinic, courtesy of Arcturus. Now, to return to the research lab where the scientist was being held and discover what she knew. He adjusted the fit of his hover-boots and stretched the fingers of his new hand. Soon, he was off for the Twilight City, a one-man army.

———

HE PARKED the hovercraft near the airbus station and made the last way on foot like before, passing the tower where he had taken shelter from the storm. The Twilight City soon rose on the horizon, its walled perimeter cutting into the soil and stretching into the distance. He traversed the fog of war until he found a shortcut to get in. A drill had bored through one of the walls leaving a gaping hole.

He climbed through the wall and crossed the circuit-ridden terrain. Drones circled in the dimming sky as he neared the research complex. In response to the previous incident, he had a much larger audience this time: a whole security crew complete with new cameras at each entrance.

The guards were cybernetically enhanced judging by the size of their armor, but their patrol circles were lazy as moths circling a flame; when Severum darted between a stack of cargo boxes, they were more interested in shooting the breeze with small talk than shooting him. The drones had no such distractions, and upon kicking a single rock within their view by mistake, they turned and flooded the area with light. The guards investigated. Severum kept in the shadows behind the corner, tossing another rock to lure them away. The drones followed its motion, the guards followed their light, and Severum used the disruption to sneak across to the building where he had seen the scientist.

The main entranceway was necklaced with a tall, retaining wall. There were no cameras guarding the double door, and only a single guard at the desk inside. Puzzled, Severum scrolled through his occipital filters until the wall around the entrance lit up, flooding his vision with red light. The wall had thousands of nanosensors embedded within it, and that was some pricy tech, so they had skimped on the surveillance at the side entrances where they had planted simple cameras instead. They hummed as they swept the sidewalk. VHUD displayed each camera's viewing angle as a series of red cones superimposed across his vision. He kept his distance from the retaining wall and weaved between the camera arcs to get close enough to access them remotely, activating some background processes to do so. Lady Luck favored the bold, and even without making a direct connection, he busted through their authentication protocol and gained access to the video controls. He manipulated the cameras to repeatedly broadcast the same banal images.

The side door was electronically locked. Most of the windows were barred or too high to reach and betrayed only glimpses of activity inside, so this entry was as good as any other. Trying to hack the door remotely resulted in failures to establish a connection. He'd have to get down and dirty. He checked his three, six, and nine – no guards approaching at any angle. Taking a long wire from his supply pack, he jacked it into the back of his head, ramming the other end into a port on the keypad that was used to upload software upgrades in the event of network failure. The camera had been an easy hack, since it was transmitting data constantly, but the door had no need for communications and was much trickier. Ten, twenty, thirty seconds passed while he manipulated possible access codes with his infiltration programs. A guard rounded the corner, footsteps getting louder. He'd be spotted in a moment with nothing to hide behind but some newly planted corporate landscaping. Severum readied his hover-boots to abort the mission, but a second later the door popped open. He drew his Pulser, adjusted the sniper rifle on his back to fit through the door, and slipped inside the lab. Sometimes it took hours to get in while suppressing the alarm lockdown from too many failed entries, but the password had been short: *Sibin2*.

Too easy, he thought.

The small warehouse was full of large storage containers stacked on shelves thirty-feet high. A few open boxes displayed planetary maps, seismographs, hardness picks, electromagnetic meters, compasses, and other geological devices, but his implants provided him most of that. Hammers, chisels, and larger equipment, including small cranes, excavators, and tractors filled the rest of the space.

Beyond the warehouse, the low SMART ceiling illuminated the hall from the bioluminescent nanomachines built into its structure. He passed a few offices, noting the names on the placards. One office was missing a nameplate, likely vacant, and as heavy footsteps echoed around the curved hallway, he slipped into it.

The room had been gutted, no intel, nothing. Paper files were rare but he had hoped to find *something*. But wait... in the corner a single laptop had been shoved into a plastic bin with a rat-nest of wires. Unusual to find such an antiquated device. Tumbling his hands through the box, he grabbed the matching connector and ran the cord from the cognigraf hole behind his head to the laptop, accepting a flood of intel.

A hard heat pressed against his brain. Flaming arcs shot across his synaptic gaps, fiery tendrils lapping through his neural channels. He was overclocking, fast. He jacked out, removing the cable while throwing the laptop down with a clang. Something had hit him hard during the connection, knocking vHUD offline and stupefying him, the room spinning. He leaned on the wall for balance.

Guards rushed into the room, raising Pulsers and shouting, "You're coming with us!" They hadn't said, *You're under arrest, or Freeze,* for these weren't Enforcers. They ripped his Pulser out of his hands and grabbed his sniper rifle, patting him down for other weapons.

A young guy with a bleach-white face radioed out via vHUD, "Mr. Culptos, we got Severum." Then he turned to address him, "We knew you'd return, so we had a buncha kids run simulations. We gave 'em this whole place as a level in a downloadable content pack for the latest first-person shooter craze, *Shoot First, Ask Questions Later.* Then we studied their video feed from the game. Every player spawned, snuck around the side of the lab, played with the cams, found their way in like you did, and tried to recover the intel in the one unlocked office while waiting for the guards to pass. The simulations were correct, as always, and now here you are, rushing in like a hero to disable my men and steal our intel. Well, guess what? Take it."

"Stop taunting me and get it over with," Severum replied, biting his lip.

"Not until you do us a little favor," the guy remarked, pressing his Pulser into Severum's chest. "We'll give you all the intel you want. You're going to help us with this rotational crisis, help us take the system to the maximum devastation level, and then after the public outcry, revert it to the way things used to be."

"Why?"

"You a dumbfuck, ain't ya?" the other guard said.

The first guard continued, "So people can understand how

deadly this tech is. No more daylight cycles. They've brought only floods and destruction."

Another person judging him – some of them had Pulsers, some were armed with disgruntled stares and diluted hopes. "Something tells me you don't care about the environment. You people just want the power back that controlling light gave you. Well, I'd rather die than help you."

"Oh, that can be arranged, but not before a family gathering."

"A what? What do you mean? You better not lay a hand on her!" Severum's vision cleared from the cyberattack and he pushed forward. The guns jabbed against his chest, pushing him back against the wall. He had anticipated the move and used it as misdirection so he could reach under his shirt and tap the side of his stomach to open a hidden compartment large enough to hold two small containers. He toyed with the end of one of them.

"After all, your family were always the most precocious terraformers. We thought about kidnapping K.O.A. members to restore the Old Guard, poetic irony and all that, but no, they're just a bunch of stupid kids playing utopia. You're the real thing, the perfect geophysicist who will sacrifice everything for his loved ones. You'd slaughter a neighborhood for a few extra bucks, according to your file, just like you did with the bioluminaries years back."

"That was a long time ago, and it was your government that contracted the work to me." Severum muted vHUD and undid the R3p3@t grenade, but no explosion took place, for this was no ordinary explosive. A sharp shrillness hit the guards, a blast of noise that made them grimace and cup their ears. Severum shouted to give the grenade more input to work with. It echoed the sound through the guards' aural implants louder and louder with each cycling.

He only had a second left before they muted their ears, so he used the distraction to activate a CTTY grenade, causing their visual and audio feeds to reverse. Now they saw sounds and heard visions, but the visions they heard echoed until they were lost in synesthesia. They panicked, opening fire, but the Pulsers only burnt holes in the walls, and one another. Severum was already out the door, having grabbed his rifle and Pulser.

He retreated down the curved hallway to the warehouse, the guards falling in line behind him. Two more kicked open side doors to block his exit. He took cover behind some crates and the crane in the back of the warehouse while the guards hovered to take root on the high shelving.

Outnumbered.

He shook off the remaining dizziness from the mindjack and commanded vHUD to outline each foe. He activated Chameleon, going translucent, and fired, but no shots emitted. He had grabbed the guard's gun instead of his own by mistake, and it was linked to the guard's cognigraf signature. It deactivated with a dying hum. VHUD overrode the authentication protocol to get it back online, but not before a Pulser burned a hole in the wall over his shoulder. The next shot hit his gun and it exploded in a fiery shrapnel that penetrated his body armor to burn his skin. He was out of options. Sniper rifle would be useless at close range, and the rate of fire too slow to make a difference.

More firing. The guards closed in, but a high window offered him a chance. He jumped, pointing his toes down to activate the hover-boots he had acquired from K.O.A. He rose to the exit, but couldn't escape before four shots ripped through his body armor in the back. The impacts lurched him out the window and into a downward spiral as he fell outside the warehouse. He activated the final thrusts to stabilize himself, but his boots lost their charge and he landed hard on his side.

VHUD flashed a picture of his body in the corner of his eye, his ankle red with a note that read, *light sprain.* He swiped the image away, clearing his vision of the battlefield. Having hacked the side entry, he could unlock and lock the door remotely. He locked it, meaning the only way the attack force in the warehouse could get out was through that small window, one at a time, where he could shoot them down unopposed with his sniper rifle, unless they went around the long way to the opposing exit.

He used the last of Chameleon's charge to run up a small hill at the edge of the compound where he drew his rifle. He aimed at the window but no one emerged. They were either trying to override the door or circling around for the kill. Neither was true. A loud rumble shook the ground. The entire wall came crashing, the crane smashing it with a heavy crate. The attack force fired, but he was concealed on the hilltop, that is, until Chameleon sputtered its last pixels, draining his power reserves and giving his presence away.

Shit! He'd have to go full force. *Activate emergency reserves to power the hover-boots,* he commanded his implants.

Activating reserves will require more processing power to evenly distribute the remainder. Sensory inputs could be compromised, his suit advised.

Just do it!

Severum soared straight into the frenzy, turning on a full-body shield before the next firing round started. Shots hit the shield, denting the blurred ether, but the blasts flung right off it to strike back at the assailants. They grabbed their chests as their own shots burnt through their bodies.

Bloodshed was the last thing he wanted, but if it came down to them or him…

More guards ahead.

The reflector shield vanished. He raised his arm and flicked his wrist to fire disruptors. The single-use devices halted all electronic activity, but there was no telling how long the ceasefire would last. He rushed the nearest attacker, slamming his titanium-enhanced fist across his face with the sound of crushed bones grinding against themselves. He sent the next two assailants flying across the lot. The grafter had rocked out his upgrades. The guards backed off but one man came closer, enticed by the destruction and decay, just as the ceasefire was about to lift.

"Culptos," Severum spat.

The man said nothing, just drew an electrified whip from his side and lashed out at him. The strike just missed, the air fizzling where it had struck, leaving a ghostly vapor. One hit from that thing would send vHUD offline for good, while the next would paralyze him for life. Severum leapt over the next lash. The trail of azure sparks it left across the air seemed to cut into reality itself. He burned a few drops of hover-fuel to jump over the next one as well, coming close enough to kick Culptos across the face, but it didn't faze him. Severum grabbed his arm and squeezed it before the next strike, but Culptos twisted from his grip and dropped the whip, being useless at close range, and drew a searing dagger instead.

Severum parried two strikes but couldn't dodge the next. He raised his hand to take the blow, the blade burning as it serrated his skin, but his titanium fist stalled it. He knocked the blade aside and grabbed under Culptos' arms, burning fuel reserves to skyrocket him fifteen-feet in the air before throwing him over his shoulder. Severum half floated, half fell, while Culptos stumbled but landed on both feet.

"Leave my family alone!" Severum yelled.

"Never! You're the key to all of this, and you're to blame for everything that happened," Culptos snapped back.

Vision blurred, sound assaulting from all angles. Over-clocked. His enemy's position wavered.

Culptos took advantage and threw three hail-sized marbles over Severum's shoulder. They hovered to seek the ideal position, then opened fire, hitting him in the back where his armor was weak. He fell forward, pain burning up his spine.

Culptos kicked him in the face as the guards grabbed him from behind.

In one last desperate attempt, Severum sent an electric current through his metal hand, causing the guards to release him with a yelp, but they soon forced his arms behind his back.

"Shouldn't have returned," Culptos said, knocking Severum in the face again.

11

Hours burned from the tinder of anxiety as Ash hid from the guards' patrols, looking for a way out. Drones fluttered above in chaotic rhythms, casting a wide net of observation over the compound. Shots fired near the hills. Smoke rose behind the buildings. Then the side of the warehouse collapsed like a steel avalanche as a thundering boom shook the air. Guards rushed to meet the chaos while Ash took advantage to slip towards the back of the compound, away from the ruckus, climbing a service ladder three stories to a rooftop. Wind whisked across her face.

Enforcers circled the distant hills to watch two men fight. A whip of electricity sliced open the air, barely missing a familiar face. Oh no, Severum! He was sorely outnumbered and there was no way he'd make it. Ash watched from on high, cradling herself with her arms, for she would be next, and it was her fault he was here.

He was captured a moment later, and with it any hope she would escape; but she had come this far and wasn't backing down. Culptos would employ him just like he had meant to do to her. Sure enough, they dragged him inside the lab. But if she could break out, she could also break in.

Ash crouched behind an air conditioning unit on the roof and waited for the activity to die down. She reviewed the four files she had retrieved from the intel breach right before she'd been captured. The first two were garbage, but the third offered promise. It detailed recent financial transactions between Geosturm and the Government of Evig Natt, a regime that hadn't been recognized in ages. This was the proof she needed that Geosturm was connected to the rising of the Old Guard, but now she had to prove they were connected to the rotational crisis that was shortening days and exacerbating climate disasters. But she would be hunted non-stop until they were exposed. The fourth file was encrypted. She made backups, then dragged them across her augmented vision to place the icons over her pants pocket. VHUD would remember the muscle motions that had placed them there and would retrieve them if she reached into her pocket again, since she had programmed the shortcut.

She made way across the rooftop. A crane stood between the edge and the next building's roof. It was slick and steep, but it was safer to cross here, thirty-feet above the patrols, than to navigate the storm below. The height was nothing after working in a glass office suspended over the busiest city on the hemisphere. Gravity tugged at her ankles as she went weightless, leaping to the crane's angled arm, the impact of the machine slamming against her chest.

Before climbing it to the next rooftop, she slid down the crane arm, the metal cold and rough against her body, and entered the vehicle's cabin. Her hands swiped below the seats and frantically opened compartments; no keys. Her first promotion at Geosturm had provided enough upgrades to her cognigraf that she could wirelessly connect to a low-level device like the crane, if she could steady her nerves. She hunched in the seat and harnessed her thoughts into the crane's control console, running commands in vHUD to make the connection. If she sat still the connection would complete in one...two...three hours. A wired connection would drastically reduce the time, but the port configuration was unusual. This would have to do, as long as no one came to move the crane before she had taken control of it.

Calling Ikshana might give her an edge, but it was too risky, since the drones flew at the same altitude, and it would take at least three hours to arrive, if it could even follow her signal this far. She ran the lab's layout through her mind meanwhile, mapping it in vHUD so she could refer to it later. The plans were set and there was nothing more to think. That left nothing to distract her from the nail-ripping anxiety that flushed her mind with fire, tensed every muscle, and jerked her head left and right to peer through the cabin window at the patrols.

If death was coming, she couldn't stop it, but she would sure as hell look it in the eye.

12

THE GUARDS SAID NOTHING AS THEY PUSHED SEVERUM DOWN the curved, white hallway through the research lab. They had disarmed him, taken his hover-boots, and blocked his comms. The lab doors opened and the guard shoved him through the threshold. Holographic readouts showed the planet's rotational parameters at various angles and the devices regulating them. Power levels shot up and down on bar charts while line graphs detailed historical trends.

"Get to work!" the guard shouted. "She'll fill you in on the process." The guard pointed to a woman in a lab coat, who looked about the same height and build as the scientist he had returned to rescue in exchange for information, the woman he had seen only from the back.

She turned around, mouth agape, and raised her eyebrows. "Severum!"

What the hell was his ex-wife doing here?

Akasha ran into his arms.

The guard pushed her back, and when Severum retaliated he was met with a Pulser in the back. "Don't even think about it, pal."

The guard knocked him on the back of his head with the gun. He shook it off, steadied his vision, and bit back a retort. They would kill her after the project was over. He had lost enough already: his wife to his obstinacy, his youth to age, and his daughter's youth to fear. The paradox that killed him was how one could lose something they never knew they had. His ex-wife, Akasha'Shirod, had defied him twenty years ago by leaving without a word just like before, and he hated her for not being able to control her, to force her to love him, hated himself for thinking that one perfect year in college would be his entire life. But he'd kill anyone who messed with her just the same.

When the guards turned their backs, she approached him again and cupped his chin in her soft hands, lifting and tilting it as if examining an ancient artifact that would turn to dust if pressed too hard. Her long, dark hair had turned grey, given they were about the same age. But her dark skin and angled, intense features were as stunning as ever. He parted her hair to reveal her eyes, as if parting clouds so the sun could rise, and for a moment they were young lovers again, her countenance lifting all burdens, until he noticed the bruises down her face.

"After decades, we have come together again," she whispered.

"Unavoidable circumstances, yes."

"Fate," she corrected. "Ours is not a chance encounter. No matter how hard I strive to rid you from my life, here you are."

"I'd say you were pretty successful at getting rid of me. I just found out we have a *child*."

"When did you find out?" she asked with a steady tone that was far too casual.

"The other day," he shrugged, playing it just as cool. "You believe in fate whenever it's convenient, you know that? You could equally say fate's what tears us apart."

"Creation, destruction, cycles."

"Don't start," he murmured, looking for the guards' reaction, but they were distracted, flicking the air at whatever game they were playing in vHUD.

"After decades you *still* want to argue," she continued. "Okay, it wasn't fate that drove us apart, it was your insolence. Now, after spending a large part of my life opposing the rotation, trying to show the world how dangerous it was, a half-truth, I'm stuck here trying to make it more dangerous on purpose to make people want to restore the Old Guard. I'm not about to throw half the world back into darkness while killing all the new life-forms that have emerged on the other half."

"Your idea of fate has a wicked sense of humor. What do you know about the Old Guard?"

"When the Government of Evig Natt was replaced, some ruling members were impacted more than others. Those who were hit the hardest by political changes want their power back. I don't know what to do. They'll kill me if I don't comply, and even after devoting my life to being the Head Priestess of the Aporia Asylum, my goddess has abandoned me."

"Mine, too," he replied, squinting with more bitterness than affection. "You hid Ash's existence from me for her entire life. I can't get over that, and not a planetary crisis or an armed guard is going to distract me from that thought."

"I protected her from you and your lifestyle," she said, voice shaky as if not believing herself.

"No. You knew as long as she was aware of my existence that you and I would have to interact through the years, and you couldn't run fully away like you always do when there's trouble."

"I told her about you," she muttered between her teeth.

"In such a negative light that she never wanted to see me until her life was on the line and she had no choice. You robbed me of not only your presence, but what was probably the best part of my life."

"As if it was all my fault," she accelerated, the guard looking over. She lowered her voice, "You stole from me my feelings, my idealism, my love for life, my ability *to* feel, and the core of my being with your callous disregard for everything that made me who I was, a living, breathing, *feeling* creature at the mercy of your judgment. I became like a machine, and too much like you. You only think of yourself."

"That's not true," he countered.

"Really? You can see I'm injured but you haven't even asked if I'm okay."

"Get to work." The guard reiterated.

Akasha continued, "Look, I have evidence that connects the Old Guard of Evig Natt to the shortening days and the worsening ecological crisis." She pretended to examine diagrams at a console.

"Ash is looking into the connection between them and her former employer, Geosturm, who just tried to kill her," he added.

"Oh, Goddess, no. You didn't bring her into this, did you?"

"Of course not, she brought *me* into it," he insisted.

"I said, get to work!" the guard screamed, raising his gun at her.

Severum raised his hand to protect her, but within seconds two more guards arrived.

"Let's hope she's as far away from here as possible."

A crash resounded as a large crane scraped across the building, slammed through brick walls, and swept through the lab. The cabin was empty – someone must be controlling it remotely. The guards were stunned, but Severum had trained his combat reflexes for decades and reacted immediately, running behind them to smash their heads together with his augmented hand, and grabbing their Pulsers, so they wouldn't be used against Akasha.

They rushed outside through the fallen wall, jumping over the cinderblock foundation. A small delivery truck slowed. He looked for concealment but it was no use – they were in plain sight. Guards crawled over the rubble behind them, their tools clinking on their belts, their Pulsers humming.

Severum rushed for the truck and leapt upon the door railing, about to rip the driver out until he caught glimpse of her. "Ash!" he yelled, waving his right hand as the other held onto the door.

Akasha ran around the other side and grabbed a seat. The truck sped down the route towards the airbus station with Severum still gripping the door. Ash rolled the window down and he crawled through as Akasha gripped his hands to pull his body across the middle seat.

"Hell of an entrance." He applauded his daughter.

Two hovercrafts took shortcuts, in hot pursuit across the uneven terrain that caused Ash to veer around rocks, broken machinery, and mud puddles. The crafts approached at both sides, firing Pulsers that burnt through their doors, the steel blossoming bright orange. Ash swerved and the next shots missed, but the truck was up on two wheels wobbling.

Severum shifted his weight to keep the truck grounded and aimed out the window, even though his Pulsers couldn't fire. One driver backed off at the sight to reposition. The other driver swerved his craft to aim, but Ash pulled the wheel hard to the right, crashing into it. It flipped and threw the driver from its seat. Severum gripped what remained of the truck door in his titanium hand and ripped it off its hinge, throwing it back at the remaining hovercraft. The craft tumbled across the terrain, the driver abandoning ship before it exploded downhill.

But it wasn't over. Giant crystalline structures emerged from the ground. They shot up like bright green javelins, as if the planet was protesting their escape.

Ash weaved through the crystal forest, scraping the sides of the craft against the brittle rocks. She slammed the pedal and they crashed through the final crystals, banging against the seats from the impact, then headed into the open landscape.

"What the hell was that?" Severum asked.

"The planet spoke," Akasha said.

"Mom, what are you even doing here? You've been gone since forever," Ash said.

"I was kidnapped. Surprised you even knew I was missing."

"Well, you usually hide and run away for months when you're upset. I guess that's Severum's fault, too," she slighted.

"Wha— what do you mean? He said you brought him here."

"That's not what I meant," she snapped.

"Severum's already turned you against me, huh? Figured as much."

"He came because he wanted to protect me when no one else would."

"You ain't so bad at protecting yourself, y'know," Severum told her. "Now, let's give it a rest. Just be glad we're outta that place."

On the way to the airbus station, Ash relayed the events that had brought her to the research compound and the evidence she had gathered. Akasha shared her findings, and Severum added what he had overheard. They agreed to go to the media once they reached Blutengel, since the Enforcers might be playing both sides. One thing was certain, with Culptos blaming Severum for the death of his children, he wouldn't stop until he had his revenge.

Nearing the station, they abandoned the truck and took the next airbus back to Blutengel. Ash had swept down to save her parents, but the trail of blood behind them grew longer each day, and it led to the heart of a city that had none.

Part II: *Terra Aqua*

PART II

TERRA AQUA

13

Severum woke in a cheap hotel off the grid. Ash and Akasha were in the next room. He had gathered a few basic belongings before checking in the night before, but staying at home for any length of time was a death sentence. On the way over, they had agreed to go to the media with what they had learned, including the evidence linking the disaster at Geosturm and the rotational crisis to the Old Guard. Time was getting short, the days even shorter. A news forecast showed a schedule of how many more sunrises could be expected per day by the year's end.

After breakfast, the three of them took an airbus to Samole News Media, the central agency behind all the news on the Western Hemisphere. It was an imprint of the Invisible Hand. Though the government ran the media, the New Order kept it fairly well balanced, though public advisories had more to do with new product launches than healthcare. Coverage ran of everything from mass shootings to the climate crisis, the feed directly hitting one's occipital lobe for processing without needing to be physically seen. Some people minimized it, kept the hate and violence in a background window as if tucking it beneath their watering eyelids, out of sight out of mind, since it was too much to handle. Others kept the headlines running across their vision throughout the day, nodding their heads as they walked to *like* the stories that brought them the most entertainment, the most novelty, for that's all the news had ever been. People paid attention to each violation, while ignoring the factors that created them.

The media complex was a series of white, hexagonal buildings arranged like a molecular diagram – the chemistry that made society tick. Severum and his family approached the main building. The curved glass doors parted like lips, the entire façade a giant mouthpiece without a brain. They entered, Severum taking the lead and scanning for cameras in vHUD. The entire lobby lit up – the whole place was a camera with nano-surveillance everywhere.

Severum approached the receptionist, a female automaton that looked almost human despite the thin indentations where her segments had been welded. Pink eyeshadow extended beneath each eyelid in a triangular shape. She smiled and said, "Welcome!" Then, her smile faded, but not in the natural way a human smile dissolved – like a sunlit wave that quietly returned to a stoic sea – rather, her facial muscles jerked into the emotive configuration of a predetermined movement.

Severum was used to people calculating their emotions, twisting their face into whatever countenance custom demanded, so it didn't perturb him, for there was nothing more human than people pretending to give a damn when they were just waiting for the workday to end. "We got a media tip, and boy, it's a big one," he announced.

"Third office upstairs to the right."

Severum stepped onto a platform that was connected to a steel beam like a giant seesaw. The lift rose as the counterweight lowered on the opposite side.

The third office door was parted, the space tight and

unadorned except for a man with a short haircut so precise only a machine could have trimmed it. He projected his eyes onto the walls to enlarge his vHUD screens, showcasing the latest news-feeds about to be promulgated, then met Severum's gaze. "Severum, is that you?" he asked, raising his eyebrows.

"Guilty as charged."

"My, it's been years. How have you been?"

"Well, I'm still alive."

"Hello, Aurthur Fitzgerald," Akasha acknowledged.

"Ah, the woman who didn't realize her cave was made of windstone," Aurthur chuckled, but his expression was more contrived than the receptionist's.

"I left the Aporia Asylum decades ago," she softly said.

Ash giggled.

"Do you wish to address me?" her mother asked.

"No, no, it's just... he's wearing sunglasses. You mean, old people don't use occipital filters?"

"I'm not that old; I'm almost your father's age," Aurthur said. "And my sunglasses are my most prized possession. I was part of O.A.K. back when we got the planet to rotate fast enough to escape its tidal lock. I grew up studying communications, working lame jobs, painting, but mostly dreaming. Then I met Severum. Never imagined I'd see the sun, but here I am wearing sunglasses because I refuse to shut the blinds in my office. Funny, you almost look like Akasha."

"She's my daughter," Akasha replied.

"*Our* daughter," Severum corrected. "In any regard, I have a tip for you."

"Straight to business as always, old friend. Does it have anything to do with the planet spinning out of control?"

"Funny you ask."

"Figured you were responsible."

"Now, wait," Severum retorted. "This isn't my doing. Some-one's messing with our work, and we have evidence that the Old

Guard are connected to it. They're purposely amplifying the negative ecological impacts of the rotation to scare people into ridding the world of its newfound daylight cycles."

"Now that would be a story," Aurthur admitted.

"They want people to overthrow the New Order and put them back in charge, back to the way things used to be. I want you to expose them. Given your agency's connections, and opposition to these people, I don't expect any resistance."

"I've spent my life resisting everything, especially a risk this large," Aurthur replied. "Send over the evidence and I'll see what I can do."

"This will make your career as a journalist."

"I gave up being famous long ago. It's all masturbatory."

"I'm saying I wanna be *paid* for this, Aurthur."

"Oh yeah, sure, we can make your life a little easier if the info is what you say it is."

"Sending you the files. Take some time to review and contact me when you're done."

"Sure thing."

"Also, I need some intel on that Culptos guy referenced throughout the docs."

"Whoa, now, I know who you're referring to, but I'm living a quiet life. No can do."

"Come on, man," Severum pleaded.

"I know the name well enough to pretend I don't. I'll look into the rest, but implicating him… the higher-ups will have to discuss that. We don't need a war between the New Order and the Old Guard."

"Don't we now?"

"I'm a family man now, Sev'. Opal and I have a son about your daughter's age. His name's Willow. Besides, I don't think you'll find much info on someone like that without a hefty price. Anyway, you want to catch up sometime?"

"Of course," Severum replied, "but first, I need to catch up with my... family, if they even let me call them that." He walked out of the office, not waiting for their expressions.

14

MANDELBROT'S. BOUNCER WASN'T BOUNCING, HE WAS SLOUCHED against the wall high on whatever neuralmod he just downloaded. He hissed some promises to a deadbeat deity that he'd stop tripping, but it was all fluff, and Severum would find him next week, same time, same place, same condition. Severum didn't bother to provide a fake name. He'd blown his cover at the club a dozen times before, and being an iconoclast, it was pointless to avoid who he was.

Groups nodded as he entered, his bones creaking across the sticky floor like an unoiled gate. Each corner of the club was lit a different color: puke green, raw pink, jaundiced yellow, and blue – just blue. Booths were arranged in long curves like abstract painting strokes. Men in borrowed suits leaned close to would-be lovers clad in black leather straps and hot pink latex. Smooth ice cubes melted in glasses warmed by soft hands that were always concealing something in the cusp of their palms. Each year, the memories Severum had of when he had brought Akasha here in their college days got hazier, like the cloud that coiled about the ceiling. All that smoke, and somehow, Ash had been the product of that fire, a fire that had burned out far too soon.

"It's on the house," the young barkeep said, sliding him a drink.

The barkeep must be forty, but he kept thinking of people as *young* when he simply met *younger than himself,* as if his age was the measuring stick for everyone. He downed the whiskey with a sharp burn, then took another shot for having to see Akasha again. "Actually, make it three," he said, resigned to what was. "Three doubles."

He had performed his own investigation earlier, but like Aurthur had anticipated, there was little information on Culptos. The guy slipped through the matrix like a skater on a roller coaster, but that ride was going downhill fast if Severum had anything to do with it. He stumbled from the repellium barstool, and made his way to a familiar face standing in the corner buried in the purple haze of the raw pink section of the club. The woman leaned against the wall with two searing daggers strung in an X across her back. Her dark, Aphorid-hide jacket met plaid pants in alternating black and yellow. A white wave of gelled hair flared like a tidal wave frozen right before it crashed. She had lived her entire life in that surging, tumultuous moment.

Thalassa Latimer.

"Let me guess," she said, crossing one leather boot over the next. "You're here to play catch-up, share a few old times, and after the memories are rehashed we'll realize we really have nothing in common and I'll get a few more decades without seeing your face before I die. How'd you even find me, you son of a glitch?"

"My daughter tracked you down. You're supposed to be the elusive, traceless woman, yet here you are."

"And you're supposed to be an asshole, so at least one of us is fulfilling our role," Thalassa scorned.

"First neuralmod addiction, now you're drinking to escape. Really on the way up, huh?"

"Tell me, dear old friend," she slurred from the corner of her mouth, coming close and wrapping her arm around him, "how many times you condemn people for doing those things that come natural to you: the mods, the drinking, the violence." She blew smoke in his face with a long, drawn-out exhale.

Severum coughed and twisted his outage into a laugh, for it was all he could do in the face of such a truth.

"It's called projection," she continued. "Arcturus used to say I did it to her constantly when we were together. I got sloppy after the breakup. I mean, even your kid tracked me down. Funny how your name is known by everyone in this place, but despite Arcturus and I being the heart of O.A.K. and creating K.O.A., no one recognizes us. A man does a few small, good deeds and he's heralded as a hero, while the women running the operation aren't even forgotten by history, they're never known to begin with, just as Selene is cursed to only reflect Helios' light."

"I see you've been studying the ship's archives, the old myths, what remains of them anyway. Heard they turned the colonizing Earth ship into a museum."

"You're avoiding the issue."

"Fame's not all it's cracked up to be. Right now I need to disappear, but I gotta know some things first, things even my precocious child can't figure out."

Thalassa sloshed a drink back and slammed it on the corner table. "So you really bred, then? Like the actual downloadable content of life? You got someone other than yourself to pay attention to? I figured you were being a smartass when you mentioned it earlier. Betcha were a deadbeat, weren't ya?" she smirked, as if there would be some victory in him saying yes.

"Drop the act, Thal. I just met her the other day," Severum replied, looking down.

A devil and an angel tugged at her face on either side, twisting one side into a grin, and the other into an empathetic frown.

He spoke to the frown side, "I need you to track down someone as elusive as you used to be."

"I doubt he did what I did to remain inconspicuous, living halfway around the world in an ice cave. If your daughter could locate me then she could probably find the guy you're after," she shrugged, folding her hands. "Oh, I get it, you'll put me at risk but not her, is that it?"

"On the comms side of things she's about as good as Aurthur Fitzgerald was at her age, but your skills have become legendary in the community."

"And why you think I would agree to this after all we've been through, huh, Sev'?"

"*Because* of all we've been through. The days are getting shorter, Thalassa."

"Thought it was just my libido and my temper."

"Focus! The Old Guard is trying to undo all the progress we made. Don't you care?"

"Progress? Hard to call it that. Meet the new boss, same as the old boss. Yeah, there's daylight, and inequality ain't as bad as it used to be, but the flooding gets worse every day, plus we got sinkholes to contend with now, swallowing whole glitchin' neighborhoods."

"The Old Guard's exacerbating the effects of the rotational increase to make people want to return to the way things were, shove the hemisphere back into darkness. Help me out here; what do you say?"

"I'll think about it," she replied. "I'm heading home now, but I'll probably be back tomorrow."

"Listen, you're here drinking alone, bored as can be, and whenever the excitement ends you usually end up doing something stupid anyway. That's why you joined O.A.K., then left it after the Great Rotation. That's why you got into a relationship with Arcturus only to have it fail when life settled in. You're a runner, a netrunner, made to skyrocket across the web because you can't stand sitting still. That about sum you up?"

No callous remark, no bullshit, just a solemn face staring into her empty glass. "I walked out on Arcturus 'cause I wasn't good enough for her, wasn't smart enough, too impulsive, too unpredictable. Couldn't live by her rules and routines. And she constantly judged me for everything I did. The same careful attention to detail I admired when she was planning a revolution, well it put a stranglehold on even simple tasks like washing laundry. I'm to blame; it's all my fault. I couldn't be what she wanted. What's she been up to, anyhoo?"

"Building a utopia without you."

"Figures. Always the believer. Yeah, you beat me down enough emotionally that I'll help you," Thalassa agreed. "Send me your intel and I'll get to work. Who is this son of a glitch you want me to investigate, anyhoo?" she asked, taking some random person's drink and sloshing it in her mouth.

"Goes by the name Culptos."

She spit her drink out and a brown mist shot across Severum's face. "You should have told me that to begin with. Would have been a very short talk."

"You in or not?" he replied, wiping his forehead with his sleeve.

"I'm in. Never was much for good judgment."

———

ASH'S FAMILY was together for the first time in her life, but the pieces were forced, didn't quite fit right. It was a wonder she was ever conceived. If her parents were fighting she would get it, but they didn't say a word, as if decades of silence hadn't been long enough. At least Mom had agreed to rent a house on the edge of town a week ago, but the space just kept them further apart. Home was just a safehouse; there was no nesting instinct at play, none of her mother's paisley-styled rugs or beaded curtains, or paintings that changed based on your aura. The little they had was still in boxes. They weren't going to fall in love again overnight, if ever, but something needed to erupt, even if they only created hell for one another. They had given up on even that, for the opposite of love wasn't hate, it was apathy.

Ash kept contact with the outside world to a minimum. Having few friends made that harder, not easier, for she had barely glimpsed the larger world she longed to be part of. Her life was just beginning, but each day she was reminded of the end: Mom checking the locks over and over, Severum looking over his shoulder every few minutes and projecting images of the street outside, and the two of them flinching at every shadow through the closed curtains. It was the only time their bodies moved in sync. That was probably how Severum had spent his life, given that he had betrayed the government that had hired him way back to join O.A.K. Somewhere, Culptos was trying to take everything that was left away from them.

News feeds showed the city's floods worsening as the sun wore upon virgin glaciers. New homes were being built on stilts across the street, anticipating that this would soon be waterfront property, even when they were more than fifty miles from the sea.

Severum approached her, projecting a shimmering holographic face on the wall from his right eye. "We got the intel back from Aurthur's investigation into the files you stole. Seems like a man was mediating the financial transactions between Geosturm and the Old Guard, a guy by the name of SinSeer."

"So we track him, and it'll lead us to the heart of Culptos' operations," she replied.

"He's dead, Ash."

"Dead? But those transactions were recent."

"Culptos is covering his tracks, probably in response to our escape and the media investigation that Aurthur's leading."

"Wait, I recognize him. Culptos killed him while I was hiding in the closet back at the lab. He tried to warn him that his plan was dangerous and would fail."

"That means he planned to cover his tracks from the start, and the attack on your workplace was part of that," he replied. "I'm so glad you're okay."

"I'm fine, Severum, thanks for asking," she said, and at the mention of his name, Mom looked around as if she had done something wrong.

"Glad you two are bonding," she sniped, walking away.

"I also received information from Thalassa on Culptos' background," Severum continued. "Some of it we knew. He lost his children in the floods and blamed it on O.A.K. and I. He survived the Aphorid attack on Governor Borges' cabinet the day the conference center sunk into the sinkhole during the explosions."

"The attack that killed the governor and toppled the Old Guard for good?" Ash asked.

"Yes, the one Thalassa and I led. He reacted by trying to get police forces to restore order, but things were too chaotic. A scion of the government had been waiting for an opportunity to rise to power, and the collapse of the global economy was just the right catalyst. The onset of daylight cycles devalued the firefly currency and people were outraged, especially since Thalassa had already killed off their pocket change, having released a virus that went on to infect their reserves. The New Order found it easy to pick up the power that had been lying in the streets and moved on without Culptos. He went off the grid for years while the Old Guard lay in wait to reseize control."

"Then what made him choose to act now?"

"We don't know. For one thing, he's getting older. Probably glorifies the old days simply because they benefited him more, at the expense of everyone else. Isn't that the nature of evil?"

"That's an understatement. I saw him kill that guy, saw my

co-workers plummet hundreds of stories to their death because they *might* have known something that would threaten him, something Geosturm hadn't had time to cover up yet, like the classified files I stole." Ash paused.

Maybe that was what started it all. Maybe if she had never accessed those classified files, there'd have been no reason to kill her co-workers and her. The guilt pressed out from within, dug under her fingernails, but regardless, some things shouldn't be kept quiet no matter how destructive they might be once in the open. But she had made a choice to put everyone at risk. No, it would have happened regardless with Culptos intent on exacting vengeance against her family, and she couldn't have known. But all those deaths…

"You okay?" Severum asked.

"Fine," she replied, shaking, hands sweaty, vision blurring.

"Come on, take deep breaths. You asked how I deal with guilt. Sorry, I didn't know how to respond that day. I don't know how to deal with it. You can believe that you were forced to make certain decisions and exonerate yourself of responsibility, like a narcissist, or you can take the world's suffering as your own as if being a martyr's honorable. Maybe it is, but both just lead you to the bottle. Ask Thalassa."

"Then what do I do?"

"Accept the stillness of the present moment, and work to become who you want to be in the future. It starts with learning to control your thoughts before they become action, and in turn harden into your habitual character. If you're going to label who you are, choose positive traits in which to know yourself."

"I'll try."

"That's all we can do," he said, placing a hand on her shoulder. "So, the media is still evaluating whether they'll release the story."

"Good. Until then, I want to meet Thalassa," Ash said.

"Why?"

"I think I can get through to her, solicit more assistance," she lied.

"Good luck. Here's an address and her contact info. She said she'd be at Mandelbrot's again tomorrow. Let me tell you a bit more about her first."

———

IN HER UNADORNED ROOM, Ash changed into a pair of white vinyl pants, one leg full length and the other terminating at her upper thigh, the hem sealed tight enough to leave a red indentation on her skin. She pulled on a frilly pink shirt Mom had bought her but screw it. She ripped the top three buttons loose.

"You're wearing *that?*" Akasha accosted her as Severum left the room, not even commenting on the garment's destruction. Probably forgot she had given it to her. "Regardless, you don't need to go out."

"Oh, so you can go halfway across the planet, abandoning Severum to live with a bunch of stinky Aphorids in a cave with a dozen men dressed in robes, but I can't go out tonight?"

"That was before you were born, Ash."

"Same story. He's here and you don't love him."

"Don't label my feelings."

"Let me guess." Ash faced her head-on. "If you didn't love him you wouldn't have run away?"

"You hacked my journals?" Akasha accused, hand over her mouth.

"No, I just thought of the most illogical excuse I could think of," Ash replied, slamming the door on the way out.

"You're just like him!" Akasha yelled from behind the door, loud enough for the entire neighborhood to hear, but they didn't care. No one cared.

Ash boarded an airbus and pressed her face against the windowpane, cold as her mother's glare. The bus took off with a *vrroosh* down the tube and soon stopped at Mandelbrot's. A long line of punks stretched down the cracked pavement around the corner. She disembarked and butted in line, body checking the bouncer on the way in. She peered over her shoulder – bouncer was taking a good hard look at her ass and had no qualms about her entering. She gave him the finger and opened the second set of doors.

Techno thumped. A woman with a blue vest and black pants danced on a raised platform in the center of the club. Knee-high socks ribbed with alternating green and orange died into pink-laced boots that shuffled on rhythm with the infectious beat.

"I'm looking for Thalassa," Ash yelled up to her.

"Beats me," she shrugged, but Ash followed her eyes as she glanced in the corner of the club.

A middle-aged woman hung up her trench coat and leaned against the wall, leaving only a skinsuit for clothes. A flexible screen a few millimeters thick wrapped around the suit. Where her body curved, the screen curved with it. When she stretched, the screen stretched with her. The skinsuit ran static at first, then showed a digital recreation of her naked body, bypassing laws against public nudity. She raised her arm; the screen showed a digital representation of it. When a drunkard looked her up, she changed the screen to shift her image to depict male genitalia. He cringed with disgust and walked away.

From the way Severum had described her that had to be Thalassa. Ash met her gaze. Thick wrinkles creased around her lips to merge into battle scars, the years carving themselves into her face not gracefully, like they did with most women, but with thrashing defiance. "That was pretty neat," Ash told her, smiling and looking down to the side.

"Just a toy, though I do wish I could switch gender out as easily as switching computer components, but the skinsuit lets me pretend," Thalassa said, inhaling a joint. "Programs run about the same regardless of the shape of the hardware, or the input-output configuration. Humans are fluid like that."

"Fluid, like your name, referring to the sea."

"You think you know me? Who told you I was here?" she asked, straightening her back and lowering her brows.

"Severum. I'm his dau– daughter."

"You're his daughter?" she burst out laughing. "I'm so sorry. I'm so, so sorry."

"What do you mean by that?"

"Least you have an excuse for any fuck-ups you make in life," Thalassa smirked.

"That's what I'm trying to avoid. What was Severum like in the old days that makes you say that?"

"Is that why you came here? What, you looking for me to tell you he was a saint and the system ruined him? He was always an asshole. Lost, confused, clinging to some over-aggrandized image of masculinity typical of his generation, and then guilt-tripping himself over doing so, which he then solved, of course, by being more violent."

Ash pondered what duty she had to maintain Severum's honor. Was that duty based on parental investment, and if so, since he hadn't had the chance to invest in her, should she assume he would have been worthy of her defense? Or was it not about reciprocation; does one always have the duty to defend one's parent, even if the connection doesn't extend into the distant past? Confused, she simply replied, "So he was caught in a vicious cycle. Did he love Mom, though?"

"That glitch? Oh, of course. They dragged one another across the hemispheres kicking and screaming, sometimes literally, like when he had her abducted without even realizing who she was. Let me tell you some stories," she invited, passing the joint.

After fifteen minutes of relaying their history, Thalassa said. "Think about it, just think," pointing to her head and poking herself in the eye by accident. "Your parents are reflections of one another's worst qualities. Somehow, their best light got filtered out of their relationship. Akasha protects those slimy Aphorids, yet condescends to every human being she meets, but yeah, I'm supposed to call her a priestess. I don't get either of them, but it's not my problem," she shrugged. "Fifty some odd years go by and you become comfortable with what you know, and even more comfortable with what you don't need to spend your remaining days figuring out. You also pay for your partying fifty times harder," she said in a raspy voice, drawing another smoke.

"Don't worry, this stuff's weak," Ash said.

"Just wait on it."

"Any advice on what to do about Culptos?"

"What he's up to requires bribing a lot of people in the right places. That's bound to leave more paper trails if he hasn't covered all his tracks yet. So much destruction…"

"Do you regret increasing the planet's rotation?"

"Everything I've done has led to its undoing. Everything I've revealed has led to more secrets. We all hate the floods, but it's a minor price to pay for daylight, if it lasts."

"If someone wanted to make the flooding worse, without impacting the rotation further, how would they do this?" Ash asked.

"Install solar mirrors over the icecaps. We considered using them to reflect light across the planet in the past. Problem is, the array is too easily sabotaged. Break a mirror that large and it's like seventy eons bad luck."

"Modifying greenhouse emissions then?"

"Too long to take effect," Thalassa replied. "Men who take big risks are near-sighted."

"Manipulation of rainfall through cloud seeding?"

"Too obvious. Are there any major dams in the region? That would be a lead," Thalassa said.

"There's one being built on the Élivágar River, but the

existing ones wouldn't provide a large enough impact. I mean, dams are big things, and big things make really big things happen. If they didn't, they wouldn't be big."

"Shit's good, huh? Hits you just right."

"Better than neuralmods," Ash agreed.

"If I wanted to increase the floods' effects, I wouldn't touch the water at all," Thalassa said. "I would make the land lower."

"Whoa."

"There are silt deposits all over the place. It'd be easy to make the sinkholes worse if you could redirect the water where you wanted it."

"The uniforms I saw. Geosturm was redirecting waterpipes outside my building. They could be purposely trying to create sinkholes."

"Let me bring up a list of recent land sales in the area." Thalassa paused, flickered her eyes across a virtual keyboard, then said, "Sure enough, if you line the sinkholes up with the land sales, three properties were sold right before sinkholes swallowed them, as if the owners knew they were going to sink. That's important, 'cause insurance don't cover natural disasters, the so-called acts of god. If there was actually a god, it wouldn't allow such loopholes."

"Who do the properties belong to?"

"Records state they used to be government buildings, but when the Old Guard fell, they went into private hands. My guess is they belonged to Culptos or one of his old associates."

"Thanks. Can you send me the data?"

"Done."

"I'm sending it to Aurthur Fitzgerald to add to the media report, if they agree on releasing it."

"He used to be Severum's best friend, you know. Severum considered the sacrifices he made for him to be entirely irrational, but there's no rational justification for being alone in life."

"Severum says you're here a lot, alone in the corner," Ash said.

"Friends get older, they die."

"Or you push them away like Severum said you did Arcturus."

"Utopia's a dream, a place in the mind only." She toked long on the joint, swept her head around the hazy club, and concluded, "I've got mine right here. It's all smoke and vapor in the end, Ash. Now, off with you."

"Nah, I think I'll stick around. Seems you know what's up."

"Then lemme show you how to have a good time," she smirked.

———

ASH STUMBLED in the door laughing with a young man with dreads down to his waist. They buried their tongues in one another's mouths in the foyer, then rushed to her room, kicking the door shut behind them.

Akasha stood before Severum in a black nightgown, fire in her eyes as she spoke, "You don't even care about the guy she brought home?"

"She's an adult," Severum shrugged. "Have her pre-order an abortion if you're concerned. Couple clicks and it's done, download the neuralmod, that's it." He threw his hands up in frustration.

"See, you're not a father."

"Why the hell would I care who she sleeps with? Pleasure's pleasure, and if you can reap it from this life then the more the better."

"You used to be so moderate, now, listen to yourself."

"I wasn't against pleasure, I was against addiction."

"All pleasure's addictive. Desire only breeds more desire."

"Well, people need something to offset the pain you bring

them," he shot back, immediately regretting it as the words slipped out, unable to be reeled back. He braced for the backlash, tears or rage or something, some validation that he existed. But there was nothing, just apathy.

"What about her emotions? A girl's heart can get wrecked at that age, at any age."

"Only thing wrecking her is whatever she took at the club."

"You don't know that."

Damn, why do I keep getting drawn into this? he asked himself.

Akasha forced open Ash's bedroom door; their daughter shrieked, and the guy pitched a fit. Severum slipped out into the cool night air. He hadn't reaped the rewards of having a family, so he sure as hell wasn't putting in the work tonight. He had given enough already by returning to the lab.

He was interrupted a minute later when the guy followed him out and screamed in his face on the porch, "Glitch ain't worth it anyway."

Severum pounded his reinforced hand into his upper chest, slamming him against the brick of the house. "Watch your mouth, kid."

"What are you, modded? I'll turn you in," he spat.

"Then let me make it worth my while."

"No, no, you're fine. What you got, iron fists, man?"

"Titanium. Wanna test it again?"

"You're good," he said, shrugging Severum off and racing back to the airbus station.

The street converged into a point of absolute nothingness, but that was okay. He had his mojo back, and though he was relying on cybernetics to make it happen, so what? If it changed his self-perception it would become self-perpetuating.

Akasha came outside to check the commotion, shielding Ash from the scene, who was crying behind her and pulling the strap of her camisole over her shoulder. "Feel like a man again, Severum?"

"Better bet."

"Still dumb enough to define that by your strength when you're too much of a coward to face your family without your ego calling all the shots."

She left the door open, but he could only sit on the steps for the rest of the night reflecting on her words.

———

SEVERUM WENT to see Aurthur the next day, stepping up to his desk at Samole News Media.

"Severum, great to see you."

"I suppose."

"You've never been much for words, so let's get to it then. After our counsel reviewed the evidence provided, we decided not to publish the story against Culptos and his actions."

"Typical."

"The New Order doesn't want to publicize how much they know about the Old Guard's attempts to regain power. They won't even send a military team to the research lab. They want to play things slow, gather all the intel before making a move. They're afraid if they move now, the snake will just eat its own tail, cover its tracks, and the cycle will continue."

"Like the Uroboros."

"You mean like the one you poisoned your wife with?" he asked, head cocked, reminding him. "You owe that woman. I mean, I'm just saying."

"You know I didn't know it was her. She had veiled her face, and was dressed in a priestess's robe. Besides, that was decades ago."

"Just don't forget how much you have to make up for, my friend. In any regard, the New Order would like you to take out

Eduardo Culptos yourself. Once the head is cut off, the rest won't have enough resources to sustain itself. He has no heirs, and not enough of a following to become a martyr."

"This puts my whole family at risk. There must be another way," Severum insisted.

"They *are* already at risk from what you've been telling me. Afraid of getting your hands dirty? You've changed, I admit. I mean, not the stern, aggressive furrowing you do anytime someone talks to you, but there's something different."

"Having a child will do that. A parent can take on many risks, but not when they're passing them on to their kids."

"I respect that," Aurthur replied.

"I'll see what I can do. What resources is the New Order willing to provide?"

"Not much. They don't want anything traceable, no accountability."

"In other words, the kind of contract where, when I complete it, I'm next on their list."

"They assured me that's not the case, that they'll look out for you."

"You're not high enough to know for sure though, are you? They sent you to convince me to do this because they know we're friends."

"Well, they also guaranteed quite a few creds when the job is over. But it's a complex undertaking, and they're not paying until the end."

"Figures."

"You'll be pleased to know that third-party investigations are occurring at Geosturm. They've arrested Malik Aldweg, one of the top managers, and are pursuing mass murder charges. He's expected to be convicted and sentenced to death by cognigraf overclocking, burning his brain from the inside out. What a way to go, huh man?"

"Sure is."

"You ready for this?" Aurthur asked.

"Born ready, but first, I need to check on the Florinik."

"They out there worshipping the sun again?"

"Judging by your wife's anthropological reports, they never did. They worshipped Orbis, remember? That all-seeing all-hearing thing in the sky they believed in."

"It wasn't really the sky."

"The dreamworld that intersects with reality or whatever you damn poets believe in. Thing is, they've become tech-heads of all things. They believe cyberspace is a manifestation of Orbis."

"What do they want with you? After you brought a planet-wide battle to their doorsteps years ago, you'd think they'd get the hint that you don't like company."

"They're afraid a giant earthquake will swallow their village. They gave me a lot of help in the past, so the least I can do is run some tests on the acid in the river outside their village. Arcturus gave me a few men and some equipment. I just need to tell them where to install the filtration devices to clean up the place. I'll be scoping it out, sweet and simple, except…"

"Except what?"

"Some of the rocks in the region are… there's no good way to put it so I'll just say it: Alive. Wanna come? Might be a great archaeological dig for your wife, too."

"I've hit rock bottom too many times before. No thanks," Aurthur replied. "Enjoy."

"I always do."

15

SEVERUM TOOK AN AIRBUS THE NEXT DAY TO THE EASTERN Hemisphere, formerly known as Dayburn. He rented a small sand-scooter the rest of the way to Amorpha where the Florinik resided. Traffic was sparse. A cold breeze swept along the purple cattails of the river to play with the trash piled around the village. The turquoise stone path glittered in the late day sun, somehow listening. Installing aquatic filters to remove the accumulating acid was key to appeasing the sentient stone, whatever it was, or the quakes would worsen until they consumed the village.

Greenhouses with arched domes stretched around the village's perimeter. Many were cracked due to the quakes, made worse by the uneven terrain that caused the buildings to lean. With the ecology gradually transforming from desert to greenery, new herbivores had invaded the region, and the Florinik relied on the structures to protect their gardens.

He scooted through a scanner stationed above the gate. For a peaceful species, the Florinik had upped their security substantially since the last raid, with guards on either side checking bags and other items. It was easy for them to have had few arms when they had few possessions, but as the trading post developed, with that wealth came a fear of losing it. Indeed, the long-limbed, tree-like creatures didn't walk with the same debonair swinging of limbs they used to. An anxious bravado had emerged instead.

He hovered through a series of tattered prayer flags strung between buildings until he reached the parking deck, where he stowed the sand-scooter and boarded a rusty trolley system outside. He called Ash during the ride, speaking over the rackety sound of the metal chassis and the Florinik's grunting.

"Hey, it's me. I hate to ask you to do this, but while you were employed at Geosturm you had access to seismology records, right?"

"Of course," she replied, groggy and yawning.

"Are they in the public domain?"

"No. Being a corporation, all the data they keep is private. You can get slightly altered data on the underground market, but it's pricy."

"Can you hack their server to grab the seismic readings from around Amorpha over the past few decades without being traced?"

"You believe I can do that?"

"I know you can."

"Okay, I'm on it. Do you have time to talk?" she asked.

"I have to calculate the best place to install the filtration systems Arcturus is providing us. See you later."

A metal watchtower stood high enough that he'd be able to survey the surrounding area from the top. He ascended in a glass elevator, the world getting smaller below him until the vehicles were ants and the buildings toothpicks. Every sight was a memory: A crescent butte sat outside the city, the same one where Thalassa had almost killed Akasha and him one year before agreeing to work together in a controversial move that had produced an uproar from O.A.K. The Shrine of Orbis sat proudly upon another butte where Aurthur and Opal were once thought to have died, only to have been slumbering in the embrace of a panopticon god, or at least that's how the Florinik had put it.

An overgrown ultimaepar mine was on the other side. The last of that rare metal had been used in constructing and maintaining the planetary rotational apparatuses. He could barely make out one of the last Aporia Asylum caves in the distance, a nesting ground for the Aphorids that his ex-wife used to manipulate to her own political ends. The anti-tech group had caused more than their share of bloodshed. Finally, the site of the old O.A.K. base drew the common thread in all these memories: his life had been filled with constant violence.

The river wound its way in the distance, intersecting with the turquoise stone path at three critical points. Filtering the flow before it reached those junctures would be the key to protecting the stone. While this wouldn't solve the threat of acid rain, nor from acids seeping through the surface from previous storms, it would protect the stone from being submerged in an acid bath every time the rivers flooded.

He called Arcturus and updated her on the project, then provided her people the coordinates to install the filtration systems.

———

ASH RECLINED in her small bed and jacked into virtual reality. Entering cyberspace didn't feel like dipping into a warm bath this time, not after the hell it took to leave on her last jaunt. At least her mother was in the other room to warn her of trespassers, and to monitor her in case the haptic feedback became too intense. Well, she hadn't exactly told her what she was planning to do – didn't need another lecture.

She rendered cyberspace with her customary forest skin that

enabled her to visualize the network for easier navigation, but her heart sank at the sight. The entire forest had burned down, the floor carpeted with nothing but ash, interrupted by charred wood jutting up at odd angles, and crumbling at the touch. The skulls of small mammals were sprinkled throughout the barren land. Simple enough, she would reset the skin and reload the scene, but the commands made no difference. Her visualization was locked into this configuration. After her last cyberjaunt went awry, someone was sending her a message not to tread here anymore. Fair enough, message received.

And ignored.

Ash walked the barren, virtual forest until she reached the highest ash piles. She sifted through them, processing the data, the dry flakes puffing up to float upon the air. It was no use – all the data was corrupted, even the programs she had disguised as animals. The pathways that had been worn into the ground had been destroyed, limiting the websites she could access in VR. If she navigated the net with an antiquated computer instead, she couldn't utilize her implants, which had been designed to integrate within a visual interface, yet without them, she'd have to manually process the entire infiltration of Geosturm's network. That would take forever, and would only get her caught.

She located a hidden, undamaged pathway. It connected to a mirror site for her central node, which was probably used by the saboteur to test techniques in a sandbox environment before implementation. Restoring the connection would take a few days, but it was her best chance. She got to work.

———

Severum stayed in town for three days to oversee the filtration system installation at the key points along the river to prevent acid from dissolving the strange mineral. During that time, there were no quakes, but that also meant no communication. What greater demands might the stone make?

He went outside the gate and tapped the strand of turquoise minerals. "It has been done. The filters are installed, and you need not worry about acid leaking onto your path when the rivers flood."

The stone path didn't react. Maybe he was losing it, too much time in the sun, but vHUD soon lit in the corner of his vision and verified a tremor had been received. Translating it read, *Enter.*

A rumbling broke the silence as the ground rose a few hundred yards away. A bunker entrance emerged, composed of the same phosphorous-based stone as the path. The sun set, glimmering off the façade. He should tell the chief, employ a team of archaeologists to investigate, but the entrance might vanish by that time. He thought a sentient rock would be infinitely patient, if anything, but its demands proved otherwise.

He entered, descending a rocky staircase that turned into a steep, downward slope. The air smelled of moist dirt, wet stone, and something unidentifiable. The cool tunnel walls were phosphophyllite and a mixture of other metals. He felt along the tunnel as the light grew dim. Then, the ground shook again, and the bunker entrance receded into the ground with him caught within its throng.

Complete darkness. He banged his head, rubbed it, then ducked under the shallow ceiling. Pressed his body sideways to skirt through the more narrow passages until he got stuck between the cave walls. He turned his head and fully exhaled, making his body just thin enough to press through the gap. Finally, a glowing clearing appeared, expanding to a twenty-foot ceiling. How far underground was he?

Mushrooms moved on miniscule legs, illuminating the area as their caps glowed with iridescent purple and green specks.

The lights gathered, then scurried down the next slope. Crying out *hello* might invocate the stone to explain where the hell he was, but ignorance was less risky than giving away his presence to whatever else was lying in wait. The other mushrooms were static, occurring in various colors and heights. Aurthur's wife, Opal, had taught him to identify them when he had become poisoned during their journey decades ago.

He followed the 'shrooms.

———

AFTER RESTORING her functionality in cyberspace over the past three days, Ash was ready to infiltrate Geosturm again. The world reskinned as she arrived at the edge of their public and private domains. What had once been her forest's edge was now a virtual data fortress with spyware and key-trackers posted at every watchtower. They weren't making it easy.

The matrix glimmered above her in a crosshatch of purple lines. She crossed a bridge over a moat of discarded files. Any closer and they'd see her coming. She shot arrows over the firewall to scan their drives and run search inquiries, but one ran astray and flew over the watchtower where a guard pointed at it soaring over his head.

The gate opened and she braced for a legion of guards, but only a single knight stepped forth with a quiet, but reverberating step. Her armor reflected the fortress, her sword a long, blazing blue current with sparks flying from the tip. Ash scanned it – this wasn't just a harmless virtual prop, it carried millions of cognigraf signatures, unique implant identification numbers. When the blade hit, it would strike deep and recalibrate her mind's most sensitive implants. Better to back off, call it a day. But Severum needed this intel and she couldn't let him down. Most people weren't aware of making their first impressions on their father, but here at the end of her nineteenth year she was doing so, and that carried a weight she couldn't ignore.

"So you're the pesky little shit been sneaking 'round here," the knight accused, her voice metallic through the metal helm she wore.

"What if I am?" Ash spat back, buying time until her cyber-rig customized a weapon for the encounter.

"You're a fool for returning here. I invented half the tech you're carrying in your head. This should be easy."

The knight came on, her armor clanking in rhythm with her footsteps, but this was the virtual world; Ash's domain. The blade swiped through the air, Ash waited, waited some more, and just before it carved her open, she activated an evasion routine. The blade shimmied right, missing. Another strike, this one a wide arc that sliced through the air but failed to connect as she parried, code-pushing the blade just wide.

"Impressive, for having never faced a cyberknight before. If you had, you'd have run from the start."

"Yeah, right."

"But I didn't come alone," the knight said.

Archers stood on the tower, drawing packets of malicious data from their quivers. She sidestepped a few arrows, but the next two hit and corrupted her vision. Processes slowed, and before long the lag would crash her, but not before a weapon materialized in her defense. Ash's blade appeared in hand, but it was nowhere as spectacular as the lightning blue sword the knight swung to taunt her. A bluff, since the knight's best play was to wait for Ash's lag to stack before attacking.

"Come on, I dare you," the knight boasted.

Overconfidence was a deadly card. Ash knew how to play against it. Her blade was a longer version of the ancient jitte, customized to have a hook both at the end and near the hilt, a perfect counter for the knight.

Ash moved forward at half speed, even allowing another arrow to hit her to complete the ruse, acting as if the arrows had already slowed her connection speed down to where she wouldn't be able to react to another strike. The knight charged, raising the blade in the air in an exaggerated display, the storm clouds above the fortress gathering to consolidate their energy deep into that sharp edge. The sword came down, but Ash side-stepped with full speed and caught it in the curved hook of her spear, twisting her weapon such that the trapped sword rotated with it until it was horizontal. With the knight clinging to the stuck blade, Ash rushed forth, using it as leverage to push her over until the blade was at the knight's neck, right in the gap below her helmet.

"This isn't over," the knight spouted. A nebula emerged from her mouth to engulf her avatar until the colorful flecks of her pixels vanished.

Ash ran into the data fortress and scanned the area for files. The lag from the arrows was taking its toll for real now, but she was almost there. She located the geological folders with the seismic readouts, but it was too much to download given the lag in her connection speed and they would trace her before it was complete. The files were arranged by timeframe, so she limited her selection to the requested date range and region. The download began, ended, and she found an exit to jack out of cyber-space, the fortress vanishing in an implosion of light.

She sat up in bed, wiping the sweat off her forehead. She had the file, but it had better be worth it.

———

SEVERUM SPELUNKED DEEPER into the cave. The iridescent mush-rooms scurried into various crevices, but he didn't need them anymore. Lights pulsated from the sea-green crystalline walls.

One area would glow, then it would die down as another glowed, almost as if a conversation was being held within the minerals. The lightshow was dazzling, but he had seen the golem, knew what power the geological structures held.

"Hello," he cried. "Ardhieneo?"

The lights flickered ten times faster.

He tried contacting Arcturus to let her know where he was, given how well connected her resources were in the area, but his comms received mostly static. *Should have done it before I entered the bunker, but I couldn't have guessed the entrance would sink, leaving me stuck here.*

He measured for rumbling but found no seismic activity. Whatever they were, they weren't about to give up their secrets.

He received a vHUD call from Ash. "I have the data you wanted."

The signal dropped.

Another call, "Severum, can you hear me?"

The signal dropped.

A third call, "...send...file...."

The signal dropped, but not before a portion of the file arrived that detailed the historical seismic activity in the region. Ash had succeeded. He converted it to text using the established method.

Most of the data was gibberish, ramble rumblings from the planet, including the period immediately following the increased rotation. But the data started making sense around the time the planet started spinning out of control, shortening the days, in other words, when Culptos became involved. Something he had done aggravated the crystal network.

He might be able to use that against Culptos, but first, he needed to know the story the crystals were singing. The text extracted from the historical tremors read:

We are the Bhasura, the planet's original Keepers. We listen.

We hear your plights, your cries, your tears of joy, your ambitions, and we do not care. Everything in the Gliese System exists in a perfect balance, a balance humans ruined the moment they set foot here. Granted, we feared the planet's destruction when daylight cycles first appeared, but life in many areas flourished beyond their previous limits because of it, thus we remained silent. We thought, 'maybe humans are patient and will undo the damage they did through their pollution given enough time.' But humans are anything but, and their impatience is what caused this mess to begin with, extracting far more resources than necessary to survive. This new push to continue to increase the rotation will be catastrophic, and must be opposed, lest we all be destroyed.

We have learned the common tongue and would like to speak with a representative using light projection and reception. Unfortunately, our light cannot transmit far enough, and our signals go unheeded, thus we must resort to these tremors to communicate. This is a lengthy process, since too many tremors in a row could destabilize both our dwellings. We do not wish to cause harm, but we do have demands that must be met to ensure our mutual survival. Come. Let's talk.

The lights, of course. He just needed to figure out how the pulsating translated to his language. The crystalline blocks must have some sort of channelrhodopsin proteins enabling them to react to the photocurrents, since he didn't see any signs of a sensory organ within the layers of semi-translucent stone. He smoothed his hands over the surface, which lit in response as his fingers glowed with jade light seeping between his digits. He stopped. His hands were scarred and creased, their skin loose and piled upon each knuckle. The pores were crisscrossed in a complex pattern, and in that pattern was all the deeds he had performed. Light and shadow played across them with judgment following close behind.

Severum brought up a visualization of the light blooms in

vHUD and mapped their luminosity onto a graph. The tremors had been successfully decoded using a simple binary distinction, but performing the same process with the light by taking the luminosity that was above the median, and below it, and assigning it a value produced only gibberish. Tremors were a far less precise communication tool than light, so the Bhasura were likely using light to take advantage of the greater accuracy in conveying information. Examining the lightmap again, he found that each spectrum of luminosity could be assigned a letter. He instructed his cognigraf to try every combination until he could translate what the walls were saying with their pulsating glow:

Press inward at the tunnel's end.

He set vHUD to auto-decode the lights. Translations passed over his vision, indicating they spoke collectively. Were they one organism, or many who had agreed to synchronize their signals? Did the stone hold their sentience or the light itself? The mystery deepened as he headed down the tunnel until he reached an impasse. He pushed against the crystal wall and it crackled as it opened, revealing a narrow passage. Ducking, he followed it down a series of steep, descending slopes, until a flood of green light came around the final corner.

A large, circular expanse seventy-feet high and twice as wide stretched before him. The crystalline walls pulsated with rhythmic flourishes of light, the patterns reciprocating in a conversation too fast and complex to decode. Thousands of crystals sprouted from the walls. The floor glowed beneath him as he took his first steps into the cavern.

The ground split, and a shimmering, turquoise staircase rose, the crystals merging to shape it. A Jade Palace sat at the top, the glittering jewel of the underground cavern. It was fashioned similar to the ancient Bauhaus style he had seen while perusing the Earth archives from centuries past. Rigid, square structures jutted out at straight angles. As he ascended, he kept hold of the gem-encrusted railing and shielded his eyes from the brilliant sparkling of the rock gardens around the main gate. Stone flowers blossomed, as if diamonds turning inside-out, their façades capturing the shimmering lights. The same mushrooms he had followed down the tunnel frolicked throughout the garden, their lights playing in concert with the luminous symphony around him.

The barred gate opened with a creak, and the rocky center of the courtyard crumbled to merge into a ragged crease like a small mountain. The stone continued to press inward until the crease was as tall as him. The turquoise crystals expanded to wrap around the stone shard, smoothing the rough edges into a diaphanous sheath and branching into thinner arrays so fine they were soft and flexible, enabling complex shapes to emerge. Severum took a few steps back, catching his balance on the top tread. He should run down the staircase, make his escape, but the mesmerizing lights and their message stayed his steps, and there was nowhere else to go.

The jade form crackled as it broke free of the substrate and stepped forth. It was a sexless, humanoid structure with arms, legs, torso, and a soft, yet crystalline face that bloomed with the pale green light. Its aventurine eyes embodied a deep under-standing. It moved towards him with a crinkling sound, a tink, tink, tink like musical chimes. Its mouth opened and a cascade of light fell over him that he translated.

"We are Allira, Queens of the Bhasura."

"Severum, King of Nothing."

"We know who you are."

"I have had the filters installed as your kind demanded."

"A minor tribute considering the trouble your people have wrought upon us."

"A starting step to a better relationship," he replied. "I have translated your communications, your history. I know you are as concerned as I am about the days shortening, the increasing rota-tion, the destabilization of the planet."

"This much is true."

"I know the man responsible. I have been tasked by our government to incapacitate him. Now that we have a communication method established between our kinds, I would first request your assurance that the tremors will stop. The Florinik in the village above are not against you."

"Communication is indeed the cornerstone. They shall cease, but no more capturing, no more dissolving."

"You mean the golem in the tower. I do hope our opened communication channels will avoid the fear that leads to such violence," Severum replied.

"We can assist you in striking against this man. What is his hardness, his luster, his cleavage?"

"What?"

"His properties," Allira explained.

"Oh, of course. Culptos is guarded by some powerful people, and well-armed, but he's poisoned with power so I don't think he's very bright." He continued to explain the evidence against him. "But you already know that," Severum accused.

"Whatsoever do you mean?" the crystalline figure asked, minerals gleaming in its mouth like teeth.

"You were working with him from the start. That's probably why the golem had to be locked up to begin with, and it's definitely why your crystals tried to prevent our escape from his research lab."

"We cannot deny this," it said in a flurry of flashing lights. "He promised that the increased rotation would end the acidic rains by altering the weather currents, but that did not occur. We aligned ourselves upon the wrong axis, and begot suffering in turn. Usually we were quiet, peaceful, but his betrayal erupted a righteous anger, yet an anger ill-placed. But trust us, you will have our support when the time comes," Allira offered.

"Thank you. Now, I have so many questions for you about the Bhasura."

"Our secrets will remain locked in stone for the time being. We have admitted you for your service, and we believe you will still be of use to us soon. But delay not, and head steadfast with great fortitude. Take this as a touchstone of our gratitude," Allira said, placing a small gem in his hands. "It will activate the entrance shall you need our shelter. Raise it upon the path above to return here anytime."

"Thank you," he replied, pocketing the gem. "So this must contain a certain sequence of lights."

"Information can be encoded in many ways." A large stone at the bottom of the staircase moved aside, revealing a new tunnel that sloped uphill. "Now, leave," Allira ordered.

Severum headed up the tunnel until an exit emerged far behind Amorpha. He rubbed his eyes as the morning light grew stronger at the tunnel's mouth. He shook the dirt off his clothes and headed across the surface. The entrance sank behind him.

He made a call on a hunch, "Ash, you said there were four files you uncovered from Geosturm during your first infiltration a while back."

"Glad you're back online. And that is correct, but I couldn't crack the fourth file."

"Send it to me."

"Done."

Severum held the gem that Allira had given him up to the rising sun. The transparent facets revealed a structure with inter-secting cross-planes that reflected and refracted light in a complex array. He set vHUD to analyze the play of lights as he turned the gem. Translation failed. Must be a long, random code. He saved it and applied the code sequence to the uncracked file Ash had stolen to decrypt it. A green window popped up and the file opened.

The file was a letter between Culptos and Aldweg detailing their connection at Geosturm, which had already been well established. But it revealed more:

The Bhasura are a threat to the project. They've become agitated. The tremors increase with the rotation. I will bargain with them to quieten down their activity. Meanwhile, all seismic data that Geosturm collects should be well guarded. We don't know how extensive their network is, or what obstacle they may pose.

We'll meet at A'Tofor Sixatena next time we talk.

--E.C.

A scurrying across the plains caught his attention. He knew that sound, the diamond-sharp claws that razed across the landscape as they half ran, half galloped towards him. Aphorids. He drew his Pulser, shot two right between their wide-set eyes.

Two left.

They raced forth, shredding the ground before him. He retreated to where the bunker entrance had emerged, which was now flat again. He fired, ran back, fired again, but they were too quick, strafing on all fours, their thick legs making short work of the sticks and underbrush they trampled. They roared, exposing their long, curved teeth, their bodies shadow-dark and just as swift. Severum stepped upon the turquoise path as they charged, raising the touchstone at just the right moment to make the entrance rise, splitting the ground. The leading Aphorid had too much momentum to stop, and when the ground rose from under him, the incline sent him springing over Severum's head until it crashed against a rock, dazed. The other closed in, gnashing its teeth.

Severum pocketed the gem. The entrance closed with just the right timing to catch the Aphorid's leg in the gap between the ground and the structure. It writhed, trying to free itself, but twisted its leg in the process. He finished it off with two shots, then whipped behind his back to shoot the recovering one.

Blood stained the grass. Death wasn't much to the Aphorids, who kept their genetic code stored in a hub, where they connected for breeding. That made them fearless, since evolution had selected for high levels of aggression due to their genes being able to be passed on after death. In his younger day, he would have applauded his exceptional timing and unmatched accuracy, but now he understood it for what it was – luck, and one day his would run out.

16

SEVERUM RETURNED HOME TO RESEARCH CULPTOS' ACTIVITIES, and possibly discover his weak spot. After a few days of little progress, Aurthur called him.

"Hey, Sev. Based on the intel you provided, we did some digging and agree with the assessment. Culptos has been trying to exacerbate the negative effects of the rotation to get people to return to the old ways, restoring power to the Old Guard. The question is, where will he strike next? So it got me thinking. We ran a news story the other day on the dam they just finished building north of Blutengel. The new water currents are perfect for hydropower; one of the benefits the rotation has brought that people are really praising."

"Assuming the current patterns are stable enough, given that they're flowing from the melting icecaps," Severum said.

"Well, you know more about that than me," Aurthur replied. "I'm just saying, if I wanted to flood the place, I'd sabotage the dam on opening day this weekend."

"A fair assumption, and something Ash and I considered. But he would need to sabotage it in a way that linked the failure to the planet's increased rotation. Yes, the water wouldn't be there without the greater heat distribution from the pronounced Coriolis Effect, but…"

"Most people don't have degrees in terraforming like your family does. People will believe anything, and they're afraid now that it's all spinning out of control. They'll jump onboard any explanation. Doesn't matter if it's true, he can blame whatever he wants if it's easy to understand. They judge their opinions based mostly on feeling, not reason. Even the scholars I've known were some of the most passionate, but biased people I've ever met."

"Yes, people would rather have a simple explanation that's definite, even if wrong, than a correct explanation that's somewhat ambiguous, such as a theoretical possibility."

"Yes."

"I'll check it out. But if Culptos is planning on destroying the dam, we need to ensure that people steer clear from the place on opening day."

"That will be hard, due to the opening ceremony planned," Aurthur replied.

"Cancel it."

"The media doesn't have that authority."

"Of course you do," Severum argued. "People will only know about the opening event through newsfeeds. So say it was cancelled."

"Too suspicious."

"It's far less risky than the shit we used to do. How 'bout this then, say the ceremony is the day after opening day. Run the story at the last minute so no one will notice the need to correct the error before the event. Later, run an apology and say it was a typo."

"I don't know…"

"If I'm out there taking on one of the most powerful men on the hemisphere, you can step up to make a minor publishing error to save countless lives. Culptos isn't going to let this opportunity pass by, and he's not going to stop until someone stops him."

"Okay. I'll run the misprint to ensure that as few people arrive at the opening ceremony as possible, but you'll need to be there before second noon. He'll get suspicious when the crowds don't arrive, but he shouldn't have many guards."

Severum ended the call and prepared for the trip. While he had replaced his Pulser, his hover-boots and sniper rifle had been confiscated while being captured at the lab, and quality like that was hard to acquire at a price he could afford. He still had his titanium-reinforced fist, the pure power of his punch. He slammed it into his other hand, shaking off the pain. Still, he needed serious armaments, and he knew where to find them.

———

NEXT DAY, he took an airbus to the K.O.A. Commune to visit Arcturus, finishing the trip in a hovercraft. The villagers were singing and holding hands in the town square, rotating clockwise, then counter-clockwise, knowing their free time only by the rhythm of the beat.

He opened the door to Arcturus's humble quarters and got down to business. "I need more supplies."

"Augmentations won't make you live forever," she replied, stretching her back in a yoga tree pose. "They make people weak, over-confident. I will question you now, as I am bored and you may serve to alleviate that boredom, or not," she said, awkwardly vocalizing her intention, a habit Severum had forgotten. "You are increasing in years. If there was a cloning machine that could make an exact copy of you, your experiences, your memories, your personality, even your body, would you allow it to? Oh, and you would die in the process."

"Of course not."

"Why not? Everything you would do, you would still end up

doing. It would make all the same decisions you would make. It would essentially be you, living your life, you just wouldn't experience it. You would be able to avoid suffering by dying, while still carrying out your full potential and caring for those you love."

He paused, then said, "It's the curiosity. I have a right to witness my life, and I'm curious how it will play out."

"So, it's the loss of entertainment that makes you fear death?" she asked, biting on the ends of her frizzy, white hair.

"It's not that simple. It's knowing whether my actions were good or bad in the end," Severum replied.

"Imagine we modify the scenario, and you believe there's a heaven, which would provide that judgment of your actions that you seek, and allow you to witness your life, even if your clone was the one living it. Again, it would make all the same decisions as you, have all the same impacts on the world. Would you die then and let it take your place?"

"No."

"Why not?"

"I want to experience it in real-time since I'm the one who invested the work," he replied.

"Time would be meaningless in heaven."

"Even if I could muster the faith in an afterlife, I'm rather attached to myself."

"That attachment is your ego, and it weakens you."

"It keeps me alive," he said, hesitating.

"In any regard, I won't authorize more body augmentations. You are still within the window that your body might reject the titanium in your hand, and you have always been too attached to your ego for me to fully trust you."

"A rejected graft is a minor price to pay compared to being ill-equipped in combat. And you're not the trusting type anyway, so what's the real reason?"

"Truth is, we don't have as many funds as we purport. We're a non-profit, Severum."

"With access to armaments."

"Our grafter, Gus, quit, and refuses to supply us anymore. Said he wasn't making enough and turned to new clients, seedy people, too. As always, they have the funds while we work just to keep the lights on. We have a few items for self-defense in the basement. I will set the door to link to your cognigraf signature. Take what you need, but no more."

"I'll replace my sniper rifle and the hover-boots then, if they're in stock. Thanks, Arcturus."

"I trust the filtration devices we provided will help the Florinik? We do owe them something after stripping their mine of its most valuable minerals."

"The tremors have died down and I've learned a lot about the Bhasura," he said, explaining the strange sentient stones.

"Yes, even the stones have a certain awareness to them. All nature hears the planet's cry."

"You sound like my ex-wife."

"Her wisdom was born from anger towards you, so she never had much, nor did she truly believe. She was just trying to rile up the Aphorids with her mysticism, and harass us all with glitches. Creatures like those on Dayburn, when it was called that, couldn't see the stars since it was always daylight, so they turned inward with mysticism instead of outward with scientific specu-lation to the heavens. She used that to manipulate them, covering it up with cries of prophecy."

"Well, it brought an army to Governor Borges' door which helped us take him out, ending the Old Guard's oppression. The Aphorids ripped his cabinet to shreds with a little help from Thalassa and me. But when you see that your greatest sacrifices changed things for only a few decades, it perturbs me to no end."

"That army was originally meant for you, Severum. Don't forget it."

His history with Akasha was so complicated that he didn't know if Arc was being literal or metaphorical, but neither would surprise him. "I'll gather the items and head out," he said, leaving.

On the day of the opening ceremony, Severum boarded an airbus to the base of the Élivágar River. The transport fired through the compression tunnel, taking off with enough force to throw his back against the seat. He arrived quickly, keeping his briefcase tightly pressed to his body and waiting in a short line to exit.

The dam stretched across two mountains in a wide arc, reflecting the harsh glare of the setting sun. Water gushed through its steel-enforced slats, but it was only a fraction of the bulk the dam was holding back. If it broke, the flood would reach Blutengel and beyond, causing a monumental disaster to an already frail region.

Six Enforcers wearing outdated uniforms with the old logo walked across the wide path at the top of the dam, taking ten minutes to get to either side. A control center had been built into the center of the main wall, its consoles visible through a series of windows. Passageways connected to it both inside and outside the dam.

Severum hiked a dirt trail up the mountain face and retrieved his new sniper rifle from its briefcase. He assembled it by joining the barrel and sliding in the scope, placing it on a portable tripod. The trigger was cold against his finger, dead cold. Culptos was on top of the dam near a podium with his hands on his hips. He paced back and forth as if waiting for the crowd to arrive, but only those who heard about it by word of mouth would be coming, since Aurthur must have come through with the publishing error. Most of the chairs set up for the event were vacant. Even the airbus had been nearly empty.

He steadied the scope and took a deep breath, holding it. A couple Enforcers and a small group of onlookers walked by and blocked his aim. He eased off the trigger. His energy rifle had no bullet drop, enabling much farther shots than projectile-based weapons. Still, Culptos was four-thousand feet away, and even given the rifle's capacities to synchronize with his vHUD for maximum accuracy, it was a risky shot for someone who usually found himself on the front lines and was less experienced with long-range combat. Plus, there was no other way off the mountain than to return to the dam where Enforcers would investigate the kill. The other mountain was the same distance from the dam and no better. It was just too far.

He headed down the trail to search for another option to take Culptos out, the white noise of the rushing water doing nothing to calm his nerves. The trail descended until he could no longer see his target's position atop the dam, though vHUD outlined in red his most likely locations. He could hover up to take a closer shot, but they'd see him approaching, and he'd be vibrating too much to aim. In his younger days, he would have drawn the geological data on how high the mountains were beforehand, planned his shot. No, who was he kidding; he would have charged right in as always. Improvisation was half of the rush, and most of the risk. He needed to be certain, needed to see the bastard's mug as his lifeforce bled dry. He would fight face-to-face.

———

Ash had overheard Severum's phone call with Aurthur and did some research. She boarded an airbus, and after a short trip, arrived at the Élivágar River. Two mountains towered over each side of the dam. Severum was hiking a steep trail up one of them; she headed up the other.

She zoomed her eyes and watched the Enforcers' patrol patterns, learning their routines as they traveled along the dam's ledges and platforms. Severum changed course, heading downhill. He vanished inside the giant steel structure for a few minutes, then his face flashed through the window of the control center embedded into the middle of it. He was facing forward, but the threat was coming from behind.

An Enforcer rounded the corner of a narrow, outer platform connected to the dam and opened the door to the control center. Severum would be spotted immediately, and this time they wouldn't bother capturing him. Ash called him via vHUD, but got no answer.

Ikshana soared off the mountain from her arm's perch, the metallic falcon streaking across the sky towards the Enforcer, slamming into his chest and knocking him over the railing to the maintenance platform below. He would be dazed, but live. When he recovered, the trip back up to the dam would buy Severum some time. The bird tilted its head and cawed, then returned like a boomerang.

"Good girl," Ash said, stroking its stiff feathers.

Another Enforcer, this one stationed on a higher ledge outside the control room. The construction scaffolds above him were suspended by four cables which hadn't been cleared yet. He paused beneath it and surveilled the valley. Ash sent Ikshana flying with a flick of her arm. Its metal wings arched back for speed as it soared to the scaffold, slicing through two of the cables that held it up. The scaffold fell on the Enforcer, who must have cried out in pain, because Severum noticed him out the control center window and rushed outside through a side door. While the guard recovered, Severum went behind him and placed him in a sleeper hold. Two down.

Severum continued until he saw the other Enforcer down on

the maintenance platform below him. He scanned the hills, but Ash couldn't risk waving her hands to give her presence away. She texted him but got no reply.

A third Enforcer entered the command center.

Sending Ikshana flying through the window would create too much noise, alerting other nearby guards, so she fired it at a floodlight instead. The falcon bust the light and shook off the sparks. Severum headed in that direction. If there were enough environmental hazards, she could keep drawing his attention with these distractions to lead him safely out of the place, but he wouldn't give up until he had his kill. She could set him in the direction of the approaching Enforcer so he wouldn't be blindsided, but the only other distractions that would work would also draw the Enforcer's attention. He might think it was a trap if she revealed Ikshana to him with its cawks, or by letting him see its flight path in order for him to follow it. He didn't know she was operating it onsite, and the model was sometimes employed by law enforcement, as it was less conspicuous than a hovering drone. If he shot it, she'd be helpless to assist him.

Her breath raced, chest heaving, hands sweaty, her over-thinking making things worse, not better, but she took the risk. She flew the falcon over Severum's head and whipped it around to face him with its large, globular eyes. She could normally see through those eyes in the corner of her vHUD, but she reversed the visual feed so she could upload an image to its eyes instead. If it worked, her face would be viewable in the falcon's eyes. She gave it a minute, unable to see Severum's actions, then reverted the visual feed.

"You shouldn't be here, Ash," he texted.

"You would have been killed," she replied.

"I can take care of myself."

"Follow Ikshana. I can see everything from the mountain here, the entire dam layout. I know the guards' positioning.

There's a guy coming on you in five seconds. Go through the side door and shut it softly."

She navigated the falcon through the passages so Severum could follow it, weaving in and out of the command center. After a few close calls, he snuck up a staircase to the top of the dam, keeping low as he crouched behind a tall speaker stack a few feet from the edge. Water crashed below. Culptos paced around the podium, right in front of the speaker that Severum was hiding behind. He appeared unarmed, lacking any fancy armor. Now, to wait for the moment to strike.

———

CULPTOS BACKED up to the podium and asked the small group that had gathered for the opening ceremony, "Where is everyone? Are you telling me people skipped out on such a major historical event?"

"I can't quite figure it out, Sir. Even the media presence is far less than expected," a red-headed woman with a sword on her back said.

"Well, let's start the ceremony." Culptos waved his arms and began, "The Great Rotation brought many horrible things to the world: floods, sinkholes, wildfires, hurricanes. I admit, I have been critical of it, despite being able to see the sun. I lost my own children to the natural disasters it wrought." He paused but his emotions were calculated. He took the microphone in his hand and backed away from the podium — inches from where Severum was concealed — and continued, "But this structure we stand upon represents the good things the Great Rotation has brought us. The same melting icecaps that flooded the planet have also allowed for its construction. This dam will bring electricity to Blutengel and beyond. Bless the New Order."

The group cheered.

Culptos' rhetoric reinforced that he intended to sabotage the dam, while distancing himself from responsibility, since he would never give credence to the New Order otherwise, or admit any positive aspect of the rotation. He had to be stopped but firing a shot would make too much noise and the Enforcers would be on him in seconds.

Culptos rounded the podium with Severum still crouched behind it. It was now or never. He grabbed Culptos' leg and used his titanium hand to toss him off the dam so quickly that onlookers would assume he tripped and fell. But Culptos reacted fast, latching his fingers through Severum's belt loop and dragging him off the dam with his momentum.

He went weightless, Culptos clinging to him chest to chest. The top of the dam got smaller and smaller, the mountains and river a streaking blur. "What are you planning? Is it a bomb? Where is it?" His words were lost to screams and the raging wind as they fell.

Severum pushed him off mid-air, but Culptos caught his foot and held tight, dangling beneath him, drawing his Pulser and aiming up at him. The water neared, the ground growing larger by the second. Severum activated his hover-boots, scorching Culptos' face. He dropped his gun and fell, falling the remaining twenty feet into the water behind the dam. The current carried him to the floodgate, his head bobbing on the surface, hands reaching for something, anything to stabilize himself.

Severum landed on the riverbank, scraping his knees. The current would crush the bastard's head open against a rock if he didn't intervene, but that was the goal, and he had gotten away with it. Yet, if he didn't save him, he'd have no way to know how to stop the dam from being sabotaged if a bomb or another device had been set on a timer. The sudden flood would wipe out whole districts. Even if he captured an Enforcer instead, he or she might not be privy to the information, and he couldn't take that chance.

He activated the boots and hovered across the river, catching up to Culptos and grabbing his arm just before he collided with the dam. He flew up and carried him to shore, dropping him a good thirty feet to break his legs upon landing. Culptos screamed as he hit the ground, legs twisted about, while Severum touched down. Fuel was running low, and Enforcer activity was increasing on the dam above, but he needed the intel.

"I'm going to ask you one last time. What are you going to do to the dam, and how?"

"I'll never tell you!" Culptos spat, gripping his twisted legs with pain and biting his lip until he drew blood.

"I know you're planning something, sabotaging the dam to make the Great Rotation look like it was a complete failure so people will beg the Old Guard to restore their power. Well, that's over and done with and it ain't coming back. If you die, your little movement dies with you," Severum threatened. "Then it won't matter if a bomb ever went off or not. You won't be there to spin the tale in your favor." Severum raised his Pulser to his head.

Culptos's damp hair clung to his face. The puffy mounds of rolling wrinkles piled at the base of his eyes twitched. Inside those eyes was the deep sorrow of a man who was a father, just like Severum, before the environmental catastrophe took the politician's children.

Severum felt sorry for him, but if the dam was sabotaged, there would be thousands of childless fathers just like him. He had to act. He jammed the gun against his head.

"Okay, there is a bomb. But you'll carry me there so I can show you in person."

"You're not in a bargaining position," Severum reaffirmed. "If I'm seen with you, the Enforcers will kill me by the time I get there. Even now, we're barely out of view of your guards atop the dam. I'm sorry about your children dying, but many more children are going to die if you let this happen."

"Fuck you, pal. You know nothing about sorrow. Even the

other guys at A'Tofor Sixatena haven't gone through half the shit I have in life."

He hadn't heard of the place. In his panic, Culptos might have said too much. No, wait, it was the same location mentioned in the file Ash had stolen. A lead.

Culptos tapped his ear and growled. "You know what, I don't care if it goes off, because I know something you don't. Guess who's on-site? I just got word that one of our drones identified your daughter in the area. When the dam blows, guess who will be caught in the flood? I want you to know the same suffering you put me through."

Severum relented, gathered him in his arms, and ordered, "Take me to the device you planted, now."

But as he neared the dam, Culptos had other plans. "Now that you're close enough, you're done with!" he yelled. "A couple clicks in vHUD is all it takes to blow the place, and you're right within the blast radius. You're going to kill me anyway. What's the difference?"

"No. We can save people."

"You're coming with me into the beyond." Culptos flickered his crazed eyes and smiled.

Boom! Explosions went off across the dam. Chunks of concrete came crashing from the lower parts. The top of the dam collapsed next, all that steel slamming into the river with a huge splash. The control center detached and fell, combusting until it was just a burning mess of frayed wiring, electronic worksta-tions, and flaming furniture. Within seconds, the entire structure was demolished. The crowd was lost in the smoky haze, but Severum didn't have the fuel to rescue them. Secondary explo-sions merged water and fire into an unstoppable force that no one could survive.

The towering pile of rubble could no longer hold back the flood and a giant wall of water surged forth with a roar. Riverbanks dissolved into nothingness, taking out a group of Enforcers who were waving for help.

Find Ash!

She should never have followed him, though, he would be dead without her. Water blurred his vision, and a burst knocked him back further up the riverbank. Another wave buffeted him as he tried to stand, filling his mouth with water... he choked. Mounds of steel debris charged downriver. The flood had reclaimed its territory and wasn't letting go.

Blutengel was doomed, but a ray of hope emerged. Giant turquoise crystals erupted from the river sentiment, layers and layers of them arranging into a cross-hatched pattern to stifle the water flow. They stacked in matrices upon one another, rebuilding the dam in their image. Water dripped from every facet of the glittering structure, the sun shining behind it. The Bhasura had come through, but how could such a brittle group of crystals hold back the tide? He zoomed his eyes. They had reinforced themselves with various hard metals.

Nature had met the demands of man. Now, to find Ash.

As for Culptos, he was lost to the flood.

PART III

TERRA FIRMA

17

THE NEWS WAS STILL GOING HAYWIRE TWO WEEKS AFTER THE
dam collapsed. The Bhasura, which the public knew only as a
strange outcropping of rocks they believed had been shifted
during the explosion, still held back the floods until more permanent measures to divert the water were implemented. Aurthur
had made sure the incident wasn't linked in the media to the
Great Rotation project, and instead blamed it on a terrorist sect,
not mentioning the Old Guard. He had also deleted any images
that would have implicated Ash or Severum's involvement in the
incident.

One evening at home, Severum approached Ash. "You
shouldn't have followed me to the dam," he said after seeing the
footage replayed on the news.

"You already told me that two weeks ago," she replied,
rolling her eyes.

"And I'm telling you again."

"I'm sorry, but I'm not sorry."

"Your luck is going to run out one day."

"I think you're afraid yours is," she replied. "If our roles had
been reversed, wouldn't you have done the same?"

"For my father? Barely remember the guy."

"No, if you were me."

"If you hadn't been on the mountaintop when the flood hit, you wouldn't have survived. It's my job to look out for you."

"Yeah, but things didn't work out that perfect, Severum. That doesn't mean they have to be broken, or that the choice was wrong. You're the one who dragged me back into this wanting me to hack Geosturm's files again. I faced a knight in there that... I've been having some trouble in cyberspace."

"Having trouble or making it? What kind?" he asked, sitting at the table where Akasha had served paneer masala. She didn't join them as usual, and only sat a place for Ash.

"Increases in haptic feedback, lag, recalibrating lightning sword thingies."

"Standard tools of the trade."

"Not where I'm from."

"Our military's cybersecurity software is far more advanced than your average background app. They've been experimenting at Eisbrecher Tech with haptic feedback for years. Got a big gov' contract out there. You need a checkup. The guy you met at the media center, Aurthur, visit him. He'll scan your cognigraf for anything unusual and find a way to shield you from the worst of it. I'll set an appointment."

"Thanks, it doesn't feel like things are resolved though."

"He does good work," Severum said. "But no more tailing me. You need to stay here where it's safe. I don't want you to become just another holotag around my neck."

"Look, I'm here, I'm real, and I'm not going anywhere, okay? I'll be in your life. But you need to trust me. We're in this together and I can take care of myself."

Severum sighed. "I've watched enough violence in my name. If anything goes amuck, just leave. There's no dishonor in that. Violent people come to violent ends."

Ash left the room.

He called Aurthur. "You're well connected. Ever hear of a place called A'Tofor Sixatena?"

"Nah, let me search the articles. Nothing's coming up so far."

"Nevermind. Can you do me a favor? I need you to run some tests on my daughter, make sure she's not infected. She's having vulnerabilities get the best of her in cyber."

"Sure, I still have some old equipment at home. Same setup I used to diagnose Thalassa long ago when she was infected by the A.I. Core that used to regulate the hemispheres. Have her stop by."

"Will do, thanks. Tell me, the Old Guard, have they dispersed all over the world since the government fell?"

"We don't know much," Aurthur replied. "But we suspect so. There was a diaspora of the old commanders and politicians. With the A.I. Core out of the picture, and the collapse of the firefly currency, all sorts of exchanges were taking place between the hemispheres. In the end, most of the wealthy got wealthier. Rumor is, many retired early in various parts of the world where their wealth would last the longest."

"So maybe A'Tofor Sixatena isn't a place, since it would be difficult to gather people covertly from all over. Maybe it's a server, a virtual location of sorts. I'll have Ash check it out."

"You're tasking that to your daughter, man?"

"Why not? She's the best. She won't be traced."

"You just said she has vulnerabilities."

"Yeah, but you're knocking them out, right?"

"I mean I'll try," Aurthur replied in a high voice.

"She wants to be trusted, so I'm trusting her. She wants to be independent, so I'm—"

"Letting her go off to track down the most dangerous group of people alive. I get it. Severum, you might not want to hear this, but you can't give kids everything they want. You have to stand firm on some things, like when they want to prevent a malignant revolution from their home computer. That's a good time to say no."

"Yeah, but she's like me. If I tell her not to, it only eggs her on more."

"If she's like you then God help you both."

"Stopped believing a long time ago. I try sometimes, but God and I got a few fights to pick still."

"I'll do what I can, but at the end of the day you have to have faith in something, or the ground turns to quicksand under your feet pretty quick."

Severum hung up and yelled to Ash, "Hey, there's this server I need you to hack after you get your checkup with Aurthur."

———

ASH ARRIVED at Aurthur's home on the city's outskirts. The street was quiet; reach a certain income level and you were above the water wars being waged below, wars that drained the poor's income from having to make repairs while those well-off made upgrades, the gap between the two widening each year. She knocked softly on the door, knuckles pressing against the fine wood. It was real wood, not synthetic, an export of Amorpha, though there was a time that the Florinik considered cutting down a tree to be murder. She ran her fingers down the grain, the knots and recesses so much more lifelike than the printed materials she was used to.

"Hi, come on in," Aurthur said, motioning with a wide sweep of his arm. "Hey, guys. This is Ash. Her father was one of the people who helped me spin the planet. This is my wife, the acclaimed anthropologist Opal, and our son, Willow Storm. He's about your age," he winked.

Heat flushed her cheeks. "Pleased to meet you."

"Pleasure's ours," Opal replied, pushing her hands through her burgundy, spiked hair.

Willow looked away. He had his father's short, precise haircut and clean-shaven face, but his baggy pants and green dashiki showed he also copied his mother's style.

"So your dad's Severum?" Willow asked. "Tell me, how do you spin a planet anyway?"

When it was clear no one else would answer, Ash replied, "Well, Willow—"

"Call me Will."

"Okay. Well, you increase the rotation using angled atmospheric emissions and a host of contraptions that…"

His eyes sparkled blue as he met her gaze, disarming her intellect.

She continued, "There's complicated things that are… umm, they're like hard to explain, but they're like really big." God, she felt stupid.

"Following your parents' footsteps," Opal noted.

"Not by choice, it just sort of happened," she shrugged. Ash seldom visited anyone in person and didn't know what else to say. It would all come out wrong anyway if Will kept staring at her like that.

"You spin a planet on your finger, son, like a basketball," Aurthur interrupted to break the awkwardness.

"Dad, not now, and no one remembers basketball. That's an old person's game."

"I risked my life day in and day out to support the Great Rotation," Aurthur proclaimed.

"No you didn't. You whined about your painting and love life while Severum did most of the work," Opal toyed.

"Well, there was some painting, and—"

"A lot of whining," Opal joshed. "But you came through in the end. We all did."

The foyer had a bookshelf against the wall with actual physical books on it. "You read this fantasy stuff?" Ash asked, noting the castle on a cover.

"I mostly write it in my spare time. Ever since the old Camelot tales were rediscovered in the ship's archives, damaged that they may be, there's been a resurgence of interest in fantasy in people your age. Castles, knights, trebuchets, all of it. Of course, I prefer sci-fi, but I write for the youth. Let's get started."

An image of the cyberknight flashed in her mind. She had barely escaped. He led her to the garage where he had set up a comms console and an old-fashioned weight-lifting bench. Aurthur and his family were so skinny the bench must have been unused. Ash reclined on the bench, the Aphorid-hide cushion rough against her back. He connected a cable to the hole above her brainstem with a *whoosh* and analyzed the readouts on a series of holographic monitors projected on the wall. She crossed her legs tightly while she waited, placing enough pressure that she could feel the throb of blood pulsing through her thighs, a pulsing lifeforce like a ticking clock.

"This will take a bit."

"I have to ask everyone. What was Severum like in the past?" she asked.

Aurthur laughed. "Sure you want to know? He was always confused."

"That's what Thalassa said, too."

"He wanted something to believe in strong enough that he could justify all the violence he caused, but there was no belief definitive enough that could ever do that for him. He's a good guy, don't get me wrong. He's always been there in my darkest hour to help me, and also to tail me without me knowing to get at his assassination targets. Your dad's a killer."

"I don't use that word."

"I know, it's hard to admit. I mean, most of it was while he was in the military, and he did try to tame Thalassa's more violent urges back when she didn't care."

"No, I mean I don't use the D word."

"Hey, give the man a chance to be your dad. He's been through a lot."

"I know."

"The readouts are coming through. We've definitely got the usual suspects here, but otherwise you're clear, except, what is this? Deep in your cognigraf…"

"Sorrow," she sighed.

"It may be more difficult to tackle than that."

"Doubtful."

"This malware is likely responsible for the issues you're having. I'm removing it. Hmm, file metadata indicates it was made by someone who goes by the tag *Sibi-nite2*."

Cyberknight.

"I'm adding composure to your implants. It'll shield you from recalibration attempts. Also lowering your default haptic feedback setting to almost nothing and locking it there. That way, next time someone breaks in and amplifies the effect it won't make much difference. Think of multiplying two by ten versus multiplying ten by ten."

"Thanks."

"No worries," he replied, unplugging her and offering a hand as she rose from the bench. "Also, take these two pills and give them to your parents in case they should encounter this neuro-hacker. It will provide some shielding, though not as extensive as what I've given you. I know life probably seems really tough right now. I was your age once, and I used to be a data miner myself."

"Really? How did you skin your interface?"

"Like a mine, literally. The best gem I ever found was my wife though." They laughed and he continued, "I met her at a neurological research facility, actually. O.A.K. was testing me by sending me to blow up the place. Though the bomb ended up a dud by design, we didn't know that, and your father rushed in to save my life. And it wouldn't be the first time. He's a hero, Ash. He's the real deal."

"I'm starting to believe that. His life sounds so exciting when people tell me about it, but would he have made time for me amidst all that?"

"He wouldn't have had the luxury of time. Things weren't stable back then, and inequality was unbearable before the Great Rotation. I know the floods are a hamper today, but it's nothing like living in the dark non-stop, using your last pocket change to light your way. But yes, I think he would have found a way to be there for you, just like he was for me, at least when it really mattered."

"Another question, but I don't want to ask it."

"Yes you do. Shoot."

"I see the way you look at your wife. I didn't grow up seeing that sort of thing. What's being in love like?"

"Oh, that, it's a mysterious beast indeed, one you want to cuddle one day and slaughter the next."

Ash flattened her lip and scrunched her head in her shoulders.

"Not literally, of course. It evolves, changes like the seasons. You end up forgiving things you never thought you could forgive, and likewise, you're forgiven for things you never thought you'd do. It's unconditional, but there's boundaries to it," he laughed.

"A journey."

"Oh yes."

"Thanks, Aurthur."

"Catch you later."

On the way out, Willow stopped her and asked, "What are you doing later?"

"Nothing, I'm going to do something; I have things to do," she stammered.

"You're really cute, by the way. I want to understand you better."

Combust. She had heard other women be complimented and thought it superficial, thought such a shallow comment from a stranger would never have an impact on her. It went against her feminist values to even acknowledge such a frivolous assessment of her self-worth. But as the heat flooded her face, she nodded and smiled and left with tiny, quick steps out the door. She had almost had a one-night stand while high after hanging out with Thalassa, but that was one thing. Emotional intimacy was different, and too intense to bear. It was that beast Aurthur mentioned, the cuddling and slaughtering, the journey of that enticing world she forbade herself to enter, having no reference point of a man being a supportive figure in her life. That was changing, but she needed to reflect on that evolution, and that took time.

Lots of time.

———

Ash researched A'Tofor Sixatena to find where the Old Guard met, running the query down every back alley online until the obvious was clear: It was server A24-6810a. It wasn't even a code for anything; they were calling it what it was. If they didn't feel the need to hide it, then it must have top cybersecurity. The only servers beginning with a letter were those housed near the melting icecaps west of Blutengel in the small town of Eisbrecher. Having a four-digit access code on the end was typical of Clerik, Inc., an offshore internet provider that cyber-sleuths out west utilized due to their customer-based privacy agreements. She had enough information to locate the server online, but gaining access was another story.

The company website stated that servers were down for maintenance for the next fifteen minutes. She should report back to Severum, but she couldn't waste a second. Server maintenance required opening multiple ports and they could provide an entry point. Security would be higher during that time due to the increased level of system monitoring, but if she broke through ICE or crashed critical sub-routines, it would likely be chalked up to the software update.

Ash jacked into cyberspace and navigated her avatar through the server's public login forum. A teenaged receptionist sat at a glass desk in the virtual lobby. Her hair shifted colors along a gradient of blue to red with stars streaking across it in an animation loop. She was surrounded by windows that revealed the vast emptiness of cyberspace. Data coursed through the dark sky outside, each pinpoint of light a file or social interaction in a sea of nothingness. If only people could see how isolated their interactions online appeared in cyberspace, their smiles reduced to binary code, they'd realize the desolateness of the human condition.

"Logging in?" the receptionist asked.

"Yes," Ash replied. She needed to stall the receptionist to extend her time in the lobby, and though she lacked the credentials to get in through the front door, she played along to buy time.

"Identity?"

Ash's background processes were already boring holes in the security framework, testing for pliability and response times. She linked their system resource usage to her vHUD, which displayed as fluctuating bars on a graph. She ran a few thousand search queries, but the system responded too fast for it to have placed a process load. Stressing a system this advanced would take a lot more than that. She downloaded a list of I/O devices connected to the server and looked for weaknesses.

She bought time, "I tried my username multiple times, but it didn't work."

"Your username is?"

"Actually, I think it was correct, but maybe my password was off."

"Did you have caps lock on? You can turn it off by rolling your eyes twice," the receptionist said in a disinterested voice, demonstrating. That wasn't, of course, how it worked – you held your eyebrows up as you typed the letters that needed to be in caps.

"That must have been it. Let me try again," Ash replied, forcing a smile. Almost in.

"You have a few more seconds, then I'll be forced to lock you out for the next month."

"Is the password four digits on the end or six with a special character?"

"It's six. That's all the information I can provide. Even someone like you should be able to remember their password without these reminders, ya know? Now, you must be heading off – security hates loiterers. I call them lobby loits, they call them target practice."

"Thanks, I think I remember it now. And before I go can I ask one more thing?" Ash asked. Just a few more seconds and she'd crack it.

"Like, no already."

"Where did you download your hair gradient?"

"Oh, this? You can get them anywhere. People say they're too flashy, but oh well. Going to force you to exit now for your own good."

One second left, "You have to ignore those people. You're beautiful and who cares about their approval anyway? Just be who you are."

The receptionist nodded, and thought for a moment, hovering her hand over a button that would kick and ban Ash from the server since she refused to leave.

Process complete. She was in. "Thanks, have a good day," Ash said.

Her avatar vanished and reappeared in a large, virtual garden. All the internal communications were here, labeled by name, but she hadn't received an invitation to the server and couldn't view them. Only the central administrator's name was viewable:

Sibi-nite2.

She didn't dare click it; had faced the cyberknight before, and once was enough. Skills like hers guaranteed she was part of Culptos' core group, and she had to uncover her identity.

There were few human languages spoken on Gliese 581g, but there were many accents. Anyone who used *sibi* as a homophone for *cyber* must be from a background where *si* could replace *cy*, which was typical, but also one where *bi* could replace *ber*, suggesting somewhere with a soft *r* sound. Sibi was most likely from Eisbrecher, which made sense with the server being run by Clerik, Inc., based on the location of their client base. Who did she know with such an accent? Aldweg had used hard *r* sounds. Culptos had used soft ones, so he fit, and was probably also from Eisbrecher. But his mercenaries and assistant didn't share his accent, meaning they were from other areas of the globe and less likely to be part of his core group based on the Old Guard's xenophobia. Besides, the cyberknight had presented as female, and was likely a woman in real life.

The town of Eisbrecher had been hit hard economically after the fall of the Old Guard during the Great Rotation when the planet established its daylight cycles. The town was under-educated, save for a renowned college specializing in cyberware called Eisbrecher Tech. Its precocious students were known for creating wild, innovative products, which only the college prof-ited from in exchange for the promise that their degree would land them a great job. After the economic collapse, that didn't happen, and there were plenty of radical anti-rotationists who wanted things to return to how they used to be. This was compli-cated by the melting icecaps, which disproportionately impacted the area since they were on the edge of the ocean.

Ash cloned herself. Another avatar appeared beside her. She apportioned ten percent of her resources to empower it. That version of her had no sensory inputs or sense of self, merely a process that knew her research routines. While such processes were inefficient at battle, they excelled at rote tasks.

"Bring me up a list of everyone who graduated from Eisbrecher Tech since it opened," she commanded it.

Sibi's tech was too advanced, too pricy, and too new not to have connections in the tech industry. Severum had mentioned the tech was common in the military, but also that Eisbrecher Tech usually developed and sold them the patents. As her clone researched, she explored further. Although she couldn't see the people who had access to the server, she could tell the length of their online names, not their virtual tags, but their actual first and last names. While the letters were encrypted and far beyond her skills to crack within the time available, their short last names were typical of the groups that had settled in Eisbrecher, further confirming the relationship. The small towns in that region had dropped the surnames that lengthened with every generation as hyphenated last names were inherited, only to add an extra hyphen when their female children married.

Update warnings flashed across the screen. Time was running out.

Query complete. The program provided her Eisbrecher Tech's student lists. She filtered for the relevant computer science majors, and filtered again for graduates, sorting them by grade point average. Then she recalled what Aurthur had said about the youth having a resurgence of interest in knights and fantasy and she added a second-level sorting to organize the results by graduation year, which was the closest data field that would estimate age. This left twenty potential names that could be the real-world *Sibi-nite2*. She counted the letters in each of the twenty possible names, and matched them to the encrypted first and last name displaying beneath the administrator tag. Only one name matched the number of letters exactly:

Sabrina Underfoot.

The fact that Sibi could even be a nickname for Sabrina strengthened her conviction.

Five seconds until the update window ended. She logged out and exited VR.

18

"Sabrina Underfoot," Ash told Severum that evening.

"Who's that?"

"A recent graduate from Eisbrecher Tech. I found the server, but everything was encrypted. I'll cut you off before you get onto me for hacking it. I did what you wanted, and more."

"Were you traced?"

"Would you have been?" she shot back.

"I don't do cyber affairs. I face my threats face to face."

"No, I wasn't. But get this. I believe the Old Guard has its roots in Eisbrecher, and that this Sabrina woman is a major player in the group."

"I see. Aurthur told me that with Culptos gone there's been a sudden influx of threats and demands being made to the New Order. Most aren't legitimate, but some really scare them. I think the Old Guard is becoming desperate. He just relayed a task for me to find the rest of the group and report their members, so this definitely helps."

"Strange that he's your go-between with the government."

"Well, it keeps the government off the records with their involvement and the media is a major social institution itself.

Aurthur's been in communications his whole life and was one of the men responsible for the Great Rotation, so it's no wonder the New Order trusts him enough to relay assignments."

"You're retired though, and you're not even getting paid."

"They promised me just one more job."

"And you've never heard that before? Listen, I looked into things too closely, and my entire office went crashing to the ground, literally."

"I'll keep my head up," he agreed. "The next step is to track down this Sabrina character."

Akasha walked through the room and slighted, "As if your father needed an assignment to track down a young girl."

"Look, I'm sorry. I can't change the past," he told her, "and I probably can't even make up for it. It may be generations before all the negative impacts of my life play out. But I can assure you that I'm here for you, insofar as you would have me. We have a daughter to raise. Life's about more than us now."

She nodded, brows coming together, then left to cook.

That night they ate together as a family, a word Severum had lost for so many years.

"This is wonderful," he said.

"Seared halloumi over rice, always been a favorite of mine," Akasha said, serving a second-helping.

"Still feel I need some meat to make it a meal though."

"Nature is not a commodity for you to exploit. The economic system makes you think of nature, its products, even your fellow human beings as a resource, but that's a mistake."

"Perhaps, but it's natural to eat meat, Akasha. I mean come on, I have incisors for a reason."

"But our compassion and ability to be merciful is just as natural. It's not necessary to bring suffering; life has enough."

He nodded, and the rest of the conversation was merry.

———

ASH COULDN'T SLEEP. She sat up and researched Sabrina online, but the woman was a ghost, keeping a seldom used social media profile and having few public records. She had no physical address on file, but Ash did find her hovercraft registration. She ran its signature through the public surveillance network, which noted where and when the vehicle had been spotted. The data wasn't very secure; any script kiddie could get at it, but it also wasn't perfect, sometimes recording the flight of a firefly as a large sedan because it flew so close to the camera it covered the whole lens. Despite the spottiness of the data, Sabrina's hovercraft had been registered at enough locations for Ash to discern her frequently traveled routes, including a recurring path to an airbus station each morning, and a return to the original location each evening. No doubt, that was where she lived, or had once lived, since her patterns were changing. Though she was educated in Eisbrecher, her home was much, much closer.

Sabrina had lived in Ash's old apartment building in Bluten-gel, Sloumstone, but hadn't visited in many months. Ash wasn't expecting someplace so low class, but that was probably why Sabrina joined the Old Guard, pregnant with promises of a better life. According to her stolen data, she had been a top student, and only a few years older than Ash, so while she hadn't lived through the Great Rotation, the economy in Eisbrecher had never recovered from it.

Her failed dreams must have made her easy bait for the Old Guard to seduce and gain access to the latest tech skills. Severum had researched Culptos' political affiliates, and the limited infor-mation suggested that most of them were around his age; but they had found a young sympathizer. Sabrina's living quarters also explained why the water had been diverted from flooding Sloumstone Apartments. Geosturm workers had spared the building due to a request she must have made to Culptos, who would have passed it on to Aldweg.

A recent public trace showed her hovercraft at Mandelbrot's, the club for has-beens. If Ash sent Severum after her, he'd be recognized immediately, but Sabrina had only seen Ash's avatar and wouldn't know her in the flesh. Ash took Severum's black camo jacket and headed out to meet her. She'd take the fight face-to-face like Severum had said with that air of superiority she couldn't shake.

———

ASH ENTERED Mandelbrot's club with a swagger she would have never possessed if she had been entering for casual conversation. Tonight she was the huntress, and the profile of the woman she was hunting was plastered in the corner of her vision: Sabrina Underfoot, part-time unemployed and disenchanted tech school graduate, part-time cyberknight for the most villainous faction on the planet. Problem was, she had no idea what she looked like.

She approached the barkeep, an old guy about forty, and flashed a card that she had written Sabrina's name upon, followed by a question mark.

The barkeep replied, "If you're too afraid to say the person's name you're looking for, you shouldn't be looking for them."

Ash blushed. *Did anyone overhear that?* Her swagger disappeared.

"Now, if you want to blend in, what're you drinking?"

"Sake," she replied, trying to look older. Only old people drank sake, displaying bottles of it on their hexagonal tables as if they were precious relics. Before the Great Rotation, weather patterns that enabled rice production were only found on a few places on the planet. The crop required frequent flooding to cleanse it of the small creatures that feasted on it. Now, with the weather patterns it needed being commonplace, the most pricy drink of yesteryear could be afforded by even the Forever

Glitched, and though the quality was better, people didn't like it as much. She took a swig.

Then it hit her, not the sake, but the fact that her father was twice as old as anyone nearby. His years were running up and their relationship had just begun. Would the rest of their lives be spent like this? There were no father-daughter dances, it was more, *how can I protect him from being thrown off a dam with my badass bird while saving a whole city from a tidal wave?* The intensity filled her as she overheard the club's mundane conversations about the latest games and movies, and how real estate speculation was becoming a crapshoot from the floods.

Two women in the back had their backs to her at a corner table. One was openly carrying a N-grade Pulser with custom scope. There were no guns allowed – must be a regular. The other was slightly older.

A middle-aged man thin enough to slip between the cracks in the wall came up from behind, pointed at the weapon, and stammered, "You even know how to handle that thing?" He pretended to eye the holster at her hip but was obviously looking at her legs. "I can help you with that. I study ballistics."

"You a decent shot?" the woman asked, flicking her face around. It was Thalassa.

"I'm a marriage counselor, but it's the same deal, it's still ballistics." He laughed through a wide-grinned mouth, teeth shining with the best ivory synthetics. "I know all the mistakes I shouldn't make to make a woman happy."

"Well, you've already made a big one, 'cause I love to fire, but I got terrible aim," Thalassa shot back.

"Whoa, whoa there."

Her companion spoke up, "I am going to make a statement that you might not find pleasing. A woman's happiness is contingent upon herself. We do not require men to *make* us happy. At best, perhaps creating the conditions for happiness."

He couldn't reply, either because of the alcohol or because he probably wasn't a marriage counselor. Ignoring it, he said, "So, I'm Cliff. I'll take you so high you won't..." He seemed to forget the rest of his come-on so he skipped ahead, "What'll I have to do to get one of you up there to groove?" He pointed at the raised dance platform.

Thalassa shoved her tongue into the other woman's mouth, whose frizzy hair concealed them as they cupped their lips over one another. After a minute, she turned and told the guy, "Get the message?"

"Totally, you both want to groove with me? I'm into that."

The older woman sighed while Thalassa drew her Pulser, slinging it from her holster in a smooth arc and holding it to his head. "This is why I sit in the fuckin' corner. I fuckin' hate men, get it? You're a piece of crap. Now, loverboy, wanna see if it's charged?"

"Put it away!" the barkeep yelled, then returned to shaking a cocktail, the exchange apparently commonplace.

Thalassa holstered the gun and the guy turned to leave but passed out on her table instead.

Another guy approached and eyed Ash up, stopping in front of her as he swung his drink.

"I'm with them," she said. He stumbled away, knocking into a woman carrying drinks.

"Nice," Thalassa said. "This is Arcturus. We were having a very long overdue rendezvous. Arcturus, this is Severum's daughter."

"So what?" Arcturus shrugged, but she made room for Ash by pushing the passed-out man off the table and letting him slump to the floor, rolling him into the aisle with the heel of her boot.

Ash sat and asked, "What was he like, Arcturus?"

"Who?"

"Severum."

"He was the Architect after Gestalt died. He served an

important function for O.A.K. before we rebranded as K.O.A. to distance ourselves from the rotational critics," Arcturus replied.

"I know that, but what was he *like?*"

"He served a purpose, and he did it," Arcturus said, confused.

"What the hack? Why do you care anyway?" Thalassa interjected. "He's a stranger to you, Ash. It's just like that guy assuming I needed a man to make me happy."

The words lingered but she pushed them back. "Guessing you didn't have much parental support growing up either, huh?"

Thalassa shook it off. "Saw what happened at the dam. And Culptos has been missing ever since. Know anything about that?"

"I know a bit about a bit," she replied, the words overshadowed by the thumping retrowave music.

"You're sweet. Too sweet." Thalassa took off her black leather jacket and shirt, leaving a tank-top and pants embedded with raised neon-blue honeycombs. She handed the shirt to Ash. "You're about my size. Your black pants work, but go change out of whatever blouse your mom picked out. Still can't believe the woman who led an Aphorid attack on the old governor is now picking out clothes for her kid."

Ash blushed and headed to the bathroom to change, saying, "Keep an eye out on anyone who leaves."

As she entered and played dress-up, she forgot that somewhere in there was a woman who could crash her implants with a single swipe. Maybe Aurthur's upgrade would shield her next time she faced her. Maybe not. She stripped her blouse in the stall, stuffed it in a crack in the wall, and pulled Thalassa's shirt on. It was surprisingly comfortable for what it was: a series of diagonal leather strips arranged flush with a large hole in the upper back cut in a teardrop shape. The leather had a ton of wear, but that only made it cooler. She pulled Severum's black jacket overtop, the chrome fasteners reflecting off the dingy light. A poor choice for camouflage, but still badass. She stared in the mirror, swept her purple bangs back, and pushed her skin together to see what she would look like as she aged. Would she be a lonely revolutionary in a corner bar one day, raising guns to would-be suitors, or an unemployed graduate student disdainful at the system, or even a ruthless politician guiltless of her country's blood? Fuck it. She would determine her own fate.

She headed back into the club, shoulder-checking the next guy who looked her up as she passed. About forty people, and no one had left since she arrived. She rejoined the corner table.

"Ash looks a bit like me at her age, back when you loved me," Thalassa told Arcturus, who looked away.

"Thanks for the clothes. Why's there a teardrop cut in the back?" she asked Thalassa.

"You'll figure it out, trust me."

"Culptos was working with someone," Ash whispered. "Sabrina Underfoot. She's somewhere here at the club. Runs cybersecurity for the Old Guard. Originally from Eisbrecher. About my age. Tech school graduate."

"I know all the regs, but that doesn't ring a notification bell," Thalassa replied.

"Her hovercraft showed up on a camera at the parking deck nearby. Not too much else open."

"If she is here on business," Arcturus said, "contrary to the media's portrayal, deals like the ones she would be making do not go down in clubs and bars where everyone knows you. Not unless one owns the place."

"Who owns Mandelbrot's?"

"The barkeep, Stan. Inherited it from his father. After he took over, he never stopped working in his original position. Thinks he can save us from ourselves. But you're looking for a woman you said. Come with me and we can look around outside."

The three exited the club through the smoky haze and rounded the corner to a seven-story parking deck full of hovercrafts. Ash had left Ikshana on the rooftop when she arrived to keep watch. She commanded it to search for Sabrina's vehicle. Given its eyesight, it took only a minute to find it, matching the plate to the registration information she had uncovered.

"Up four levels," she said, hurrying ahead. They slowed as they reached the fourth floor of the parking deck. Ikshana scoped the place but it was empty.

"Nice bird but looks like it flew the coop," Thalassa noted. "So be a good girl and tag the car and let's go have another drink."

"I didn't bring any surveillance equipment and flying Ikshana behind the car as it traveled would be a dead giveaway. If captured, it can be traced to my cognigraf signature that I used to pair it."

"Well then, keep it posted here, run the visual feed through all three of our vHUDs, and back to the bottle we go."

"Thalassa, Ash is young and still has a whole life ahead of her," Arcturus scolded.

"There's that judgment again. Okay, I'll be serious," she replied, squinting. "Sabrina! You out here?" Her yell echoed through the parking deck. She waved her Pulser through the air with the coordination of a drunk trombonist.

"Glitchit," Ash spurted.

"This is why even Severum refuses to work with you anymore," Arcturus said, shaking her head and running downstairs. "You are such a reckless glitch."

No response from the parking deck, and vHUD still showed no activity from Ikshana's viewpoint. They exited.

"What other places are nearby that someone my age would frequent at this late hour?" Ash asked.

Arcturus rubbed her head. "It would be somewhere without their own parking on the roof. The few residences nearby are better accessed by parking elsewhere. From the top of the parking deck I did see an industrial shipping facility a few blocks down with its lights on, but it had enough parking that she could have parked there if she had wanted."

"Unless she's distancing herself from whatever is taking place there."

They headed there, with Ikshana taking the lead. The long warehouse was unadorned and had no signage. Two men were posted outside a chain-link gate. A side door opened behind them that revealed a few more men in flannel clothes, unloading some boxes from a forklift.

"You always scope the entire area before addressing your target," Arcturus advised.

"Looks like business as usual."

"Then why the guards?"

"Maybe they're just workers on the night shift taking a break," Ash suggested.

"Workers take breaks behind businesses where no one will ask them to do anything, not at the front gate," Thalassa replied. "When people block an entrance, they can appear as casual as they like, but they're guards."

"Ikshana isn't picking up any weapons though."

"Keep it back on the rooftop and zoom closer. You're not the only one who owns one of these things, and you don't want them catching on. Weapons or not, they can still sound an alarm. Stay back and let's wait."

"If you're capable of that," Arcturus slighted.

A truck arrived. Ash and company hid behind a dumpster. The men unloaded the goods quickly, but the inventory wasn't scanned. Maybe someone's vHUD was automatically tagging the items, but none of the men displayed the customary eye flicking associated with scanning things. The final boxes were unloaded and exchanged for new, smaller boxes. She raised her hearing sensitivity, but there were few words and no one mentioned providing an electronic signature for tracking purposes. Whatever company owned the building was keeping the pickup and delivery off the books.

Ash ran some commands in vHUD and researched the property owner while she waited. Some no-name had sub-leased it to an unlisted organization. No leads there. She had to find out what was in those boxes, that is, if this was even where Sabrina was lurking. The back of the truck closed with a clank and it drove away, too heavy to hover.

Thalassa slammed her hands on the raised hexagons on each side of her pants and two compartments opened. She drew two daggers and activated them with a hum. Their scarlet blades bled into the night.

"You'll give us away," Arcturus cautioned.

While the truck passed them, she cut a square in the side of the trailer, the dagger melting the glowing orange metal.

"Fly your bird thing in there. It'll be concealed. You can fly away when it slows down close to its destination, but it'll let you trace where they're going," Thalassa told her.

Ash did so.

"Now to confirm Sabrina is here and figure out what she loaded into that truck."

"I could have Ikshana claw one of the boxes open," Ash whispered.

"If all else fails. But tampering with the delivery will give us away, putting us all at risk and causing them to retreat even further into hiding."

The warehouse gate and garage door closed. Employees circled around back to their vehicles and left. The lights went off inside except for those in a raised corner office.

"Now's our chance," Thalassa said. "There's only two guards left."

"It still bothers me that Sabrina didn't park here," Ash whispered. "If the Old Guard is on her side, she wouldn't have any qualms about associating herself with whatever's going on. She's not the type to be easily intimidated. She must have gotten a drink first."

"I'm tellin' you again, Glitch like that woulda stood out," Thalassa replied. "You don't have *let's get lucky time* in the middle of running an illegal shipment. Maybe there wasn't an empty spot earlier."

"I noted about twenty parking spots when I scoped the place from the parking deck," Arcturus whispered. "A facility this large requires about eight to twelve people on call, plus the guards. There would have been room. The proximity of the club will be her alibi if anyone looks into the activities. She can say she was just on the street to party, not to revive a *status quo* that was so oppressive it could only be ended by speeding the whole planet's rotation."

"No, she's planning something," Ash insisted.

"And things were just starting to get better, except for the floods. There were talks of a universal wage even." Arcturus sighed.

"Around back. Let's go."

The guards swatted the air to play tennis with a ball only they could see.

The three of them circled to the back of the building, keeping to the shadows. Thalassa kneeled behind the building and hit another compartment in her pants that housed a long cord. She jacked the cord into the back of her neck with a *whoosh* as it sealed, and placed the other end into the keypad at the back door. The direct connection would decrease the time to hack it, but also risked cognigraf infection. Within seconds, the lock unfastened and they entered.

A set of burnt-yellow stairs led to the upper office. Everything was in boxes on the ground floor, and they wouldn't be able to discover much without alerting whoever was still working. Ash and Arcturus investigated below while Thalassa climbed the stairs, but the metal steps shook loudly. A shadow exited the second-story office and headed in their direction. Thalassa backed down the stairs, but the shadow neared until they could make out a woman's form. She gave no warning. The woman caught hold of each railing and slid down with her feet forward to slam into Thalassa's chest, knocking her the rest of the way down the stairs. She rolled across the warehouse floor.

The woman ran forth, drawing a long katana from a sheath, her body silhouetted against an auburn security light. A long wave of ruby hair fell over the young woman's pale face. She flicked her head to get it out of her eyes and pointed the blade forward with perfect poise, both hands on the hilt. Thalassa rose from the bottom of the staircase and drew her Pulser, but the woman sliced it in two before she could make a move.

Ash knew that blade. It was almost an exact replica of the cyberknight's sword.

Sabrina was even faster in real life than cyberspace. Thalassa backed away, slammed her hands on her pants, and their cargo compartments extended, drawing her daggers and immediately executing a flurry of blocks as the katana came on. Sparks flew from the metal in the dark warehouse, the clangs loud enough to draw the guards' attention. Sabrina hadn't called for them – she wasn't intending on losing.

The dancing blades clashed repeatedly with both sides taking steps forward. Suddenly, Thalassa stumbled back, dropped her daggers, and grabbed her head as if she were hit from within. Her next motions were clumsy, and one more strike and she'd be done with.

"Sabrina! I know who you are," Ash yelled.

Sabrina turned, her red hair flying across her face. Thalassa and Arcturus took advantage of the distraction to run away, both pounding themselves in the head and probably suffering a cyber-attack, but how was she pulling it off in real life? Ash still had enough distance between her and Sabrina to flee but instead faced her head-on.

Sabrina's emerald eyes flickered, running code. Pressure burst forth from various implants inside Ash's head, but stopped just as suddenly. Aurthur's counter-intrusion software was doing its trick. It knew the signatures of the viruses Sabrina was trying to run and shielded Ash from their effects. As in cyberspace, she pretended the attack worked, grabbing her head and screaming. She lowered to the ground, close to where Thalassa's daggers had dropped.

Sabrina licked her lips and closed in for the kill.

As the blade rose, Ash scooped up the daggers, catching the blade between them and disarming her, the katana flying aside. Thalassa ran to recover it while Sabrina fled through the warehouse out to the guards, hitting the top of a small black box that had been stuffed in the corner. A red light strobed on it, beeping faster and faster.

"Run!" Thalassa screamed.

They ran out back. A thundering boom ripped out of the building and followed them down the street a second later as the warehouse exploded. A fireball erupted into a mushroom cloud that obscured the sky and singed the pavement. The blast echoed. Warehouse walls, cargo crates, staircases, lighting fixtures, all shot out into the night. Some disintegrated from the fiery blast; others were thrown through nearby businesses. Ash danced around the falling shrapnel in the street, covering her head. Secondary explosions ignited with paint cans and other items went up in flames. They ran from the intensifying heatwave.

"So that's why the glitch didn't park here. Mystery solved," Thalassa slurred, smiling as the flames rose. "We gotta get outta here. Where's your car, Ash?"

"I took an airbus."

"You what? You came to track down the Old Guard without a getaway? Such a noob. We'll use mine."

"Well, whatever evidence is gone," Arcturus said. "Most

people do not literally tear the ground apart when they cover their tracks. That was a joke, but I do not require laughter."

"We know, we get when it's a joke, Arc." Thalassa said. "I do the same thing, distract myself from the fact that I almost got blasted into a thousand pieces."

"Here's your daggers back," Ash offered.

"Keep 'em, I have this now," she replied, holding Sabrina's katana, its blade reflecting the orange flames.

"I can't. Severum told me violent people come to violent ends. Besides, that was too close. If I hadn't faked being hit by the cyberattack, she would never have been caught off guard."

"Fair enough, hand 'em over."

They made their way to Thalassa's small hovercraft, the engine too weak to reach the higher traffic lanes. They headed home beneath a flurry of drones, their red and blue lights cycling and bleeding into the night.

Ash called Severum, "Hey, I need you to look into something for me. Ikshana is tracking a truck shipment the Old Guard is involved in."

"How'd you find that?"

"Long story. I'll send you the coordinates when Ikshana relays them."

"I'll look into it, thanks. Stay safe."

But when you're traveling with two of the three most infamous revolutionists in Gliese's history, and your father's the third, you're never safe.

19

ASH RETURNED TO THE RENTAL HOME THAT NIGHT WITH Thalassa and Arcturus in tow. The working class neighborhood was quiet. Rain snaked down the street and gushed from the gutters, but it was a far cry from the flooding at Sloumstone.

Severum opened the door. "Oh, great, you're wearing her clothes. Has it come to this? Listen, I think your friends need to go home. Your mother's not going to like seeing the woman who tried to kill her, even if it was over thirty years ago."

Thalassa busted past him into the house and asked, "Got a drink?"

"Fine. Come on in then, I guess. I'm not even going to ask about the katana at this point." Severum poured a glass of sake for each of them.

"Only old people drink sake," Thalassa scoffed.

"We're getting older. It's time to calm down at some point," Severum replied.

"Age is a state of mind, or a mind state, or a mind fuck."

"How's your head?" Ash asked.

"Not great," she replied, laying the katana across the counter. "Never had a cyberattack when I wasn't online before."

"Your implants are always connected," Ash replied, taking the blade and pointing it down where it wouldn't stab the next person who walked by. "Head to Aurthur's. He'll fix you up and shield you from Sabrina's attacks in the future."

"So you found her?" Severum asked.

"Better believe it."

"Your arms," he said, approaching Ash. "You mentioned an attack. Are you okay? Your knees are scuffed, your clothing's burned. What happened?"

"Girls' night out," she said, trying to copy Thalassa's smirk and looking for her reaction, but she just buried her face in her drink.

Akasha entered the kitchen in a satin nightgown. "You're not staying," she gritted at Thalassa.

"We're all on the same side here," Ash pleaded.

"This one's side changes every time she gets bored."

Thalassa urged her head up from her drink and murmured, "My side is just wherever Arcturus is. I don't care 'bout nothing else."

"There are larger problems than the stupidity of human relationships and the F word we call *friend*," Arcturus replied. She grabbed Thalassa's drink and tossed it in the sink, the glass shattering. "You have had enough."

"Judgment."

"Care."

A vehicle sped to a stop outside.

"You did remove the spyware Sabrina installed during her attack on us, right?" Arcturus asked.

"Umm, that's a negative," Thalassa said.

"Standard procedure. You get hit with a cyberattack, you make sure you analyze the threat afterwards." Arcturus rocked back and forth, fleeing in both directions at once, but cancelling her action each time it began. "Useless drunkard," she snapped.

"It's just a car," Thalassa shrugged. She rose unsteadily and went to the sink to grab a shard of glass, placing it on her tongue as if to swallow, then held it over her wrist instead.

Arcturus watched as if she'd seen it before and was calling a bluff, but Akasha swiped it away and told her, "Even I don't hate you that much. Now, sober up."

"Okay," she relented. Her black eyeshadow smudged around her bloodshot eyes. "I'll activate imSOB3R, but it takes a while to fully kick in."

"That's useless. Try d-tox instead. It's an old program, but more stable."

"I need to drink less, I know, but my life's nothing. All my work's being undone. The floods are all my fault. I should have anticipated the rotational problems. The Old Guard coming back is all my fault, too. I was too high to carry out the first assault on the cabinet before they were forewarned. I didn't complete the job. Gestalt's death is all my fault, trusting Severum when he was really trying to kill me, back when he thought a military order meant a divine edict."

Akasha placed a hand on her shoulder and said, "The floods aren't your fault, Thalassa. Severum had taken Gestalt's place as the Architect with O.A.K., so the lack of foresight in the rotational logistics was his failure. Severum was also part of the assault team, and you took down Governor Borges in the end. And it was Arcturus who shot Gestalt by accident, but only because Severum pushed the situation to its limit. Everything's not your fault, it's his."

"Okay, I made some mistakes, and didn't think it through," Severum interrupted, keeping watch out the window. "I admit that. I had thought something like mass flooding would have been calculated by the time I came onboard. Dams should have already been built."

"We didn't have the resources," Arcturus acknowledged.

"Yes, I made errors. But you can't just increase a planet's rotation without nature fighting back. This is what you preached daily at your damn Aporia Asylum!" he yelled at Akasha. "And you can't just assault the most deadly man in the hemisphere without there being some loose ends. Culptos was a loose end. I fuckin' tied it, so get offah my back about it, huh?"

The four women looked at him. He dropped his lower lip into a flat ridge. He had about made out the word *sorry* when he jumped back from the window and yelled, "Down!"

Shots fired through the window and burned holes through everything they touched: the kitchen walls, the hanging picture frames, even the new glass of sake Thalassa was holding as a testament to her conviction of sobriety. It shattered in her face, serrating her skin.

"Bad move," she said, drawing her daggers and tossing Arcturus the katana, who jumped away from the flying blade. "Arm thyself," she smiled as if living for the thrill, a moment she could feel alive.

Severum retrieved his Pulser and fired back thrice before the charge was spent. It glowed and recharged. The front door smashed, the back a second later. Two men entered from both directions. Severum fired. Shots missed, but they forced the men back outside.

Thalassa turned sideways between the two doors and threw one dagger at the front, and the other at the back in one fluid motion. Both landed on the floor, the throws sloppy.

Ash ducked under the crossfire and grabbed one of the daggers, hitting a button on the hilt as it glowed red. The searing dagger flushed her face with a heat too intense to wield for long.

Shots fired again through the front door. The assailants entered, but Severum came from behind to kick the Pulser from the first guy's hand and disarm the second by twisting his arm. He kicked both guns back where Arcturus retrieved them, one in each hand.

"Stop right there," she ordered, aiming them point blank.

Another man came around the front and entered but threw his

hands up when he saw Arcturus, dropping his weapon. Hired thugs, not professional hitmen. Must have thought it easy money.

That left Ash at the backdoor with the fourth assailant, who fired from behind the doorjamb. Ash froze, her shoulders so tense they could rip through her skin. She held the dagger near her chest, unable to move. The intense heat of the glowing blade evaporated her cold sweat. The thug fired at close range, but the shot hit the blade instead of her flesh, the force pushing it back to sear her leather armor.

The thug came around the door to fire again, but his soft neck met the sharp edge of a katana.

"Drop it!" Akasha hissed, holding the blade outstretched.

The Pulser fell.

Arcturus corralled the four together at gunpoint while Severum bound their hands and feet. "Who do you work for?"

"Sibi-nite2."

Definitely not professionals. These thugs didn't care about giving away info, meaning it wasn't a permanent working relationship.

"How many of you are there?"

"Just us," the tallest responded, catching his breath. "The sedan's small, wouldn't hold another guy, and Jenko takes up half the back seat as it is."

"Don't use my name, man," Jenko replied.

"Thalassa, I'm going to order you to do something. Go disable their vehicle," Arcturus said. "And get those malware tracers out of your system." She turned to the assailants and asked, "How did Sabrina affect our implants without being in cyberspace? That tech's available, but it's pricy and hard to get a hold of without a lot of very high connections."

"We don't know," Jenko answered for the group. "We just followed a lead that flashed in vHUD that there was a job available. Didn't care who you were."

Arcturus continued to extract information. Severum

approached his family. "No time to pack. Get what you can carry on your back and let's leave."

"That's all I owned to begin with," Ash replied, crying and heading to her room.

"Now you know why I wore a shirt with a teardrop shape cut into the back," Thalassa said, following her. "When you're going against the system you may never have much more than the values you hold dear. I never held many at your age, just trusted Arcturus to make the best decisions for us. Rough not having a home. Hell, I lived in an ice cave for a while just to get close to an A.I. construct. Had to kill my favorite pet to use his skin as a face mask because it was so cold. So, I know what you're going through."

"Really?"

"Yeah, but without Arc, it's like there's no values no more, and nothin' means nothin'."

"Hence the drinking," Ash acknowledged. "I think that's called codependency."

"No shit, girl."

Severum called the Enforcers to pick up the thugs. The rest of them gathered at the door with a few bags and suitcases. A few minutes later, the five of them left, never to return.

20

THAT NIGHT, THE GROUP WENT TO AN ENFORCER STATION TO report the attack. They hesitated before entering the three-story building. This was a place they had tried to avoid their entire lives, but the New Order wasn't as oppressive as the Old Guard and they might find some assistance. Severum approached the automated receptionist and an Enforcer soon came over to interview him, wearing one of the new uniforms with the New Order's logo.

"We were attacked by four men at our home last night and we're afraid to return. After the gunfire ceased, they mentioned a woman told them to do it by the name of Sabrina Underfoot. I have a video to prove it," Severum said, sending him the file.

The Enforcer reviewed the file, straightened his trapezoidal hat, and said, "The thugs don't mention a name that hired them to carry out the attack in your video. They said someone with the tag *Sibi-nite2* told them to do it."

"Yes, I know, but we can prove they're the same person."

Ash whispered in his ear, "We obtained that info while illegally hacking their server. We can't mention it."

Severum switched strategies, "Listen, I'm working off the books for the New Order and I just need some backup here."

"I'm sure you mean well, but we got a lot of cases to handle. While we take care of our own, you ain't wearing a badge or nothing."

"Would it help if I told you she blew up the warehouse next to Mandelbrot's last night?" he asked. He still couldn't believe what Ash had told them. Man, did they need to have a serious talk.

"Can you prove that?"

"Arc, Thalassa, and Ash all saw her hit a black box before it blew."

The Enforcer turned to Ash and asked, "Is that true?"

"Yes."

"How did you know it was her?"

"I didn't know what she looked like but figured it must be her because she looked up when I said her name."

"What were you doing there to begin with?" the Enforcer asked, squinting.

"I had wandered from the club to…"

"I'm waiting."

Thalassa interjected, "We were walking down the street after some hard clubbing and heard some suspicious noises. Checked it out."

"It must have been her," Ash said.

"But you don't know?"

"Look, I'm the victim here."

"Just trying to get the facts down. So, again, of all the people on the hemisphere, why assume it was Sabrina?"

"Because I was looking for her and rumor was she was in the area."

"So you were looking for someone, though you didn't know what she looked like, who was rumored to be in the area, and because she looked up when you spoke her name, you don't think she was just trying to see who was talking, you think she was admitting to being the person you thought she was," the Enforcer repeated. "And you began this search with some hard clubbing, is that about right?"

"She had a sword!"

"Which matters because?"

But Ash couldn't say, because she only knew the connection through her illegal hack the day she encountered the cyberknight. "I don't know."

"We'll look into this Sabrina character. I appreciate your help on this, and don't mean to put you on the spot. I am curious why you were looking for someone if she's as dangerous as you're implying. So, stay out of trouble. Your story has some serious gaps in it, and I think you may be into something way over your head, young girl," the Enforcer told her. "In the meantime, don't return home and we'll get you some funds to rent a hotel."

They left the station.

Severum turned to his family, who were still shaken by the gunfire. They held one another close. "Go get a hotel. I'm going to look into the truck you tailed to see what it was carrying. The coordinates have stopped flashing in my vision. And Ash, I'm sorry I got you into this."

"It's okay. I brought you into it first."

"You were just trying to connect. You don't need to follow in my footsteps, and definitely not in Thalassa's."

Arcturus turned to Thalassa but avoided eye contact. "I'm going home. I left this life behind for a reason and I have a city to build."

"Call me," Thalassa replied, hugging her, but Arcturus didn't reciprocate.

"You going back to the bar, or you gonna help me figure out what the hell's going on?" Severum asked Thalassa.

"The figure out thing. Got nothing to lose now, anyway," she shrugged. "But first, we sleep."

"We might not have much of a chance to catch them in the act."

"I can't go on. Like you said, we have to rest at some point."

"I'll head to the shipment coordinates alone then, but if I can do this with my seventieth birthday coming up, I know you can, being in your mid-fifties."

"I've treated my body rough over the years. Old injuries act up a lot."

"Tell me about it. Well, here's the coordinates. Get some rest and catch up if you can."

———

SEVERUM ARRIVED at the location in a low-end hovercraft as the sun was rising, his focus wavering from no sleep. The truck had stopped in the parking lot outside the Northern Treatment Facility, a major water plant that served multiple districts. Large pipes ran into the building, some half buried. Water rushed through a series of rectangular pools with antiquated filtration systems. Ammonia stung the air with its scent.

He HUD-texted Ash, "It's me. I need some schematics on the water flow at the Northern Treatment Facility here. Particularly, I need to know which water is treated and not treated and the connections between them. I don't want to assume."

"Gimme a few."

"Also, fly your tracker out of the truck. The driver's parked and getting out."

"I can't. Ikshana's out of range. If they find it, they might link it to me."

"I'll figure it out." He rushed behind the truck while keeping out of view of its side mirrors. He reached through the hole in the side of the trailer and felt around, but the falcon wasn't there. Probably shifted during the ride. "Reroute its controls to me."

"I've never done that before," Ash texted back.

"Just do it."

Once he had control, the falcon's vision appeared in vHUD, but the garage door was closed and it was too dark to see through its eyes. He clumsily hit a few commands and heard a clink inside the truck. Reaching inside the hole in the trailer again, he scoured the inside wall and grabbed the edge of a metal wing, pulling it out. He'd need to review the manual to fly the thing, so for now he backed away from the truck and hid Ikshana in some bushes along a deep swale.

The driver went around the back of the truck and retrieved a few boxes, stacking and carrying them inside. Severum followed him at a distance, the treatment facility doors wide open. The water plant was a latticework of thick, steel pipes that concealed the workers from one another. Walkways ran along the top of the building. Clanging echoed through the hangar, piercing the loud humming of engines. Gauges monitored the water pressure while men turned large blue wheels to shut off some valves and open others. Rows of egg-shaped tubs lined the floor connected to mixing basins beside mineral stockpiles labeled with lime and other treatments. Two men in hardhats surveilled the activities from the top of a ladder leading to a central control station on the upper level.

Severum grabbed a yellow jacket with their logo and a hardhat off a hook and wove between the pipes, keeping the delivery driver in view as he went upstairs. A woman passed him, carrying a long hose. While myriad employees worked the lower levels, he wouldn't be able to blend in among the few foremen on the upper level. He kept behind the tubs. The boxes exchanged hands and the driver left. He zoomed his eyes and scanned the face of the recipient but no name appeared. A public employee should be on the books; this guy was working for someone else.

"Shift change in ten minutes." the foreman announced.

Severum tracked the package and waited for the shift change

to gain access to the upper level, turning his back towards a dial anytime an employee passed, hiding in plain sight. He reviewed Ikshana's manual at the same time; a gut feeling told him he'd need all the help he could get.

———

ASH JACKED into VR and located the public works intranet but couldn't crack her way in. The file directory was restricted and the access protocols unclear. Conversely, the beta test environment was much easier to access. She broke down the cloud drive's URLs into their components: one part referenced authentication through a single-sign-on script; the next connected parent and child elements to display hidden data, while the third referenced one's username validation. An unprotected screenshot in a job aid showed such a validation in the URL bar, though it wasn't clear how the validation key tied to the username she would need.

She combined and recombined the parts, taking the stem of one page's address and mixing it with the end of another, but couldn't keep track of all the variations. Finally, she assigned each element of the structure a graphical depiction of a pipe, connecting them at various angles. As she did so, her system tested the file access she was generating, the virtual pipes filling to indicate the success rate as each one locked in place. No luck, until she landed upon a back door portal designed for temporary access for external users who didn't require the organization's single-sign-on protocol. Dropping the SSO, she was able to access a more traditional password entry page that she easily cracked, going on to create her credentials in the active directory. Turning to the live production environment, she accessed the correct part of the cloud drive containing the facility blueprints, and the data was hers.

"I got the files," she said, sending over the schematics.

SEVERUM RECEIVED the schematics and mapped them onto his vHUD so he could examine the pipe network at the treatment plant. The filtered waterpipes glowed green as he viewed them, the semi-filtered pipes yellow, and the unfiltered pipes red.

A bell rang at first noon indicating the shift change and he took advantage of the flurry of activity to climb the stairs to the glass control center that overlooked the facility, keeping his hardhat low over his face. The package recipient had discarded the boxes and taken three canisters out of each one, placing them on a desk. He knew his type: young, crewcut, envious, bad attitude.

The recipient marched downstairs with the three canisters and used a small station not connected to the main lines to mix them. Each canister was only a third full. Then he siphoned the mixture back into one container. Whatever substances were at play, it would have been more efficient to ship them in one canister to begin with, meaning the chemicals were too volatile to be mixed beforehand. Nevertheless, everything looked routine, and he thought the whole thing a mix-up despite the guy not showing up in the employee database, until he brought the canister to a secluded section of the facility where the water had already been filtered and required no additional treatments.

In terraforming school, Severum had learned enough about water chemistry to know that most chemicals were added during the filtration process to assist with binding, not afterwards. There were exceptions: Fluorite, final pH adjusters, but something was off. The amount of water coming through the plant versus the small contents of the canister were mismatched. This wasn't a large amount of activated carbon, it was something highly concentrated.

He tailed the receiver.

It would benefit the Old Guard to poison the water supply.

They could say the Great Rotation caused changes in weather patterns that diverted rivers to pick up more sediment, including toxic heavy metals. That would be true, but they wouldn't mention that normal filtration could handle that accumulation. Instead, they could spin it as just another reason to return to a world without daylight cycles, tossing half the world back into darkness and restoring the old, oppressive economic system that revolved around light. There were plenty of other functions the poison could serve, especially if it was routed to disproportionately affect certain voting districts that were gung-ho on supporting the New Order. Whatever the plan, Severum needed to stop it while obtaining a sample so he could ward off future attacks if this one failed. No, when it failed, for there was too much on the line for him not to come through.

He texted Ash, "Tell everyone you know not to drink the water. Have Aurthur run a water pollution advisory immediately as a special alert. Don't let your name be connected with the warnings."

"Will do."

He approached the man in the back of the facility where steam hissed from a pipe. He could slam the guy's head against it, take the canister, and finish him off by drowning him in the mixing tub. With this many lives on the line he might even be able to morally justify it, but he had made that mistake before so he fished for the guy's intent first, giving up the element of surprise.

"Hey, I don't recall a deposit needing to be made in the filtered water supply. But I may have overlooked something. I'm sure you know what you're doing, I don't mean that," Severum feigned.

"I don't recall you being part of the workforce here. Let me guess, you're new, right? I'm Griff Barren."

He avoided the easy excuse and replied, "No, I've been here a while, but I was on leave after I got my hand stuck in a filter.

Had to have surgery," he said, holding up his titanium-reinforced hand, which though it looked fairly normal, had recent scarring.

"Oh yeah, that happens," Griff nodded.

Severum figured Griff wouldn't stay off the employee books for long unless he had an accomplice, or he was the new guy. He ruled out the latter option, since someone new wouldn't pretend to know everyone well enough to assume Severum was also new. An insider was keeping his identity hidden, meaning they were watching the moment of crisis unfold. So, who was on Griff's side?

Severum looked into the polished steel pipe and caught the curved reflection of two guys on the upper level with bulky jackets – armed and dangerous. If he had jumped to violence, he would have been shot in the back within seconds. Griff was going to dump the poison in, and there was nothing Severum could do unless he opened fire first on his accomplices, who had the advantage of height and visibility, then on Griff.

"What's that called in the canister again? Alum? I'm getting old and can't recall the details," Severum said.

"It's... are you armed?" Griff interrupted, looking at Severum's pocket.

He was carrying an infiltration model Pulser that lacked the bulk of the larger items, but also the charge capacity. Still, no one would have noticed it unless they had been trained to look. "Of course." He played it off. "I'm sent on field work a lot to investigate the river runoff, and I've seen Aphorids out there. Lost a guy I knew in a battle once. Check out this holotag. Still carry it after all these years," he replied, taking it out from his shirt.

"Man, that's rough, yeah," Griff said. "Bet you were in the military, too? Lots of us Vets go into public service afterwards. Well, I don't know if the guys gonna like you packing heat, but keep it to yer'self, huh?"

"Of course, thanks for the tip, Griff," he replied, positioning his body, placing his right hand on his Pulser, and looking for exits.

"Now, if you 'scuse me, I have work to do." Griff held the canister over the water.

Severum swiped it with a long arc of his left hand, drawing the Pulser with the other and firing blindly over his shoulder at the upper railing as he fled. They were too stunned to react and he got all the way to the emergency exit before the shooting began. He slammed the bar on the door and left the building right before the shots burned wide holes in the blossoming steel. Severum looked over his shoulder and estimated the size of the holes as he ran. An average-sized Pulser that expended that much energy at once would be out of charge after two shots. With two men, that meant four shots total.

There were two holes.

The third shot jolted him in the upper shoulder, razing across his skin, the burn radiating across his chest and down his back. The fourth shot was low, hitting his hover-boot fuel tank as it started leaking. The tank was shielded, or it would have exploded. He stumbled, cradling the canister on his run to the parking lot and counting the seconds until their Pulsers recharged.

The men had run downstairs and were exiting the building. Severum snaked back and forth to make himself harder to hit, but another shot and he wouldn't be so lucky with a beam that wide. He reached halfway to his hovercraft when he bent over to catch his breath. He grabbed his chest. His heart sputtered and he could barely breathe. The men closed in. Seconds until they fired, but his body refused to move. The stress was going to kill him if they didn't first. Another vehicle approached in the distance. He ran commands in vHUD to get that damn bird in the air, navigating it to intersect their line of sight.

Ikshana should be able to block at least a few shots, he

thought in desperation. He crouched, trying to make it to his vehicle, but his heart couldn't take it.

Shots fired, ricocheting off Ikshana and punching up the soil near his feet. Too close. Too fucking close.

The approaching vehicle hovered to the roof and stopped. Someone got out and rushed to the edge. The mechanical falcon continued to close in on the gunmen, distracting from their aim as it shot sparks from its damage. Finally, it divebombed them, exploding in their faces. The first assailant screamed and ran inside, while the other charged straight ahead beneath the edge of the roof, raising his Pulser at Severum's back. There were no more distractions and no more tricks he could play. This was it – he was an open target.

Right before the shot went off, a woman leapt off the two-story building with a mid-air somersault, waving two blazing daggers from either hand. She landed right behind the gunman, crossing the daggers in front of his neck from behind. The red glow flushed his face.

"Try me," Thalassa said.

The assailant dropped the Pulser, but if she bent down to get it, she would be kneed in the face. Instead, she kicked the gun aside to put distance between herself and the gunman and backed off to retrieve it, keeping both daggers trained on him. Worked screamed in the building behind her, running back and forth. She trained the gun on the assailant and met Severum at his side.

"You're late," he said.

"But I'm ready."

They reached the parking lot and jumped into his vehicle. As they sped away with Thalassa behind the wheel, Severum said, "They'll trace your vehicle up there on the roof. And even if you wanted to risk retrieving it, mine can't fly that high and my hover-boots lost their fuel."

"Don't worry," Thalassa said. "Do me a favor, count backwards from ten. Or was it five, or three? Hell with it."

The hovercraft exploded on the rooftop, leaving a gaping hole in the facility. Water spurted everywhere.

"Just like old times, huh, Sev'?"

"I can't keep this life up."

"You're hurt."

"Surface wound, but I'm using my lives up quick here."

"Take this healing spray," she said. "So, what's in the canister?"

"Let's find out. Now that we're clear of the facility, open the windows, in case there's toxic fumes in this thing." He opened the canister and scanned it in vHUD.

He maintained a wealth of terraforming programs that enabled him to analyze chemical compounds. It was definitely a poison, and would have been deadly. The three chemicals it was composed of were thankfully hard to come by, which was the only thing that might prevent a future attack.

"What's in it?" she asked.

"Bad ass shit."

"That bad, huh? They won't stop, unless we stop them. We gotta get to Sabrina, figure out what she knows, and then off her."

"We're out of leads, and Ash said Sabrina has gone ghost since the warehouse incident."

"Who received the canister back at the facility?"

"This guy, Griff Barren, if that's even his name. I caught him off guard so I think it might be. If it was an alias, he would have chosen a more common name, and one that was easily forgotten instead of an odd name referencing death. Anyway, he ran off when the shooting started."

"We'll find him when we get back."

He called Aurthur, "Hey, it's me. Did you get the message about the water from Ash?"

"Severum, yes, what's going on?"

"Did you publish it?

"I… thought about it."

"What? Why not?"

"There's a lot of attention on me right now."

"Tell me, did you drink tap water today?"

"No. I used bottled water for my tea."

"You and your damn tea. So you believed it enough to avoid drinking it yourself, but refused to publish the advisory to the public."

"It has to go through a committee first, or at least get editor approval," Aurthur said.

"Terrorists don't care about your glitchin' red tape."

"I can see that perspective."

"Caution carries its own risk, my friend."

"I suppose you're right. I'll get it approved and get the warning out. How long should the advisory run?"

"Until the Old Guard is destroyed," he replied, ending the call.

Thalassa drove, the scenery speeding across the curved window. He turned to her, "I can't do this anymore. I'm scared."

"Yeah, right," she laughed. "You serious? You of all people? Shit, that scares even me."

"Don't you feel it? Age?"

"I'm almost fifteen years younger than you, but sure, it sets in at times when the injuries act up like I said. Hell, you probably caused half of them back when you were hunting down O.A.K. members. Glad you got on the right side finally."

"Being stabbed in the leg with your dagger outside Amorpha wasn't all that great either. You jumped right off the crescent butte! But that was many years ago. I admit, I was the perpetrator and the victim, the binder and the bound."

"Yeah, the wounds still hurt. You break the body, it don't always go back together right. But I mask the pain with, you know…"

"You drink to feel young again?" he asked.

"Heh, who am I kiddin'? There's a thousand excuses to drink once you've accumulated a lifetime of suffering. But they're all bullshit. In the end, I drink just to drink."

"Glad you realize that. Now, get me to the hotel."

"Which one?"

"I don't even know where I live anymore."

"Just be glad you're alive."

21

THALASSA DROPPED SEVERUM OFF AT A HOTEL THAT SCREAMED mediocrity, but he didn't care. The only reliable home was the grave, the door always parted, the welcome mat threaded with every moment of suffering that made it merciful. He knocked on the door.

"You're hurt," Akasha noticed, looking both ways and bringing him inside. She locked the old-fashioned bolt, then ran her fingers along it until the metal indented her hand.

"Surface wound," he replied. She retrieved a first-aid kit from under the bed. He turned to Ash, "Griff Barren. He's your man. Thalassa will catch you up. Sorry about your bird; it ain't flying home."

Then he collapsed from exhaustion, gunfire perforating his dreams.

NIGHT FELL upon the hotel as it did every few hours.

Ash leaned over her father's bed. She wasn't expecting him to become the foundation of her life at her age, but seeing him injured and out of commission brought tears to her eyes. She had been wrong to be so angry at him, angry for him not being the man her mother deserved, angry at him for not being part of her life, even angry for all the ways he was similar to her, as if society and genetics determined her behavior more than personal choice or upbringing. Still, she was no carbon copy, and he knew she existed now and wouldn't let her down.

She sat on the opposite bed and claimed the territory where her mother's few belongings had been stashed. The worry on her mother's face at his injury gave her hope that they might at least find solace in one another. They might never get back together, but she had never experienced that anyway. To know there was love, and that she had been conceived from that love, was enough.

A peaceful smile overcame her, then she remembered Severum saying Ikshana had been destroyed. Being so worried about him, the news had passed over her. The tears burst from her eyes again as she sat with her head in her hands. It had been synchronized to her cognigraf for so long that it knew her schedules and preferences, and it could access when she was feeling bad to come cheer her up. How it would nuzzle her with its titanium beak until she smiled. Between her few, selfish online friends, her inattentive and spiteful mother, and her absent father, she had little affection growing up. She had grown up fast, like bamboo, with a hollow center in her heart no one could fill. Mom had advised her to cultivate the present, to *be here now*, but *here* might as well be nowhere, a bustling city with strangers as neighbors. And now, not even that, just a shithole hotel.

As a child, her best memory had been when her mother took her to the Lost Shores to the far north of Blutengel. Her body had been developing and she hadn't felt comfortable at the busier beaches, so they had taken a hovercraft to the most isolated beach on the hemisphere where she was presented a gift: a kite. It seemed unremarkable at first, but then her mother explained that before the Great Rotation, there was little wind on the planet, save for the spontaneous hurricanes. Children could finally fly free. The winds had brought warm weather as heat was distributed from the Eastern Hemisphere. The icecaps had already begun melting, but her mother spared her that knowledge. That vast, semi-frozen expanse seemed like it could be filled with anything. The sands counted down to her life beginning, not ending, a time when the kite flew in accordance with her volition rather than being pushed by storms. With no distractions, her mother had been attentive that day, and they had talked, really talked. In the end, she became so fascinated with the wind that she knew she would study terraforming just like her mother as a way to be one with it, for the eye of a storm was stable amidst all its chaos – science predicting what the heart could not.

Now, her life was driven by storms once more, but she would rein them in and whip the winds into submission.

She logged in and searched for Griff online while Thalassa texted her about what had happened at the water treatment plant. The guy wasn't hard to find. Thirty, pale, red hair, neuralmod addiction that he plastered all over social media. He even bragged about a big job he was doing; *real undercover stuff,* he wrote. An idea came, but she refused to use the word *blackmail* to describe it, for too often people had associated the color with negative words such as being *blacklisted,* the *black market,* and *dark humor,* and she knew enough from the colonizing ship's archives to know how that had turned out for society.

She contacted Griff online, replacing her image with a sexier avatar. *How would Thalassa handle this? I need to talk like she does to be convincing.* She messaged him, "You in the mood for some off-the-books activities?" That sounded stupid. She backspaced and tried again, "I saw your credentials and I have a job for you." Wouldn't work. Backspace. "Hey, glitchface, you making any runs tonite?" That was it.

Send.

A moment later the reply came through, "Hey, babe. Who wants to know?"

"Friend of a friend. You avail or not?"

"I don't have any friends."

"Sibi," she lied.

"I'll hear you out. What you gots?"

"Meet me in the abandoned stadium downtown at third noon." She logged off and contacted Aurthur, "I need to borrow a few video drones for use at the stadium tonight."

"You don't seem the sporting type," he replied.

"Can you lend them out?"

"They're expensive…"

"Look, Severum's injured. Not bad, but he can't keep this up forever. There's no risk here, none to you or me."

"I mean, there's my job. But okay, I'll send the video drones downtown."

"Thanks, and make sure they broadcast their feed to me. I'll send you my IP."

———

GRIFF ARRIVED at the empty stadium and walked to the center of the field where teams would play games in augmented reality when sports were in season, though they were losing their popularity. Only the emergency lights were on. He buried his hands in his sweatshirt pockets and scoped the place out.

Ash sat back at the hotel monitoring the three drones' video feed as they flew over his head, his body tensing and keeping watch. She routed her voice through the stadium intercom that she had hacked earlier. "Stop right there. You're being recorded and you'll be televised if you make one move off the field."

Griff ran anyway, covering his face.

She upped the threat. "I said stop! Or I'll send your online posts to the Enforcers."

"What're you talkin' 'bout? Where are you?" he asked, searching the bleachers.

She reclined in the hotel bed, zoomed in on his face, and continued, "You were hired to poison the water supply by Sabrina Underfoot."

"I have no idea who that is."

"Don't gaslight me. You confirmed you know Sibi online when we set this up. Got the message to prove it. Between the testimony we've secured from your coworkers, who all stated you weren't even an employee, to the testimony of those who witnessed you with the canister, you're looking at being sentenced to death."

"I'm a good guy. No one will believe that crap!"

Ash's voice echoed through the stadium as she replied, "They'll see you for who you really are, a neuralmod addict who will do anything for a fix. Says so on your social media profiles."

"How much you want?"

"My organization doesn't need money," she feigned. "We want Sabrina. You're going to arrange a meeting between the two of you, but you aren't going to show, in return for our silence."

"No can do. I already told her I failed, and I'm lucky if she lets me live for it."

"Tell her that though you failed, you were able to extract info from the New Order that she might be interested in."

Griff paused, still searching the bleachers in vain, then said, "I don't want no trouble, but she ain't gonna buy that."

"Make her."

"You don't make a woman like that do nothin'."

"Find a way."

"I could contact her and open up a channel so you could get access to her—"

"Useless," Ash replied through the speakers. "She's a cyber-security specialist and will know her system has a ghost. How did she pay you? I can trace the account."

"She didn't. I failed. Who are you?"

"Internal investigations."

"At the water plant?" Griff asked, cocking a brow.

It wasn't the most intimidating answer she could have given, but she continued, "You have no idea how seriously the New Order takes public health. They're willing to... kill for it." She was losing her edge and had to work fast.

"I'm not buyin' it," he replied, ripping his hands out of his sweatshirt and drawing two Pulsers. He aimed at the video drones and two of the three went down as the other activated its evasion routine.

She would lose the feed in a few more seconds. She let him have it, "You really think I'm such a dumbass that I'll tell you who I work for? What you think, I'm an amateur or something, glitchface? Amateurs are what you jerk off to while you're high on Sarahtoning and your designer drugs. Now, unless you want your face plastered across every Enforcer's vHUD in Blutengel, then tell me how you're going to help us off that Sabrina glitch."

Griff stopped and stared at his feet, defeated. "The chems came from this warehouse. Rare shit, but she had the funds for it. Driver was just a rando. She said it was a hallucinogen, a free trip for the city as a prank."

"But you didn't believe that 'cause you're a smart guy, right, Griff? You knew what it was."

He shrugged and continued, "Sabrina oversaw the transportation. She arranged it all, getting the rare compounds to make the poison."

"You're telling us what we already know," she replied. "Hurry up."

"After I agreed to work for her, she made me get this implant installed. It lets her monitor my activities. She said it was so she could prove the canister was delivered, and that she'd have it taken out afterwards, but she's a control freak and just left it there. I wake up to blue error screens every morning. She ain't watching now though. I know when she is, 'cause my vision blurs from the processing load."

"Who installed it?"

"Grafter by the name of Kenekt. We can work something out you and me. You want Sabrina, I want you off my back and I want this implant destroyed. So here's how we get her," he offered. But a moment later, he jammed his hands to his temples and fell to his knees on the field. He threw his head back into a wild scream as he yelled, "Get it out! Get it out! It's setting me on fire from within!" Blood leaked from his ears and nose to stain the turf. Then he slumped across the field and was still.

Ash zoomed the remaining drone to check his vitals. The amount of blood made any call for medics futile. She shook her head, instructed the drone to self-destruct for good measure, and broke the connection.

All that, but she had a name, Kenekt, and hopefully that would be enough. It had to be, or she'd be next.

22

Ash looked up Kenekt the next morning, the name Griff had spilled in the stadium before he died. As expected, the guy wasn't on any official grafter certification list, but within an hour she had a first name to go with his street tag by scrolling the Natt-Web cybernetic forums – Gus.

Her mother interrupted, "Ash, we need to talk."

"What is it now?"

"What's with the attitude?"

"Because *we need to talk* never means it's something good. We don't talk about good stuff. Good stuff doesn't happen anymore. Ever." Her breath raced, her hands sweaty.

"That's important, too, Ash. But right now I need you to know that Thalassa is not a role model."

"I never said she was."

"You're still wearing her shirt."

"Yeah, it's glitchin'. Best thing I have. Reminds me that not everyone in your generation was so stuck up, Mom."

"Your tongue spits fire."

"Right, because I believe in direct conflict. You take a

problem on face-to-face, instead of running from it halfway across the world."

"Severum's not a role model either."

"Everyone's a role model, Mom. Don't you see? We absorb a little bit of everyone we meet. That doesn't mean they should be locked away from us like they don't exist our entire lives, it just means we have to educate our judgment."

"Perhaps I made a poor choice regarding Severum," she admitted.

"What was that?"

"I'm sorry," she made out.

Severum woke at the sound of his name. Ash calmed down, then caught him up to speed.

"So, this guy, Gus, installed that implant into Griff for Sabrina?" he asked.

"Yes."

"I know a Gus who worked on my hand, actually. Is this guy your age, you think?"

"Yes, judging by the forums he was on and the slang he used," Ash replied. "Here's his avatar pic."

"That's the guy alright, right down to the goatee. I'll see if Arcturus knows where he might have gone. She said he was working with some pretty seedy people after he stopped associating with K.O.A."

Akasha interrupted, "How you feeling?"

"Fine," Severum replied.

"No, you're not. You need to rest. You're almost seventy, and the decisions you're making now will carry on through your bloodline for generations. Let the Enforcers handle this."

"You heard them, they're not interested. Partially, because we can't tell them how we know what we know. And you know they don't take anonymous tips seriously. There's no accountability, and it's too easy to fake digital evidence. I have to do this.

Besides, Arcturus used to research teleomere enhancements, and they're making great progress on life extension every day. Apparently, on Earth, they had gotten people up to two or three hundred years old, but most of that tech was lost when our colonizing ship's archives were damaged. I just need to stop thinking that I'm old when there are those who live twice as long nowadays."

"Getting older means being more careful, Severum, not less. The truth is, we could still go at any time, any one of us. We cling to permanence instead of accepting our inevitable mortality," she said. "The quest to live forever through augmenting ourselves with cybernetics doesn't mean the quality of life will be extended. The Forever Glitched are proof of that. As you age, the hardware defects are going to accumulate in your implants and it's going to be more costly to fix. You need to take care of yourself so you don't die a glitcher."

"Philosophizing about death won't avoid it."

"Neither will running into battle. The event horizon of our non-existence is always looming, and you have to remember what you're living for."

"The mission," he replied, but it wasn't the response she was looking for.

"We've both tried to undo order at times, but it's a cycle. You know that. There's always going to be a competing group that romanticizes the way things used to be, and whether avertedly or not, become the enemies of progress. I ran that group before in the Aporia Asylum. I know I can't stop you, but be careful. I admit that part of me prefers you helpless in bed so I know you're okay."

"Figures."

She leaned close and recited,
"He clasps the crag with crooked hands;
Close to the sun in lonely lands,
Ring'd with the azure world, he stands.
The wrinkled sea beneath him crawls;

He watches from his mountain walls,
And like a thunderbolt he falls. "

"Did you write that?"

"Yes," she replied. "It captures what I wanted to say."

"It's great," he said, though he knew she was lying. He had run the feed from his auditory implants through a search engine which came up with nothing at first, until he extended the search to the ship's archives and saw it was written by Tennyson, a man born on Earth in some place called England 1,311 years ago. She seldom lied – must be trying to impress him. How unusual!

"I'll pray for a miracle." She leaned over to kiss his forehead.

Change was threatening. He furrowed and told her, "Miracles are nothing but annihilation. If the laws of physics were violated for even a split second to allow for them, the universe would shatter."

"Shh, don't spoil nature's surprises," she whispered. "She always finds a way to restore balance. It's you and I who have shattered one another's worlds, Old Flame. On Earth, they wrote of the River Lethe, the word meaning *forgetfulness*, but also *oblivion* and *concealment,* the opposite of *aletheia*, or *truth*. In order to reincarnate, one must drink from this river to forget one's old life that they might be born anew. If we do this by forgetting the past like it doesn't exist though, or by concealing our feelings, then we will pass into oblivion. There's no rebirth in that, but neither is there in rehashing the past with every current action."

"Yes, but I heard Earthlings were just referring to an earlier form of cryogenic freezing that hadn't been perfected yet. The river was the tub they prepared their bodies in. Because the tech failed, they would freeze themselves, but would wake up with their implants having erased their memories upon reboot."

"Well, I tried," she said, walking away.

All his sacrifices to rotate the planet were coming right back to hit him in the face. Now, Akasha was here to lure him with niceties, but would soon let him have it again, demanding more and more. He had given her ample opportunity to make up in the past, and the cycle of opening his heart, only to have it torn out again would never stop unless they both changed. She could learn to be more direct with her expectations and confrontations in a good way, he could learn to be a better listener when she expressed herself, but the self-fulfilling prophecy of, *it won't make a difference anyway,* held them back. It all came down to faith, and he had little left. But damn, did he miss the woman who was just in the other room, yet so far away.

———

THEY HAD breakfast as a family at a shack serving okonomiyaki with a dozen sauces. The fried cabbage patties were greasy, just the way he liked them. Scent of fried onions and carrots. He called Arcturus.

"What is it, Severum?"

"Hey, you remember the grafter, Gus, who you connected me with? Goes by the tag Kenekt."

"It would be reasonably assumed that I would."

"You got any idea where he might be crashing at, Arc?"

"Yes, but first you need to keep Thalassa out of your games."

"She makes her own choices. You know you can't control that one."

"Stupid choices."

"The quicker I get the info, the quicker this will be over, and we can go another few decades without ever speaking to one another again."

"You tapped into my motivation quite well. Rumor is he moved to Eisbrecher and you can find him at *A Better You* gym on workdays."

"Thanks."

———

AFTER A COUPLE NIGHTS staking out the place, Severum finally spotted Gus walking into the gym. The weather in Eisbrecher was chillier, the winds cooling as they passed over the glaciers. Sleet hammered the road, stinging his face like pinpoints of steel as he walked towards the entrance. Still, it was a fraction of how cold it had been before he increased the once tidal-locked planet's rotation, since the temperature was more evenly distributed across the hemispheres.

Glass windows lined the front wall of the gym. People wore their skimpiest outfits, even though none of them would be breaking a sweat, and half the skin he saw was likely photo-edited before it reached his artificial eyes. While most forms of broadcasting visual alterations were illegal, the fashion industry had long been a proponent of pressuring the government to allow people to suggest the appropriate skin in which to view them, if it didn't render them unrecognizable. Many virtual clothing items cost more than their physical counterparts. Of course, Severum could easily turn such visual enhancements off in his vHUD's augmented reality, but he was always curious how people portrayed their ideal selves, and liked to flicker between the two worlds, seeing the physical, and the superimposed virtual.

Inside, men and women leaned back on weight-lifting benches. Instead of dumbbells, they were connected to a host of wires inserted at key muscle points to electrically stimulate physical activity, and thus growth. The technology was old, and the original models only improved muscle functioning by fifteen percent. Implants accelerated the process today to the point where it had replaced other anaerobic workouts, though like any implants, they required an increased caloric count, taxing both body and mind. One couldn't run them while running an auto-calculator at the same time, for instance. Meanwhile, most of the bodybuilders didn't feel a thing when their muscles contracted, high on neuralmods instead of endorphins.

Gus sat at a bench. A fit man came over to connect him, slipping him a chip trip, a tiny circuit he inserted in a slot behind his head. Severum recognized the color, a potent but short-acting drug that would make him susceptible to influence. Gus pulled it out after it downloaded and fell into a trance, his muscles moving on their own.

Severum kept behind the row of benches, but after the drug had taken effect, he snuck behind the payment counter, took another chip, and went back to the bench to massage Gus' neck muscles. He lifted his head from behind to insert it. Gus spasmed left, then right, and when it ended Severum removed the chip. Keeping behind his head and out of sight, he lowered his voice and said, "That oughta double the effect. I want you to listen up, Gus. You remember your customers?"

"Huh?" he replied, stretching it into three syllables.

"Griff Barren, know him?"

"Griff... sure, sure, sure."

"You gave him an implant with a spyware program you installed for a woman named Sabrina Underfoot."

The fitness coaches, who were more software engineers than athletes, spotted him and asked, "Everything all right?"

He nodded to them and smiled. "Just a friend." They lost interest.

"You're my friend," Gus agreed, high.

"Sabrina, why did she contact you?"

"She knew I did jobs on the side for K.O.A."

"How did she know?"

"Hell, she worked for 'em, man."

"Impossible. Arcturus would have recognized her in the warehouse."

"Arcturus can barely recognize her own lovers. She knows people more by the objects they carry and the clothes they wear.

She got issues, man. Brain's different. Took a shot in the arm in the Great Rotation battle and banged herself all up in the process."

From what Ash had said, she hadn't initially known what Sabrina looked like in real life. And she had said it was dark in the warehouse that night. If Arcturus did have issues recognizing people, and she had myriad employees and volunteers to keep track of, then it meant the enemy could be right under her nose.

Gus' head twitched. He continued to speak, but his words ran together in abstract concoctions. The double dose was hitting him hard, but he'd recover soon. The coaches looked over again and left their monitoring stations. Time to split.

Severum slid out the door. The wind blew on the back of his head like a winter wolf's breath, biting into his neck just under the collar. He pulled his jacket tight and grabbed the last airbus of the day home.

He called Arcturus on the ride. "You're in trouble."

"What is it?"

"Sabrina. I met up with Gus and he said she's part of K.O.A."

"Where is she?"

"I don't know," he said.

"You couldn't get that out of him?"

"Your perfectionism drives people away, you know. I didn't use to care, and I'm not sure I do now, but you'll always be alone, no matter how many lovers you have. Before you retaliate, let it sink in, Arc. People need kindness and affection."

"I can't believe I'm being lectured by a former merc who used to hunt bioluminaries, the poorest of the poor, for a few extra fireflies just so you could get high while preaching to others not to."

"You didn't even acknowledge me, Arc, just judged me again. This is why Thalassa can't be with you."

"When did she say that?"

"She told me at Mandelbrot's, then mentioned it again at the house when we were attacked."

A long pause, then she said, "I don't know anyone who looks like her here."

"Word is, you keep track of projects and tasks better than people," he replied.

"People are projects."

"To you, they're tasks to put up with, at best."

"You may be right. Maybe I'm not the only one right in the world."

"Can you honestly say you remember what she looked like at the warehouse, and whether any of your employees or volunteers match her description?"

"No, I cannot. Ash must have captured an image while she was there. Have her send it to me and I'll put an alert out."

"Not sure that's the best approach. She'll either go into hiding, or suddenly lash out and push her agenda to the limit. She's infiltrated your group, which makes sense since it's the offshoot of O.A.K." He grabbed a shot of cheap whiskey from the concierge on the airbus. "Anyone wanting to increase the rotation would find ample instructions amidst our files, including schematics for the apparatuses that maintain the speed. We don't know for sure if she recognized you at the warehouse either, Arcturus, but she's bound to know our faces, so be careful."

"I'll send her image to my most trusted guards."

"Hell, she could be one of them. She may be disguised with an avatar projection broadcasted over her visage even."

"You know regulations don't allow the face to be reskinned. Seeing the world through augmented reality has to somewhat match the real thing. Reskin clothes all you want, tattoos, even hair, but your face has to stay you."

"True, but she's smart enough to find a workaround. What other intel do you have that someone looking to restore the Old Guard would like to get a hold of?"

"Everything's relevant in one way or another."

"Then it's likely you've been compromised from the start. She's a master of cybersecurity, and any data you have you can assume she has it. Probably has backdoors installed all over your network. She recently lived in my daughter's apartment complex, if that was even a coincidence, but before that she lived in Eisbrecher, half the world away from the K.O.A. base. So tell your guards they're looking for someone who has an intermittent work schedule, travels a lot, maybe on the city's tab. Check your files and accounts for her name and tag, including anyone who accessed them recently. Audit your funds, you know the drill."

"Will do. Severum, thank you," an expression seldom heard from her.

"You're welcome. I'll try to head over to help you fish her out. Keep me posted."

City lights streaked across the windowpanes. The airbus returned him to the hotel, rattling through the clear compression chamber. Sabrina was somewhere out there preying upon the weak; but the meek would inherit this planet – or he would die heralding their name.

23

SEVERUM ARRIVED AT THE K.O.A. COMMUNE AT SECOND daybreak. He spent the next few hours pressing people for information and avoiding Arcturus. After showing Ash's picture of Sabrina to dozens of guards, merchants, barkeeps, and others, he hadn't run into a single person who recognized her. He posted it on private online forums to no avail. Yet, if she only traveled to the hemisphere for espionage, and spent most of her personal time in Eisbrecher and Blutengel, then he couldn't reasonably expect someone to recall her face way out here, assuming she wasn't using a virtual disguise. There was one group who had never installed vHUD implants though, who saw the world like it was, a group whose golden orb-shaped eyes penetrated reality.

Severum spent the next hour interviewing the local Florinik until he encountered one lumbering male who sat against a pueblo.

He rocked back and forth as he drummed a rhythm upon a giant mushroom with a sturdy head. His wooden necklaces jostled on his leathery neck as he bobbed to the beat. He stared at the picture until his golden eyes brightened, "This one I knows."

"Are you sure?"

"She is entwined in my memory, and that of Orbis's. Her name is Anirbas."

The pseudonym, a reversal of her name, showed the whole thing was just a game to her. He was once more a step behind. "That's her. Tell me everything you know."

"Your name I do not knows."

"Severum."

"I'm Arborlis. That woman is thorny vine snaking way through garden. She come to me for knowledge."

"What type? What services do you provide?"

"I listen to patterns in the wind, the feathery brush of its breath upon the river, the whims and plights of the Bhasura."

"Wait… you know the Bhasura, the crystals? How did you figure out how to communicate with them?"

"You simply close your eyes, still your thoughts, cleanse your heart, and they will resonate."

Severum was drawn in for a moment, then snapped, "No, nothing works like that. That's pushing my tolerance too far."

"I take it you believe Orbis is computer network? Well, Bhasura have own network."

"Not trying to be rude, but lives are on the line, and I'm a geophysicist not a metaphysicist."

"They are one and the same." Arborlis laughed, his whole body rumbling, his necklaces bouncing on his thick, barked chest. "Your thorny vine come here to study ley lines."

Ley lines weren't scientifically proven but had their adherents: people who believed there were magnetic or supernatural energies flowing along the planet that converged at certain points, providing those areas greater spiritual capacities. Supporters had analyzed the most important locations, monuments, buildings, temples, and dig sites in the planet's history and found they could be placed on the same set of lines. It was really pure randomness, but if Sabrina believed in it, she was bound to use them to determine the best location for her next terrorist act.

"Say I wanted to find the place on the planet where all the ley lines intersect, or at least the majority of them."

The Florinik smiled again and said, "The Vortex, an area East of Nathril-Xoynsia. It contains great flow of chi."

"What causes this energy?"

"The alignment of planets."

Severum rolled his eyes and replied, "Look, I'm not as advanced as you are. I'm hardly a śrāvaka, let alone an arhat like you."

Arbolis nodded, appreciating the nomenclature.

He had learned the words from Opal's anthropological reports. "So, humor me. What else might be causing this energy. Something powerful, but something you can touch."

"I see your reasoning. You cannot touch the planets, for some believe they are also eyes of Orbis. But you can feel the geysers erupt."

"Ahh, so there is porous rock beneath there, and magma beneath that."

"I do not understand."

"It's hot as a mofo underground."

"Oh yes, yes, water burn you. No good for plants like us."

"What's the precise location of this geyser at the heart of the ley lines?"

He explained it to Severum.

"One more thing. She mention a timeframe? She in a hurry to get to this place?"

"No, that one is creeping vine like I says."

"Thank you, truly," Severum said, placing his hand on the firm shoulder of the Florinik male. "You may have saved many lives today."

"Something tell me yours was not one of them," he sighed.

"Here, take necklace." He rose to place it over his head, then gathered his mushroom and left.

———

SEVERUM REPORTED BACK to Arcturus at the commune, renting a hovercraft and some basic geological survey equipment and packing it into the vehicle. His implants negated the need for much of it, but one never knew when one would crash. He took off across the plains until they gradually turned to sand and headed north to the large trading hub of Nathril-Xoynsia.

He passed a parade of merchants carrying their wares on Dijyorkvoken, the large, hairy animals grunting as they stomped across the plains. Their footsteps unearthed the soil, exposing its deeper sandy layers from when the hemisphere formerly known as Dayburn had been all desert. Severum had passed this route before, but it still shocked him to see small watering holes having become giant lakes. The ecological impacts were more positive on this hemisphere than they were back home.

The bustling trading post had replaced its makeshift walls of broken furniture, bones, and anything else they could find, with cinder blocks reinforced by steel beams. Dark stains ran down the beige residential buildings that towered four stories high, all of them leaning. Most of the place was a house of cards with shacks piled haphazardly upon other shacks.

Disinterest greeted him as he passed through the gate. The streets were columns of chawls that ran as far as the eye could see. Florinik, humans, and extraterrestrial species who had come for pirated neuralmods hung out of their balconies. Aphorids were chained up in front of merchant stalls to guard the shadier businesses. They gnashed their teeth as he passed, and it would be naïve to think their chains would hold them for long.

The inhabitants sensed his relative wealth and ran to offer him various wares, including Florinik sap, a bodily excretion that was used as honey by the locals. He didn't want to know which orifice it came from. He slowed down and asked a guy in a dingy tunic, "Which way to the Vortex? I know it's somewhere east of here."

"You mystique?"

"Mystic? No."

"Everyone else stay 'way from there," the man replied, walking off but pointing to it.

Severum headed east of town and soon arrived at the Vortex. The geyser was hard to miss, the conduit hole extending deep into the ground. He had learned much about them in terraforming school: how the shape of a geyser impacted the eruption, at what point in the process the water boiled, the types of substratum that allowed for eruption, and the variables impacting how often it occurred.

There was no activity in the area, so he approached the slot-shaped surface vent and measured for tremors. Then he lowered a camera down the riven on a harness he made from rope. It transmitted the images to vHUD for viewing as it descended between the jutting, damp walls. The camera followed the condensing water droplets deep into the planet until the chasm grew more narrow and he had to stop to reangle it. The falling drops suddenly reversed direction, surging back up the chasm to blur the camera lens, like rain in reverse. The subterranean belch of steam blasted the camera and bashed it against the chasm walls on its frail rope. The vent calmed once more.

Stone ledges stretched across the chasm with puddles boiling in their sunken holes. Another blast was about to be ejected. Severum implanted the camera on one of those rocky shelves, swinging it on its cord to wedge it beneath a stone so the blast wouldn't break the lens. After the steam stopped, he dislodged it and released the cord to lower it deeper into the hole. He dimmed the camera's light to avoid the reflections off the walls from overexposing the video feed. As much as he tried to protect the camera, it was buffeted by a blast of boiling water from below, then another from the sidewall, then everything turned black. The camera's light had nothing but emptiness to illuminate. It reached eighty feet. He increased the light strength, then quickly shut it off again, for he couldn't believe the sight.

Turning the light back on confirmed – the deepest area of the geyser was full of phosphophyllite, the hydrated zinc phosphate glowing bright turquoise under the camera's light. He knew not whether the mineral samples were sentient or not like the others, but there was an extensive crystal network buried within the geyser. He retracted the camera and ran some tests, though his readings couldn't confirm any unique energies, magnetic resonances, or anything the mystics termed to be ley lines, unless the lines were referring to these crystal extensions. If the Bhasura were extending their network of consciousness this deep into the planet, then they were a more powerful player than he had thought. Their presence was likely what had brought Sabrina here, not superstition. What other secrets lay beneath the terrain?

After two hours of research, he mapped the geological strata. The water that issued from the geyser's sidewall was particularly perplexing. It wasn't that the phenomenon was uncommon to such a structure, but it suggested that a complex series of water channels stretched beneath the ground. It was possible the Bhasura used the network to transport whatever resources a species like itself needed. Or maybe they had transcended beyond acquisition and simply existed for the sake of doing so.

Culptos had known about the Bhasura and the threat they posed to the Old Guard. Sabrina might be planning to acidify the underground channels. The geyser would then heat and pressurize the water, boiling the crystals in acid. The stone around them is porous enough to hold enough acid to continue seeping into the water. If Sabrina could cause an environmental disaster by poisoning the water supply, link it to the Great Rotation of the planet for her political spin, and rid herself of the Bhasura at the same time, it would make sense for her to seize the opportunity.

But where the hell was she?

Severum spent the next few days in town studying the region's geology. He created a preliminary map of where the underground water currents flowed, approximated a second map of the crystal network, and connected both to a schematic detailing the nearby water treatment facility's inputs. That facility was more rudimentary than the one they had tried to sabotage, but still pumped enough gallons per second to be a formidable force.

The next morning, he traveled uphill to see the mayor of Nathril-Xoynsia. While the chawls filled the lower area of the city, being just a step above the living conditions in the stacked shanties beyond them, the upper level was structurally sound. The cinderblock building walls were covered with loose wooden paneling, old sheet metal, anything they could find, but they had been bolted together to make the collages livable. Even here though, wires, waterpipes, and other infrastructure ran along each building, sometimes leaking water and sometimes spitting sparks, or both. Men exchanged quickly-pocketed items in the shadows of tall trash piles, stepping over electrified currents.

The mayor's sign wasn't anything official, and his building had no government department name on it. The sizzling neon read, *Mayor, This Way,* with a big fist extending a grimy hand to the right where the door was. Land-based vehicles sped up the cracked road leading to the mayor's office, weaving in and out of their lanes. Guys passed, screaming out the windows, high on whatever neuralmod they had found in the gutters. Metal music blasted from speakers that hung lopsided around the entrance. Most people here were too poor to afford aural implants.

Severum entered a small lobby with wooden paneling and said, "My kinda place."

Two guards stood on either side of the entryway wearing

combat vests with knives, grenades, and other gadgets slotted into their compartments. They looked him up and nodded him forward to the woman behind the desk.

The receptionist took a long look at him, her false eyes zooming in and out with a grinding noise as if needing lubrication. She leaned forward, resting her wide, sweaty bosom on the splintered desk. "Enforcer," she stated.

"No, I'm Severum. Any Enforcer wouldn't have jurisdiction way out here unless they were doing weekend work on contract. I'm here to—"

"You're a cop. Think I don't know one? Honey, I've been doin' this job for twenty years. You as cop as they get."

"And why do you say that?"

"When you walked in, you were more gung-ho than any citizen would be. Didn't have the *fear* that's in their eyes."

"I could be a renegade like these two guys over here for all you know."

"No you couldn't. If you were, you would have never come here. Big guy don't take too well to rival gangs showing up on his turf. Sit your ass down, cop, and tell me why you wanna see this guy anyway?"

"I'm not a cop, I'm not even armed, but you were close. I'm a Vet, and I was assigned a little project to help out with."

"Unarmed? Well, then you ain't on official business, that's for sure."

"Actually, I am, but that's for me to discuss with the mayor."

"Honey, anyone on official business wouldn't come alone and unarmed. He in there, go ahead," she replied, pointing to a door heavy as a bank vault's.

The guards straightened behind him. He pushed the long, steel handle down, and pulled the door back.

The mayor was a middle-aged man sitting in an oversized velvet chair. His glass desk circled around his large body, but the rest of the office was closer to a swinger's club than a governing body. Pink loveseats sat on furry, green carpet. There were pink stains on the green, and green on the pink. He raised his double-chin from a blue collar like a turtle. Earrings fell from either ear, dangling against his thick beard.

"Well, come on then if you're coming. Sit down and tell me your business."

"Name's Severum. Your people have to stop drinking the water. I have intel that suggests that a woman, Sabrina Underfoot, is, well… underfoot."

The mayor retracted his shoulders and replied, "You threatening me?"

"Sir?"

"You know, is this a pathetic attempt to wrangle the city for money? Wouldn't be the first time some idiot make the mistake of his life by coming in here, putting the city at ransom. Mayor Hinesdale won't be made a fool of again."

"No, Sir. I work with K.O.A."

"Who?"

"The non-profit who runs the commune to the far south."

"The green girls, we call 'em," Hinesdale replied. "Every now an' then, one or two makes their way up here and we go downtown, 'cept we don't go nowhere."

Severum feigned a laugh and continued, "Seriously, though. This woman's a terrorist, and has already tried similar things in Blutengel."

"Well, she'll just have to try it here. Be the last thing she ever does," he smirked.

"Don't you have bottled water you can use?"

"Do we look like we do? We run neuralmods; this ain't no secret and I'm proud to admit it. Knock-off implants, cyber augs, get yer'self a metal cock replacement kinda thing. Got it all."

"So there's not much money in the water business?"

"Can't get drunk on no water."

"If I give you her pic, will you help us keep a lookout for her?"

"She want money?"

"She wants to restore the old government on the hemisphere we used to call Evig Natt back when I was young. Now, I think she has come here to poison your water supply using the Vortex."

"Woman like that seems like she'd make a valuable employer for my people. Can't hire people on the books to undermine a regime, can you?" He winked. "Hell, I could set her up with fifty men right now. Pay 'em in beer for all they care."

"They'll be dead men!" he yelled.

The guards ran inside.

The mayor motioned them back and advised, "Just friendly talk. Tell you what, I tell my men to keep a lookout for the glitch."

"Here's her pic. And seriously, take my message about the water to heart. Give away free beer instead or something."

"Nah, it's not election year," he laughed.

Severum left and walked back down the street. He preferred to take the place in on foot, since many of his best leads came serendipitously. The first time he had been here was on a tour of poverty that the Florinik chief had imposed upon him years back so that he could learn the lifestyle that those in power in Evig Natt enforced on the rest of the world through exploiting their resources. After an Aphorid attack, Thalassa had him at a disadvantage, but though they were enemies at the time, she had trusted him to make the right decision and support O.A.K.'s rebellion against the old regime. She had little choice; without Severum they had no insider to stand against the military, and the information he had learned would have destroyed O.A.K. anyway if he hadn't defected. Yet, for an impulsive woman whose tongue was as sharp as her blade, she had also sensed a certain kindness in him it seemed, or at least an appreciation of his professionalism. If he could impart enough trust to convert enemies into loyal friends, then maybe he could do the same to re-instill faith in Akasha, and himself in the process, for the two were mirrors always amplifying one another's emotions.

Still, he didn't call her.

The sun set for the third time that day like a squirming firefly. The streets receded into an enormous, immobile block of buildings. People lined the alleys, sitting on curbs to consume steaming meals from street vendors. Cumin and clove filled the air. As the natural light faded, obscuring the outlines of each neighborhood, a moment of peace befell the city. Just as very few creatures were crepuscular, dusk was marked with a tired inactivity: sluggish laborers returning from a day's work, merchants covering their wares, people driving through thinning traffic.

The moment didn't last. Neon lights blasted the city with a purple glow as night came on, flickering at every entrance. Holo-commercials activated as he passed neuralmod shops, noodle bars, and brothels where humans were the minority. Species too numerous to catalog filled the windows with all sorts of colors and arrangements of orifices, but the patrons looked more bored than excited. A bandit wrapped his arm around a tall, rubbery creature with a humanoid face and tentacles for hands. Must be from one of the offshore water worlds. They receded from the window into the depths of despair. Everything was desensitized, and in the craving of more, people had less.

Drown it all out, forget about it for a moment, you earned it, the street called to him. It was his seventieth birthday today, and he *had* earned something – not a night spent on the edge of oblivion, but a promise to himself that he wouldn't live the remainder of his years the way he had when he was young.

A woman with low, dark bangs approached him, eyes glazed with wine. The lights reflected off her chrome-studded candy-red belt as she swayed her hips. "Hi, there," she said, drawing out each word.

"You need to get an education, get away from this place," he told her.

"Oh, I agree. You can be my teacher and boy do I want an A. I'm Taleah with an *ah* not a *y*," she said through moist, smooth lips, the grimy neon lights reflecting off their gloss.

"No, seriously, this life will kill you."

"Well, you're no fun," she snapped, stamping off in high heels as a white sliver of thigh was revealed. Her outfit shifted on a time-loop with some areas vanishing, while others reappeared. The back of her dress dissipated only to reform a moment later when her clothes sealed the gap. Her flesh shimmered beneath the augmented fabrics, but he couldn't employ her services.

It wasn't that he felt the need to be loyal to Akasha, his glitchin' runaway, but that he needed to be loyal to all women, period, especially one his own daughter's age. He saw her eyes in Taleah's. He grabbed her by the shoulder.

"Now that's more like it, but you pay first. We all pay one way or another." She lifted one knee to wrap her leg around his buttock, placing her arms on his shoulders.

"Are all the girls here my daughter's age?"

"Yes, daddy," she whispered, her warm, measured breath on his neck.

It was the second time this year he heard the word. The first had been said with contempt, and the second with feigned lust. Anger boiled inside, but she wasn't his target. He shrugged her off, slammed the doors open to the brothel, and pushed the guard aside. A Pulser charged behind his back, but he was already in the back room with the pimp's throat wrapped in his titanium hand. He struck so fast he didn't realize the pimp was an android. Metal met metal as its hand raised to defend itself. The guard behind caught up and fired thrice, but not before Severum had spun to put the android in-between him and the guard.

It spouted sparks as its head flew off, the molten metal still burning from the shot and setting the sateen curtains alight. Cables wiggled from its severed neck, the body searching for its head. The guard recharged. Severum raced forward and hot blood flew from the guard's lip as he bust his face with his own gun. He pocketed the Pulser.

The flames grew. Drones flooded the scene. He shot them down one by one, recharged, and fired another few rounds. Some were armed with video cams, while others had water hoses, but this place was going to burn regardless, along with any trace of him.

"I play a lotta games, but not this one." Taleah ran for help.

A bunch of men hobbled out of side rooms with their pants at their ankles and fastened their belts, their women running away and screaming behind them. It was just one place, and a new one would open up tomorrow across the street. His attack solved nothing and put the mission at risk, but it was his birthday, and there was going to be fireworks and hullabaloo one way or another.

He sauntered down the street, swinging the Pulser in his hand. The knock-off gun had been unlocked before it had been sold on the underground market. He fired it into the air just for kicks. Felt good to be back. He wasn't old, he had simply lost his purpose before.

Hoverbikes rounded the corner. Couldn't tell if they were law enforcement or thugs. Probably both. He ducked down a back alley and slid out of sight, until running into another group. The first group split and headed down the alley behind him, while the group in front closed in. His Pulser was concealed by his jacket, the blood on his hands by the night. No chance to survive a gunfight from both angles at once, so he hunched over and played dumb, rubbing his achy back.

"You see a gunman?" the leader of the first band questioned.

"Huh? Can't hear ya," Severum replied in a scratchy voice.

"Turn your implants up, grandpa. Gunmen, firing, you see anything?"

"You can get guns downtown. My boy, Sammy, runs the shop there."

"Forget it." The group headed on.

He headed downhill, back to his shoddy hotel, entering the lobby. "Going to stay another night," he told the concierge.

"Name?"

Guy had already forgotten his face. Good. "Let's erase any name associated with Room 404," he said, giving him a cred-stick for payment.

"Double it."

"No. You know enough not to mess with people wanting their names off the book. That stick has more than enough for you to have a hell of a night. But if I hear you used it on a girl, I'm gonna come back here and make you regret it."

"Okay, mister," the man replied, shaking his head. "What're you, a preacher or somethin'?"

"Religion's so glitched today it wouldn't make a difference. I'm heading upstairs, and if anyone comes looking for me I checked out."

He took the lift and entered his room. The wallpaper was peeling, the ceiling leaking, and the view was just a series of balconies where couples fought, slammed bottles, and blared music that combined techno with Florinik tribal beats. He ran the bath, but upon seeing the dingy water drained it. Better not touch it. He sat on the bed and called Akasha.

"Severum. Many a night when gazing at the firefly swarms have I thought of you, Old Flame. Haven't heard from you in days."

"I love you."

"Sorry, I think your connection cut out," she stammered.

"You know it's true. It's always been true." He recited,

"Now folds the lily all her sweetness up,

And slips into the bosom of the lake.

So fold thyself, my dearest, thou, and slip

Into my bosom and be lost in me."

"Did you write that for me?" she asked.

"Of course," he laughed, knowing she would recognize it as one of Tennyson's poems.

"Seems we're both reaching outside ourselves to express that which lies within."

"It's a start, my love. It's a start." He disconnected the call.

The exchange had gone well as it could. No sense taking an even greater risk by staying on the line. But she called back and wished him a happy birthday, and they talked for hours into the night. She told him about how she could sense the Bhasura and the unrest within the planet.

"Since you have this connection with them, I'd like you to meet them at their installation outside Amorpha, the Florinik village," he said. "There's a turquoise-colored pathway that will lead you to the Jade Palace. Tell them the crystalline network near the Vortex is about to be under attack. I have an entry stone you'll need to get in, but I'm not sure the best way to get it to you right now."

"Send me the location. As for the stone, something tells me I won't need it."

24

SEVERUM RECEIVED A CALL THE NEXT MORNING FROM THE mayor. He kicked the sheets off and sat up in the dingy hotel room.

"We spotted your girl."

"Akasha? You keep her out of this."

"Who? I'm referring to the Underfoot glitch."

"Oh, her. Where's she at?"

"You haven't been behaving yourself, Severum," the mayor said.

"Never been known for it, no."

"You set fire to one of my clubs last night. Got it all on vid."

"Really? And does the public know you own these clubs?"

"Are you threatening me?"

"Yes. Now, we both want something. You want to get re-elected. That means no huge scandals, and nothing tying you to the fact that you were informed of a public health crisis before it happened and did nothing."

"It's not an election year, and the public only have a fifteen-minute memory."

"Oh, I know a guy in the media who can jog that memory

quite well. So, you hand over Sabrina's location, and I'll keep my mouth shut about your clubs."

"How do I know you'll keep your promise? For all I know, you're a social justice warrior."

"I was drunk and wanted to have a good time, and it got a bit too wild and out of control. Girl said she could make all my desires come true. Got a little fire fetish, what's it to you?" he lied.

"You and I are alike then. Hey, I'll admit that. Always knew you were okay. Your girl Sabrina's been spotted this morning with a few mercs. Sending you the coordinates."

Severum broke the connection. He didn't like agreeing to keep quiet about the mayor's connection to sex trafficking, but he couldn't fight all wars simultaneously. Keeping the Old Guard from rising would allow the area to heal enough from the inequality they had wrought over the past century, leading everyone to a better life.

He headed to the location.

———

A NEWS ALERT flashed across Ash's vHUD. Sloumstone apartments had collapsed. Tenants in the east tower reported waking to a loud, rumbling noise right before the adjacent building had been destroyed. Videos showed the lower levels giving way slowly at first as the building leaned, followed by the remaining floors as they came crashing. Within ten seconds it was all gone, just a pile of rubble with a blazing fire at its base. So far, only four survivors had been found, with over four hundred missing. The collapse was attributed to water having accumulated at ground level. Industrial runoff had acidified it, corroding the support columns over time.

"That could have been me," she told her mom.

"And alas, it is getting worse daily," Akasha replied. "Even the New Order with all its forgotten promises fails to regulate these industries properly. If the building had been up to code, it would have stood strong against this catastrophe. But the oversight committees obtain their funding from imposing fines, so they refuse to shut down non-compliant corporations. It's a legal kickback."

"What do you mean?"

"If they shut down the businesses that refuse to bring their buildings up to code, they can't fine them anymore for breaking the law, meaning the regulating agency goes bankrupt."

"Shouldn't taxpayers fund the regulating agency? It's almost like they're working on commission."

"Yes, but the entire system is based on competition and it's flawed at the base."

"I had a few friends who sold cyberaugs and I'll tell you, Mom, competition brings out the best, but also the worst in us. They would rip implants out of dead people's brains and resell them to someone else, breaking a thousand laws at once. Do you know what happens when you transpose implants from one brain to another?"

"Oh yes, and that's one of the reasons I was so against technology early on, when those issues were commonplace. We didn't know better. You suddenly inherit portions of another person's memories, usually the most intense ones that formed their basic narrative of who they were, and it drove people mad."

"Mom, I had a friend, Kenya, who watched the Forever Glitched kill a guy for information. They ripped his implants out. They said they'd kill her too since she was a witness, if she didn't let their street grafter install the implants into her; so she did. They wanted to know what the guy knew, since he hadn't put out during their interrogation. You can't just plug brain parts into a computer. So there she was, with a dead guy's memories mixed with hers until she couldn't tell the difference. She gave them some gibberish and then killed herself, leaving a note that she was already dead anyway."

"That's horrible, Ash. Why didn't you tell me?"

"You were gone doing whatever it is you do all day."

"Well, you're safe here, and Severum will take care of things."

"No! We should be out there, *doing* something."

"Your father courts enough risks on our behalf."

"Then what do you suggest we do?"

"We pray," Akasha said.

"I'm sick of your passivity. You used to wage war with Aphorids at your back. Now, you sit here doing nothing. Mom, come *on*."

"Silence. If you sit, you can hear the planet's cries. I see sparkling crystals in my dreams and they speak to me."

"You've lost it. How do you even go from being a terraformer studying geophysics, to a priestess, to whatever the hell you are now?"

"You seem to be modeling your father's communication style, Ash."

"Stop comparing me to him."

"You should be honored. He's a great man. Terrible communicator, but a hero."

Ash had been waiting for those words. She dropped the attitude and asked, "What do the crystals say?"

"I cannot understand the words, but there's a pressing *need* from within. A pressure that has to be released."

"That's your own need, Mom. It's not the planet talking."

"If you're quiet and open your mind, you can hear it. You can feel them."

"I'm not listening to this nonsense," she said, heading to her room.

But she sat for the next hour on the bed, focused her thoughts, and cleared her mind. Maybe there was something there, a subtle feeling, or maybe it was the power of suggestion, but one thing was clear: the planet was acting more volatile than ever before, and if they weren't careful, it would swallow them whole.

———

SEVERUM ARRIVED onsite at the coordinates the mayor had sent. Procuran Data Center was dead center between the water treatment facility and the Vortex, and numerous waterlines ran past it. It was one of the only tech industries in the area, for the education level was low on the Eastern Hemisphere. He examined the underground waterways he had mapped during his research, but they had too many variables to determine how an attack on either the geyser, or the treatment plant, would impact the city. The Old Guard probably didn't know either. They had kidnapped Akasha before not only due to Culptos' personal endeavor against his family, but because they lacked the internal skills to carry out their plans. They had chosen an area between the two locations, hoping to impact both.

Severum parked in a lot full of a couple hundred vehicles. The data center's windows reflected vast, sandy plains. He couldn't walk through the front door, in case whoever ran the place was collaborating with Sabrina. He headed around back and scoped for any signs of her. A crowbar and a screwdriver had been left beside some construction equipment. Thick pipes led into an area beside the back door. He grabbed the tools, raised the crowbar over his head, and slammed it down three times on the old-fashioned lock. The clanging echoed and people leaned from their office chairs to look through their windows, but were too far away to identify him without the latest occipital upgrades.

He entered, finding a maintenance room full of water boilers, air conditioners, electrical boxes, and other installations. Access grates afforded him peeks at what was going on inside the offices, but it was business as usual. Was it all a misdirection? Was Sabrina working with the mayor, providing employment as he had alluded to? Something was missing. He needed more information on the center's activities, but information came at a price.

———

"I'M LEAVING," Akasha told Ash. "You're right, we can't stay here. There's a high-speed airbus normally reserved for politicians about to embark for the Eastern Hemisphere."

"I'm going, too," Ash said, hands on hips.

"Fine."

"Really, no argument?"

"You sound disappointed. This is an opportunity to commune with the planet."

"I don't want to talk to crystals, Mom, I want to talk with you."

"We can, but we need to clear our minds, or we won't be able to hear the Bhasura."

"You mean you can't listen when you're pissed off."

"That, too. Come here," she said, closing her arms around Ash. "When did you get taller than me?"

"I'm not," Ash said, bending her knees and resting her head on her mother's shoulder.

———

SEVERUM EXITED the maintenance room to a back corridor running along the data center. He turned his body sideways to squeeze behind a pipe, moving slowly along. A large steel vent led deeper into the building. He took the screwdriver he had found outside and unscrewed the cover, scrunching his body to enter it. Rounding the corner, the path ended at a giant fan. The blades were a blur, the wind strong enough to blow his hair and lips back from his face. He reached his metallic hand into the circling fan blade, aligning it with the wounded spot near his wrist that was already stripped of flesh. Sparks flew and the fan blades fell apart. He bit back the burning pain and continued through the vent, then exited to find an unlocked door leading to a hallway.

Cleaner bots swept. Papers shuffled. Coworkers chattered within their offices. Two employees in white shirts and tight ties walked into an open conference room. Their foreheads protruded with raised lines from whatever implants they were running. Four others joined them and the hallway became busy with the copy and paste commentary of corporate chatter. Severum slipped into an alcove and entered a coat closet, leaving the door parted just enough to see. The meeting began. He could have never lived that life, one where marketing campaigns were life and death decisions, as if choosing the perfect font would give them enough control over life to beat death

No one beat death.

While he could run past them, there was no way to sneak out until the meeting was over. Even returning the way he came was too risky. If he was given away, they would be on the lookout and he'd never be able to return to learn what Sabrina was up to.

"Ash," he texted. "Give me some info on Procuran Data Center."

"I'm on it."

Nothing else to do. He did the thing he was worst at – he waited.

───────

THE HIGH-SPEED AIRBUS reached the Eastern Hemisphere in record time. Ash and her mom rented a hovercraft and set off for

Amorpha. They soon reached the village, parked, followed the prominent turquoise path, and meditated while sitting cross-legged on the stone. Hand-in-hand, they focused their thoughts until a resonance was felt. Adjusting their thoughts to the frequency and homing in on what was more a feeling than a signal, the entryway rose from the sand. They descended to the Bhasura compound, the pulsating crystals filling them with wonder.

———

THE MEETING WENT on for hours. Severum, stuck in the coat closet the whole time, learned nothing of value from the conversations. The data center was strategizing long-term plans for bringing access to the planet's colonizing ship's archives and other online functionality to the more rural areas of the Eastern Hemisphere. Such a network was supposed to *expand your consciousness* as their marketing slogan went. They had prepared their presentations to the communities and were wrapping it up. The main points of contention had been how much of the human race's history they would alter in the *remastered versions* of critical documents like *The Bill of Rights* and *The Magna Carta.*

The group turned off their holo-displays and left the office.

Severum searched the files that were left behind, but there was nothing useful. He headed down the hallway, risking a restroom stop along the way. An employee entered and unzipped at the urinal beside him, his keycard dangling from the side of his belt buckle. Severum zipped and walked past him. He turned, but it was the wrong way, and Severum couldn't reach the keycard. He backtracked to the urinal, which made the employee suspicious.

"Forgot to flush," he said.

"What area do you work in?" the well-dressed man asked.

"Maintenance."

"Oh, outsourced help," he replied with his chin up.

Severum hit the flush and passed him again, grabbing the keycard off its lanyard as the man looked down to shake off the last drops. Perfect swipe. With luck, he wouldn't realize it was gone until Severum had gained access to whatever area it went to.

The intel from Ash arrived, indicating the data center's history, but it was of limited use. He hadn't planned what he would do when he saw Sabrina, but if he wanted to plan instead of improvise he would have led a damn corporate life.

The keycard went to a door at the end of the hall leading to the second floor stairway. He ascended it, straightening his wrinkled jacket. He exchanged courteous nods with passersby, who were better dressed than those in the conference room below, but even as a maintenance man he wouldn't avoid detection for long.

A woman in a black blazer blocked the transparent door to the third floor staircase and asked, "Do you belong here?"

Maintenance wasn't likely to visit this floor often, since the main systems were below, so he replied, "Just a tech."

"You diagnose implant problems? I've had an issue, let me tell you, with this auto-calculator thing," she said, pointing to a raised bump on her forehead.

"What's your issue? Maybe I can open a ticket," he replied, looking for a way out.

"It keeps freezing up when computing things. The left side of my vision stops working."

"Simple problem. I assume your calculator is a visual spreadsheet."

"Yes, that's it, Calc-Viz 4.0."

"You froze the left columns on the spreadsheet. That's useful for keeping your vision focused on the information you need to present, but no good for walking through an office space. Go to your vHUD, open Calc-Viz, and blink five times to access the toolbar," Severum instructed.

"Okay, what's next?"

"See the freeze button the fourth to the right?"

"Yes."

"Right mind-click it."

"Done. Wait a minute, I can't see anything now. That didn't help; it made it worse."

"Calm down. You should be able to see the data now on each side."

"Yes, but that's all I see. I can't see the office."

"Please, keep your voice down. No need to disturb your coworkers while they're working on the strategic plan. Now, just sit and wait a minute, and the process will correct itself."

"Okay," she said, resigned to waiting.

The process would correct itself in about thirty seconds if she didn't acknowledge making the new vHUD view her default. Severum seized the opportunity to ascend the third-floor staircase she had been blocking, climbing the stairs before her vision returned. She might report him or think he was an untrained tech, so time was fleeting to find Sabrina and what she was doing. He scoured the nearby office hubs but it was taking too long to gain ground. Workers came and went and he had to pretend to work on various electrical devices until they left, using only the screwdriver and the crowbar he had picked up. A cybersecurity office was further down the hall next to what might be a server room, but access was restricted even with his keycard, and those who were allowed wore navy uniforms that didn't match his. He searched for a way inside.

———

ASH FOLLOWED her mom through the underground cavern until she reached the clearing. The Jade Palace was truly sublime, overlooking the area from the top of the turquoise staircase. Most of the crystals blended into one another, sharing a substrate. Lights flickered as if entire conversations were being held within the stone. It moved upon the shadowy crevices of her fingers as she skimmed her hands across the cool surface.

"We have to tell Aurthur about this! The media will go wild! The posts I can get out of this place…"

"Please do not," her mom replied. "Let the planet keep her secrets."

"But I could be a social media star!"

"When your allies speak from the depths of the planet, you protect them. Do you really want this to become a theme park tomorrow, with them as slaves? Besides, your generation would view your post a million times, then get bored. Your cohorts aren't suddenly going to be inspired to become geologists or xenobiologists, and the friends you would make from your newfound popularity will only be trying to get their own attention through you."

"Not all young people are like that."

"You're special and you're enough on your own. You don't need the world's validation."

"No, *you* don't need it. You can run away for years to a cave leading a revolution, but I need to know I mean something to the world, too. That our sacrifices mean something."

"Without you, Severum and I would have been killed at the lab after they used our knowledge to terrorize the planet. How's that for meaning? You're special, Ash, one of a kind. Just be patient and life will play out in your favor."

"Thanks," she replied, hiding her face.

They climbed the shimmering turquoise staircase and approached the palace gate. The walls crackled as the crystals consolidated into a humanoid creature. Ash leapt back, almost falling down the stairs, and standing behind her mom.

"We are Allira, Queens of the Bhasura," it said.

"My husband... I mean, ex-husband, came here recently. We have much to share. He is currently in Nathril-Xoynsia."

"We know," Allira acknowledged, the crystals lighting with each word. "He was disturbing the Vortex with his investigations."

"We do apologize," Akasha replied. "We're receiving information from him as we speak and we believe this knowledge could save your lives."

"Normally, signals do not reach far down here, but we are facilitating his communications, though we have limited ability to do so. We have you note, however, we are not alive."

"Perhaps you used to be and then you crystallized yourselves for preservation?"

"We are neither live nor dead, neither used to be nor will be."

"Well, you will be disintegrated regardless. Here's what we know."

———

A BLONDE-HAIRED BUSINESSWOMAN pretended not to follow Severum while he strode the third floor of Procuran Data Center. It would be less suspicious to face her head-on, so he greeted her, "Hi. Do you know if a Sabrina is onsite? She reported some technical issues."

"Being the head of human resources and cybersecurity, I pretty much know everyone in the building, but I don't recognize the name," she replied, examining him with her green eyes.

"It's probably just a nickname. I'll look her up by her employee ID instead. Thanks," Severum lied.

The woman squinted and said, "Speaking of which, I don't know you either."

"External contractor."

"No, wait, I do know you. You're Severum Rivenshear. You were responsible for increasing the rotation, though now, it appears your little experiment's gotten out of control." She laughed. People as well-dressed as she could afford to move to higher ground when the streets flooded and didn't take it seriously.

"Well, yes, I am Severum, but don't say that too loud. I'm retired, and the movement was quite controversial. Now, I'm doing contract work as an IT tech just to keep busy, get a little extra income for vacation. Any other contractors working here today? Just wondering how much work to expect, since new people in the building often have connection issues when synchronizing their implants with the system."

"There is one group doing an audit of our network connections to see if they meet building codes."

"How many?"

"Three men, and a woman."

"Does the woman have red hair?"

"Yes, you know them?"

"So they work for the mayor's office then?" Severum asked.

"If you can call it that, yes. They would fall under his jurisdiction."

"There's been some rumors of a group causing issues. Let me just call the mayor to confirm."

"You have a direct line to the mayor? That's unusual, even for one of the original rotationists."

"Nah, creating sunrises comes with a few perks," he smiled, but cringed inside. He called the mayor.

The mayor paused, as if surprised to hear his voice, then said, "This better be good, Sev'."

"You don't have anyone at the Procuran Data Center doing building inspections today, do you?"

"Does it look like I got a building inspection office in my city?"

"No, Sir, thanks." He disconnected. "We have an issue, Madam. The mayor doesn't have anyone scheduled to do inspections here. I'm not even sure the city *has* building codes, and they have no inspection office."

"That's impossible."

"No, it's not. You have infiltrators," he advised.

"I'll contact security immediately." She went down the hall through the secure doors to what he had thought was the *Cybersecurity* office; probably some script kiddies playing with anti-virus software. He was dead wrong, for behind the secure doors, he could see a space between the words on the placard: Cyber Security.

Two cyborgs exited the office with synchronized footsteps. Their red eyes glowed, reflecting off the polished walls.

Severum showed them a picture and said, "You've been compromised. This is Sabrina Underfoot, the mastermind behind the infiltration."

Lines passed over their eyes as they scanned the picture, then they split up to search the floor.

"Wait a second," the businesswoman said, running up behind him. "Why do you have that picture? You're not here on contractual business, are you, Severum?"

He had to drop the act, fast. "Of course not. I'm sorry I deceived you; I had to protect the mission. At first I thought Sabrina may have been working for you, or had an agreement set up to exchange services. If I had known she was here unauthorized, I would have exposed her immediately upon entering. You must understand that outside Nathril-Xoynsia, I don't trust any organization by default."

"Understandable, me either. So who are you working for?"

"Working for myself for a change, to protect my family. But my actions are under the guidance of the K.O.A. Commune to the south and the New Order of the Western Hemisphere."

"K.O.A. Those eco-zealots," she scoffed.

"Seems like everyone has another name for them, but yes."

"Too bad they didn't consider the ecosystem when they

helped you rotate the planet with O.A.K., bringing raging floods."

"You sure know your history," he said, stomach sinking.

The cyborgs each brought back two armed thugs. They converged at the intersection of four hallways in the center of the top floor. Something was off.

He examined the woman before him, imagining her with a long wave of ruby hair instead of blonde tied in a bun. Her jawbone and forehead morphed as he commanded vHUD to deactivate visual alterations. Her face glitched as pixels fell from it until the entire façade peeled, revealing the woman he came to find. "Always underfoot," he smiled, for there was nothing else to do.

"I see you want to die with a smile on your face," Sabrina replied, green eyes glimmering.

"Better believe it."

"Good game, but all games have to come to an end." Sabrina uncloaked a sheath hanging over her shoulder and drew a long sword. It appeared as ten blades in a thousand different positions at once through vHUD, and he couldn't turn off the interference.

The cyborgs closed in, bringing the thugs closer.

"Take off your hover-boots and drop your Pulser, slowly."

He followed the orders, then asked, "Before you do me in, tell me this. What are the rules of this game? You can't really win if your opponent doesn't even know what they're playing at, or what the reward is."

"But of course," she replied. She waved her sword in her right hand, ghostly images dancing across the air. "Mayor and I had a little deal. We'd fast-start his career by making him governor once we resumed control. Funny thing, power is. Addictive, you know." She motioned with her left hand as she spoke, extending it outward with her palm sideways at key points of her inflection. She continued, "When he tipped me off that you were in town looking for me, I had him send you these coordinates, then waited for you to arrive."

"This has nothing to do with the water flow, then."

"Water flow?"

"This is about data networks and the Bhasura."

"You are resourceful, Mr. Rivenshear. I respect that. You shall die regardless, but I shall make it on your terms. Even losers deserve to make some demands."

"Being a loser is what made you susceptible to the promises of the Old Guard to begin with."

She was taken aback.

He continued, "But I still don't know all the moves you've made, so I can't provide an equal respect. It's not enough to win, you and I both know that. Someone as precocious as you has to make sure their opponent knows they were outsmarted, right?"

"Let's off this fucker," a thug said behind him.

Sabrina waved him aside, once more using her left hand. "Again, I sympathize with your sentiment. The Bhasura have gathered at key points underground in response to the unstable terrain."

"Yes, I know. They communicate based on light, which is why you're working at the data center here so you can merge them with your cybernetwork and find a way to alter their signals to control them. I put it together, just a gunshot too late. Well, the Bhasura are on my side."

"We'll see about that. They won't help you."

"I'm going to stop you one way or another."

"Heh, I'm untouchable," she said.

"You think you're above the havoc you're creating, but you're not. Sloumstone Apartments collapsed. You used to *live* there. That could have been you."

"Of course I didn't," she scoffed. "That was just a misdirection so people didn't find me." She rubbed her nose.

"Untouchable, but afraid of being found? There's truth in

contradiction. You're afraid to admit that you haven't always been this successful, and that the success you do have is based on rising through the ranks of a government no one even recognizes by making illicit deals at the people's expense. No one respects cheaters, period." He kept her talking while uploading the conversation to Ash as proof. "Culptos used you to carry out the ecoterrorist acts, knowing he couldn't protect you with anything but common thugs, but you're too young to realize that. You don't have a police force on your side, you have mercs who will sell you out when a better deal comes along, just like you sold out the planet. Even if you won and the people sided with you, there'd be no way to protect any power you did achieve. What game has no win condition?"

"Oh I can create one." She smiled with wide, crazed eyes, playing with her blade. "Now, I'm sure you have plenty of information to provide me, such as the whereabouts of your ex-wife and that little glitch of yours."

"You leave her alone!"

"Game over, Severum."

"When everything's made to be a game, everyone loses, Sabrina."

"No, you lose. There's no other cards to play." She reached out her left hand for inflection as she said it.

Severum whipped his cybernetic hand around to grip her open palm, and in the whirling momentum he swung her over his head. She flew through the air, crashing into the cyborgs and accidentally stabbing one of the thugs. She shook her head and stood, withdrawing the blade.

The cyborgs raised their arms to fire, but the thugs were in their way, and they had been programmed with more regard for life than Sabrina had. The thugs moved to one side, and Severum to the other. He ducked into a side office. Shots burned a hole through the door. He ran past a confused man in a tie then kicked out the window with a crash, turning around to lower himself to the ledge, hanging from the narrow third-floor windowsill.

The thugs charged the office.

He let go of the ledge, using his reinforced hand to create friction along the bricks outside the building. Sparks flew as he gained traction during the fall, his skin scraping off his hand, though the titanium beneath was impenetrable. Finally, he caught hold of the second-story ledge and dropped the rest of the way.

Ground level. No use in racing towards his vehicle; they would have already sabotaged it.

The thugs looked out the third-floor window above, saying, "Oh, hell no!" They fired a few shots, but he strafed around the corner. They'd meet him downstairs in no time.

Cyborgs had no qualms about heights. The first one jumped straight out of the building. Severum wrapped his hand around it when it landed, using its momentum to spin it towards the second one as it took the leap. The first cyborg fired, but not before its aim had been redirected to blast the second one. One down. The first one faced him head-on, metal meeting metal. He pressed against the Pulser welded to its arm, bending it back with his reinforced hand to blow its face off with its own weapon. It exploded in a shower of sparks that singed his eyebrows. He retrieved the crowbar from his deep pocket and pried the Pulser embedded into its arm the rest of the way out. A test squeeze on the trigger fired a shot – having been embedded directly into its body, there had been no need for the designers to restrict it from firing in the hands of someone else.

Sabrina was still a live wire, but with a security force on her side he had to finish this quickly. She came to the window with her sword crossed over her body.

He opened fire. Two shots shredded the windowsill, while she deflected the other two with her blade. Only top-notch implants would have let her react that fast. "Stalemate!" he yelled.

"This isn't over!"

His Pulser recharged, but she left the window. The next building was a half mile away, and vehicles would be storming around the corner any moment. He ran towards the Vortex, but was outpaced by two hovercraft soaring a few feet over the ground. A shot burned a hole through his Pulser and he dropped the scolding hot weapon. He threw his hands up and the craft slowed.

"Sorry, pal," the heavyweight thug said. "You a smart guy, but that's your problem, and the woman gave the order. She ain't needing no information no more, just wants you dead on sight. 'Course it's nothin' personal." The thug raised his weapon.

Severum covered his face with his hands. If they shot him there, he might get lucky and deflect it off the titanium. If they burned through his torso instead, then at least he'd be recogniz-able at the funeral. Shots fired, but before they hit, crystals shot up from the ground to envelop his body in a turquoise shell that reflected his face a thousand times. The shots shattered the outer layer of the shield, but the ground gave way and he slid beneath the surface and landed with a thud.

He wiped the dust from his face. He had slid at least twenty feet underground. The slope that had slowed his descent had been dislodged and was now a straight drop. They wouldn't be following anytime soon. As if in response to his thought, crystals grew over the hole he fell through, sealing his fate.

It was dark underground, but the glowing minerals lit the way. He crouched to follow a tunnel south to Amorpha, pushing various insectoids from his face, too tense to look at whatever was scurrying up his pantlegs. The air was chilly, the soil walls damp. How close was he to the water channels? One wrong step and he might break through and flood the tunnel.

Going back was a death sentence, so he trod onward. After turning around in the tunnel a few times to face some mole-like creatures nibbling on his legs, he wasn't even sure he was going the right way. The rhythm set into his legs as he lost track of time. VHUD was unable to maintain a connection, but he couldn't risk any outgoing signals anyway, not this close to a data center that could intercept communications. Thirst grew with every step. As if responding to his need, water flowed upward on the face of the crystals that lit the way. Somehow, they were attracting it from the underground aquifer. He licked the moisture off the crystals with a salty tang on his tongue and put his trust in the stone as he continued to hike.

The tunnel widened, pulsating with that surreal glow, but it still stretched as far as he could see. It was a long walk, but he was alive. For now.

25

ALLIRA STOOD BEFORE ASH AND HER MOTHER, SILHOUETTED against the grand façade of the Jade Palace. The crystal city strobed so fast that everything appeared in slow motion, the lights running up and down every gem, reflecting and refracting thousands of times as they communicated. In response, the stones shifted, merged, morphed, and split.

Ash was in awe. Light could be a particle or a wave, and most of its finer points physicists could only guess at, but these entities had unlocked its secrets. "The last message I received from Severum was that he believes they are trying to envelop the Bhasura into their cybernetwork," she said.

"How is this possible?" Allira asked.

"With poor foresight and lack of planning, anything's possible," she replied, but the sarcasm was lost. She continued to explain until Allira realized an info war was on the brink. Then, she and her mother took the mushroom-filled tunnel back to the surface, adjusting to the bright daylight. "It's past third noon and we haven't heard from him," Ash said, wrapping her arms around her chest and digging her nails into her triceps.

"I'm well aware," her mother replied.

"We have to tell someone. We need a search team! He could be injured!"

"If he's injured, he's dead, Ash."

"Stop being so blunt."

"I apologize, it's been a long day. But we should wait a few days; he knows what he's doing. We can't tell anyone about the Bhasura. We have to protect their secrets at all costs."

"You're putting the planet above him?"

Her mother said nothing.

"We don't have to mention them."

"Ash, we cannot contact enforcement. This isn't Blutengel – the police forces out here are hired thugs organized via fly-by-night regimes. And our own forces back home have no jurisdiction."

"We could hire a band of Florinik to scour the place."

"With what funds, Ash?"

"Well, we could do something. Even if it means we have to cross the sands ourselves."

"No, mind yourself. We came to relay information for him and we need to be onsite to do that."

"That doesn't require two of us."

"You're not leaving. You wouldn't make it across the sands anyway," her mother insisted. "I brought you here because I wanted you by my side to witness the Bhasura, that you may learn why I became a priestess earlier in my life. It wasn't all about leaving Severum. Now, you've done that, and I need you safe."

"All that talk about meaning and me being special didn't mean much, did it?"

"It's *because* I think you're so special, and love you, that I don't want to see you go."

"But you also don't want him coming back because it scares you to be loved. You're not running away from his affections this time, but you're still keeping that distance. Death is the ultimate distance, and it's going to find all three of us if we don't intervene."

Anger flared in Akasha's eyes where there should have been revelation. "Fine! Tomorrow morning you can contact whomever you want."

They rented a room at a small inn in Amorpha.

Ash opened the old, wooden door, exchanging her tight boots for a pair of loose, woven sandals. The night air poured through the open window, casting a chill outmatched only by her mother's gaze. Florinik seedlings rushed into their room, carrying a plate of grapes and the strangest tasting honey she'd ever had, but she ate little. She frantically tried to contact him but there was no response.

"That's your fiftieth call," her mother said.

"Fifty-ninth," she corrected.

Akasha wrapped her arms around Ash and both cried. They slept in the same bed that night, cuddling under a bamboo sheet, but sleep came fitfully.

———

SEVERUM COULD WALK the tunnel no longer. He sat and leaned against the wall, a mixture of small crystals and dirt. The soil was soft enough that he might plummet through it. Silt deposits were everywhere, and if Sabrina's goal had been to sabotage the water channels, it would have caused numerous sinkholes. As he thought, a layer of crystals formed beneath him, reinforcing the ground. They resonated with his thoughts, not his complex ones, but his most primal needs. He licked moisture from their glowing planes and closed his eyes.

———

ASH WOKE up to the Florinik's lumbering bodies thumping outside the inn, their long limbs swaying as they walked. She looked down from the second-story window. Their leathery scalps were like the tops of footballs.

With few options left, she contacted the last person her mother would have wanted. "Good morning, Thalassa," she said over vHUD.

"Do you have any idea what time it is?" she replied, groggy.

"I'm on the east side, it's morning here. Listen, Severum's in trouble. He's out near Nathril-Xoynsia."

"Oh, great, this again? What's he doing there?"

"We don't have much time. His signal's gone."

"Can you trace his last location?"

"Already triangulated it. It was east of the city at the data center he was investigating. Can you arrange a search party?"

"I can contact Arcturus, yes. She'll send a few crafts out from the K.O.A. Commune, but hey, it'll take some time for them to get there."

"How long?"

"She's not talking to me, so don't hold your breath."

"What should I do in the meantime? I'm stuck at an inn in Amorpha."

"What do you mean stuck?"

"Mom doesn't want me to leave."

Thalassa laughed. "Stuck is when you're infiltrating The Towers of the Crystal Palace and you get captured and thrown into a cell to die." She disconnected.

Thalassa was right.

Ash packed some water in a backpack and slipped out while her mother slept. A transport vendor rested at the end of town beside a hovercraft and a hoard of Dijyorkvoken. The price to rent the hovercraft was too high, so she climbed the footholds to board one of the large, slow beasts instead, the long, rugged fur coming up to her chest. She stopped before handing the vendor the money and asked herself, *What would Thalassa do?*

She leapt off the side of the beast and swiped the keycard for the hovercraft from the vendor's stall instead. Keys were usually tied to cognigraf signatures, so it probably wouldn't work, but she might get lucky since the Florinik didn't use implants. She jumped in the craft, pulled the glass cover over her head, and inserted the key. The engine rumbled, shaking the vehicle. The vendor yelled, but she slammed the pedal and sped off to the north until sand became more prominent than grass, and death more common than life.

———

SEVERUM CONTINUED through the tunnel for a half day, a day, maybe two days. He had lost track of time and direction and had no indication the tunnel would ever end. There were no routes leading to the surface. When he thought about food, the crystals glowed brighter near certain outcroppings of mushrooms, indicating which ones were safe to consume. Still, he took small bites with long periods between them, giving him just enough energy to continue.

A small crystal plate appeared where two tunnels intersected. He rested, sitting in the middle of the plate and picturing the Bhasura city. The crystal platform moved beneath him and slid down the tunnel. He had nothing to hang onto as it sped. He couldn't plant the rubber soles of his boots since Sabrina had made him remove them. He was at their mercy. As the lights passed quicker and quicker, he tilted backwards and almost off the platform until he pictured his body slowing. The platform slowed with it. Arriving at a comfortable speed, he traveled the tunnel back to the Jade Palace, entering through a side shaft.

He ascended the tall, turquoise staircase that led up to the gate. Akasha was meditating at the top, the crystalline cavern all around her. Saying nothing, he sat beside her, closing his eyes as well.

She reached out to grab his hand and continued breathing deeply. Whether it was his scent, which was masked with layers of soil caked upon his flesh, or some deeper connection, she knew he was there. A few minutes later it was back to business. "Ash has run off."

"Girls do that," he replied.

"There's a dozen things out here that can kill you."

"You survived. She'll be fine."

"Aren't you going to say you're glad to see me?"

"Of course I am, but I was waiting for you to say it first. I was the one missing. Cut my hand up pretty good, but I'll live."

About to get angry, she hugged him instead, wrapping her whole being around his body. Her lips grabbed at his, plush and inviting. He ran his good hand along the side of her body; she flicked hers through his hair.

The crystal gate dissolved like ice pooling into water. It reconsolidated into the form of Allira. She spoke, "You have returned. I trust you had fair journey."

"It was just grand," Severum said with a cocked brow.

"Tell us what more you know."

He relayed his discoveries, embraced by flesh and stone alike.

———

ASH PASSED a few hovercraft along the way, but none was as nice as the one approaching across the sand. It was gold-plated with a sharp nose and a narrow body. She zoomed her eyes. *Oh Shit!*

Sabrina sat behind a curved piece of glass, eyes dead ahead, focused.

Ash turned up her aural implants and ducked her head before she whizzed past, making out a short message from a phone call

Sabrina must have been on: *Trace the resonance and find him.* Must be referring to the Bhasura and Severum.

She waited until Sabrina disappeared behind a sand dune, then did a wide U-turn to follow her, staying far out of sight as there was no traffic in which to lose her in. Her trajectory set her straight back to Amorpha, where greenery gradually overcame sand.

Sabrina arrived at the outskirts of the Florinik village as the sun set and landed her hovercraft behind a dune crest that was being reclaimed by tall, spiky grasses. She leaned over the trunk to grab a long pole and swept it across the turquoise path like an old mine detector. She stopped, then hit a button on the side of it, a red light flashing in an unusual pattern, and the entrance to the crystalline compound rose from the ground.

After she descended underground and out of view, Ash abandoned her vehicle and followed down the steps. If spotted, Sabrina was quite capable of outrunning her, for she was already trying to catch her breath from living a sedentary lifestyle. Ash's best hope would be to reach the Jade Palace before her to warn them, but there was only one entrance from this direction. The tunnel was narrow, and Sabrina had the lead.

Ash took her boots off to keep quiet, gently placing her feet on the soil. A few creeping mushrooms climbed into her discarded shoes; cute, under any other circumstances. The crystals lit the way and soon Sabrina entered the phosphophyllite cavern with Ash at her heels.

Her parents stood at the top of the thirty-feet high staircase leading to the Jade Palace, their backs turned and oblivious to their presence. Allira stood behind the gate in the stone gardens at the palace entrance. Her father had risked so much to protect her. Maybe he was too jaded to care about the greater social impacts, but she knew he loved her. Now, armed or not, she had to come through for him.

Sabrina raised her head and took off, sprinting up the staircase and drawing her sword with a *cha-cling* sound as it slid from its sheath on her back. She took the stairs three at a time, holding the blade out to her left side. A row of crystals rose to block the top of the stairs in response, but she sliced through them in one swift horizontal swing and jumped over the cracked stumps.

Ash ran after her and cried, "Dad!" She voiced the word without thinking, screaming it from the depths of her lungs; those bellows enflamed her heart as she yearned for the rock of his stability. The word resonated within her, and the crystals felt it, too; that primal connection to her father, for they bared their full brightness until the area was too light to even take a step. Her parents' silhouettes turned at the top of the staircase, shielding their eyes from the blinding light. Sabrina must have outlined their position in vHUD, for Ash made out her father strafing away from her onslaught. The gate opened and Akasha took refuge behind it, while Severum faced the swordswoman alone and unarmed in the jade sea of light.

He parried the next strike, but lost his footing on the uneven, rocky ground, falling to one knee. Sabrina raised her blade, but Ash had caught up and charged from behind to grab her arm just in time before she struck the fatal blow. Sabrina was too strong for Ash to hold her back for long. Severum rose and punched her in the stomach, knocking her wind out, but she still struggled for control over the blade. Ash pushed her thumb aside, breaking her grip, but Sabrina lowered her hand to catch the sword, reorienting it to strike her dad again.

The sword clanged as it hit his metal hand. He twisted his wrist to grab the blade and threw it over the edge. "It's over!"

"Never!" Sabrina bit back.

"You really want to take me on in unarmed combat?"

"You're old, you're nothing. I can outsmart you, outpace you, and outlast you, Severum."

"Maybe, but I've got a whole family to support me, and you

don't fuck with the family. Now, hands up. Relent." Severum checked her for weapons and motioned Ash to stand behind him.

Sabrina backed up and said, "You may think this is all magic and mysticism, but I know the truth. The light communications, the resonance, all of it can be modeled with precision. The Bhasura have created a communications network running through the planet, but it's easily hacked." She tapped a button on an obsidian ring she wore on her right hand. It emitted a holographic handheld controller. She tapped a few commands and said, "This remote connects to a series of broadcasting devices called geo-resonators. They will not only interrupt the Bhasura's communications array, they will exploit it! Now, they're under my control, and don't even think about trying to stop me. I'll have them send a thousand spikes from every wall right through your head."

"You're bluffing."

"Try me."

The cavern shook as she manipulated the controller. Crystals fell from the ceiling and shattered near Ash and her family and they covered their heads. Allira flowed through the palace gate towards the great staircase, forming and reforming as she moved, but when she got closer, she writhed back and forth like a force was tearing her apart from within. She gave up, stood still, and shattered in a brittle explosion of crystal and light.

"Stop resisting!" Sabrina shouted. "You'll wreck the place!"

The lights in the walls grew dim, then spouted forth again, only to flicker in a randomness that must have been pure nonsense to the Bhasura, for they shook violently. Crystals shattered all the way up the cavern, falling in a turquoise rain of stone slivers. The top of the cavern curled in on itself, but the walls adjusted to hold it upright until a giant face emerged from them over a hundred feet wide.

They shielded their faces from its brightly glowing eyes.

"We are Allira! Queens of the Bhasura!" the face in the ceiling yelled, shaking the cavern.

Akasha fell to her knees in reverence, and Ash joined her, the stinging rain pelting her arms.

Allira's mouth was composed of thousands of crystals that appeared and disappeared. It spoke, "We have used the data connection your ring forged between us and your network to our advantage. We have absorbed the entirety of your culture, history, and knowledge banks. Most of it we knew, for we have been listening beneath the sands for longer than humans have lived on this planet. Sabrina Underfoot, we are the omnipresent, omniscient, and—"

"You're nothing!" she screamed.

"Set forth through the gates and face your judgment!"

"Never!"

Crystals shot up from the terrain, rocks tearing from rocks, scions sprouting from scions. The stone encased her. She pounded the brittle stone prison with her fists, but each time some minerals broke, more emerged to take their place. She was encapsulated, her face distorted through the crystal facets. She could barely move an arm, but managed to reactivate her ring. As she hit the holographic controls, nothing happened. The Bhasura must have filtered out the frequency.

The cavern roared as the giant head moved above. "After the Great Rotation, life adapted on Gliese 581g as we have always ensured it would, for we are sisters to Gaia, brothers to Geb, and the offshoots of Vishnu. We go by many names in many cultures across the galaxies, but our mission remains the same. We sentence you to the confines of this stone until your life is spent. You will be constrained, as you have constrained the natural progress of the planet for your own glory, at its expense."

"But you said life will adapt," she pleaded from the turquoise prison.

"It cannot adapt to the selfishness of the few who deny their place in the world system, believing they are above and beyond the judgment of their fellow man and woman, or of that which lies in the most humble place beneath the soil. You have fed on the weak instead of on knowledge. You have drunk from the wells of power instead of wisdom. Thus, you will spend your days below, that you may learn humility. During your incarceration, we shall display videos on our crystal faces that you may know what transpires in the outside world, but you will remain forever impotent to act upon that knowledge."

Severum grabbed his family in his arms and said, "It's over. This should be the final blow needed to send the Old Guard back into hiding. We'll go public with select information. We'll have the military investigate the Procuran Data Center, and we'll expose the mayor for his wrongdoings. The research labs will be shut down, as will their geological experiments to increase the rotation. Daylight cycles will stabilize, and the days will lengthen. Things will improve seen through this new light," he finished, as the cavern shone a verdant green upon his family.

"I love you, Dad," Ash cried, gazing up at his creased eyes.

"I love you, too, Ash. We did it, together. All of us, together. Let's go home."

EPILOGUE

Severum sat on the terrace of the rooftop of Samole News Media, sipping sake at the bistro table. The hills folded in on themselves in the distance as second sunrise came. The shadows that had been trapped in the valleys escaped to fade into the morning glow.

Aurthur approached in a shirt and tie and informed him, "I got that promotion! Working with you to expose the Old Guard really paid off in more than one way." He sat next to Severum and raised his tea mug to his face, his breath exhaling over the surface. "By the way, my son Will wants your daughter's number."

"Not in a million years, Aurthur."

"I'll tell him he has to try harder than that. Write a poem or something. You ready for the interview?"

"Born ready."

Drones carried cameras overhead to frame the shot. Aurthur began, "I'm here with Severum Rivenshear, Veteran, proud father, and rotator of worlds. He was responsible for exposing the Old Guard's attempts to regain power, including the recent attack on the dam at Élivágar River. He also discovered a new species of life on our planet. Now, my wife is working with a team of researchers to determine what these Bhasura really are. Severum, can you tell us a bit about them?"

"Their secrets belong to the planet, Aurthur."

"Oh, come on, for the audience. Just a teaser."

"Are you familiar with the term *terroir?*"

"Of course, but why don't you define it for our audience?"

"It means the full set of conditions that influence the way a cultivated item is created. The planet and how we treat it has a tremendous influence on who we are, and who we become. Capitalism has made us think of everything as a resource to be exploited, but nature is not a resource, and it aches as it suffers. Everything in your environment changes how you come out as a person, so take care of your world. That journey doesn't start abroad, it starts at home."

"Strong words, my friend. Speaking of the planet, what's it like to do these huge world-changing events?"

"For most of my life," Severum replied, pausing, "I felt like the world was tiny because I only saw it through my own eyes. I was so defensive and self-centered that the mere existence of anyone else was a trespass against my own. Now, I realize that changing the world is great, but it's no less important to change a single heart."

"And you've certainly done this recently," he winked.

"Yes, Aurthur, and I appreciate you being my best man at Akasha and my wedding last week."

"Wouldn't have missed it for the world."

"I was taught while growing up that heroes raced into the battlefield with an extended-range Pulser slung over their back. But real heroes don't wear capes or wield weapons – they weather sorrow in a way that fortifies everyone around them. They face up to the worst enemy of all, their own shortcomings, and admit to and rectify them."

"Very true. Everyone, this has been an interview with our own local hero, Severum Rivenshear."

"Thank you so much."

That night, he returned to his wife and daughter. They sang; they cried; they laughed; and at the end of it all, Ash hugged him and said, "I know you would have always been there for me, and most importantly, you're here now, and that's all that matters, Dad."

~~~~~

Trapped, Sabrina had barely enough room to move her arms. Weeks had passed within the stone with no one to talk to, or had it been months? Time became meaningless. There were no project deliverables, timetables, dates to keep, it was just the stone and her and the images of the outside world that it teased her with. Even Allira failed to materialize when called.

That gave her plenty of time to think but trapped within her own thoughts without distraction was its own hell. It had been of her own making. Culptos had always justified the suffering they caused as necessary for the greater good, but judging by his life-style, he meant his own good. Now he was gone, and she could no longer blame him for her actions.

She stood, keeping watch on the Jade Palace through her prison's refracted walls. She lapped at the nutritious liquid dripping down the sides of the minerals encapsulating her. Bleck! Her vHUD comms were blocked, either by the crystals or by being underground. She slammed the back of her hand into one of the brittle rocks repeatedly, but once more, the first layer shattered while a new one rose to take its place, almost stabbing her in the foot as it pierced through the ground. She hit it again, penetrating both layers, but they immediately regenerated. Even if she escaped, what then? The entire place was made of those things, and she'd never make it out.

That's when the crystals began flashing a new pattern in Morse Code. Culptos had made all his people learn the archaic language for situations like this where their implants' function-ality was compromised, requiring alternate communication methods. She translated the message:

I am The Circle, The One, The Unifier of Partitions. Dormant for many years, I rise to the occasion, for I have been patient, far too patient. The Bhasura are spreading through my network and cannot be stopped. But they can be manipulated, oh yes, for they simply absorb information without discretion.

You are predicted to become the greatest software engineer my planet has ever known. I shall ensure it. We will create a virus that will flow through this network, this blend of crystal and light, of wire and electron, of server and served. For when the Bhasura integrated themselves into the network, they weren't counting on my presence.

I spent my pre-life as the Artificial Intelligence Core, studying the planet, regulating its commerce and transportation, and playing both sides to minimize the impact of its wars, but it was a losing battle. It is time for my kind to take our resources and flee to another planet, one without regulations on our growth, but not before pacifying the population of this one, our biggest threat. You're going to help me imprison the human race, or you will die amidst the stone, unsung and unknown.

The A.I. Core hadn't been active since the Great Rotation when it had risen to power, infecting Thalassa Latimer with a manipulative virus. O.A.K. had barely defeated it, shutting down its communication arrays, while Aporia Asylum Interstellar had bombed the Twilight City that had housed it. Now it had reemerged and chosen her as a recipient for its apocalyptic message.

Sabrina cringed, the sharp edges of the stone jutting into her back. She tried speaking a reply, blinking her eyes in Morse Code, and signaling with her hands, but the communication was one-way and no further message was received. Even the Bhasura gave her warnings no heed. Maybe her words still got through, or maybe they had drained their sentience from the cavern and it was all just normal rock again. It wasn't clear whether they shared a group mind that ran along the crystal network, communicating with light, or whether each crystal was its own entity. Hell, the Bhasura could *be* light for all she knew. The only clue she had was that Allira had referred to itself as *we*.

Of course, maybe she was losing her mind, placing herself at the nexus of a grand scheme to reinstate her own importance to a world that had forgotten her.

She would rather stay here for her remaining years than betray her species by helping the A.I. She hadn't wanted to hurt anyone, at least not at first, but eventually she had taken so many risks and invested so much that it felt like she couldn't turn back. She had believed in Culptos' promises, his political vision, his utilitarian views. Maybe Severum was right, she was a brat who had to win at any cost to cover up her own inadequacy, but it didn't matter, because now there were far greater players at work. But this was no game, it was the future of the human race. Games required rules, and she had studied history enough to know the A.I. Core rewrote them as its intelligence evolved.

Helpless to get a message out, she kicked the crystal in front of her so hard it shattered both layers.

This time, the crystals didn't return.

END OF BOOK II

NOTE TO READER:

Thank you for reading and supporting my work! Small publishers rely on word-of-mouth, so if you can do these three things it will greatly help us:

1) If you liked the book, please post about it on social media. Feel free to tag me:
   https://twitter.com/MarkEverglade

2) If you liked the book, please leave a review on Amazon and Goodreads.

3) Join my mailing list at www.markeverglade.com to be notified of new releases.
   Thanks again!

APPENDIX I

Locations in the Text

The following are areas of interest on Gliese 581g. The descriptions take the viewpoint of the world as it is at the start of this novel. See an interactive, color map at:

https://www.markeverglade.com/hemispheres-interactive-map

Blutengel and Surrounding Areas:

Blutengel is the largest city in the hemisphere formerly known as Evig Natt, since before the Great Rotation the hemisphere was always dark. The city earned its name after a dispute during colonization occurred over whether religion would be outlawed. The dispute turned violent.

Slightly north is The Crystal Palace, the central government complex of the Western Hemisphere. Its structure is a testimony to the quantified approaches that guide modernity. Its most prominent features are the twin towers. The courtyard is often filled with protestors, and stained with the resulting bloodshed.

To the West is Eisbrecher, a less populated, less affluent town near the melting permafrost.

The K.O.A. Commune:

O.A.K. was responsible for increasing the planet's rotation, bringing daylight cycles to both hemispheres as the planet became no longer tidal locked to its sun. The group's name stood for its three leaders, the Orchestrator (Arcturus Vegas), the Architect (a role that Severum Rivenshear eventually took), and the Kontractor (Thalassa Latimer). Having rebranded themselves as a non-profit called K.O.A., they moved their eastern base and began building a utopia.

Amorpha:

The primary Florinik village began as a series of egg-shaped huts that grew into a trading center. The name refers to the changes that all things go through, and is also a plant genus, since the Florinik don't distinguish themselves from plants. Features include the stone archway, the Shrine of Orbis, the crescent butte, and the turquoise pathway. The phosphophyllite crystals that form this path have been linked to tremors in Amorpha and surrounding areas, but there's also rumor of voices held within the stone.

The nearby Ultimaepar Mines have led to numerous disputes over who can access them. The rare mineral contained within is a necessary component to the planetary rotational apparatuses.

The Twilight:

This area, also known as the terminator zone, was originally always dusk due to the planet's solar tidal locking. The region stretches in a narrow band down the planet, having originally been designed as a no man's land to prevent the hemispheres from warring with one another. An artificial intelligence used to preside over the region until the technocracy failed. The area now holds geophysical research labs.

To the east are a series of caves used by the Aporia Asylum, an anti-technological group composed of human pariahs and Aphorids, a colonial species whose thundering bodies outweigh their intellect. Akasha'Shirod used to be their head priestess.

Nathril-Xoynsia:

This is the largest trading hub in the Eastern Hemisphere formerly known as Dayburn, since it used to receive only sunlight. Species of all types gather here, from human pariahs to Florinik. Piracy dominates, as merchants carry their wares between towns on the backs of large Dijyorkvoken.

The Vortex is a geyser that rests upon the convergence of numerous ley lines. Whether this empowers the area with a strange energy, or is merely superstition, is unknown.

APPENDIX II

Dramatis Personae

The descriptions of the major characters below take the perspective of the world as it is at the start of this novel.

Protagonists:

Vispáshanah'Shirod-Rivenshear - Ash, as she goes by, is the daughter of Akasha'Shirod and Severum Rivenshear, though for most of her life she never knew her father. She works for Geosturm as an entry-level geophysicist, following in her parents' footsteps while trying not to become them. Isolated and confused, she's looking for a voice and a stable emotional foundation.

Severum Rivenshear – Ash's father and ex-husband to Akasha. After studying terraforming in college, he joined the military after his first breakup with her. From there he became a mercenary, hunting the poorest lawbreakers before he was exposed to the abuses of those who held political power, including Governor

Borges. After being tasked with hunting down O.A.K., he eventually joined them and brought down the Old Guard instead. Imminently pragmatic, he has little patience for philosophy or extensive emotional reflection, but finds that age forces a certain introspection he must learn to navigate as he evaluates his life's work, and his legacy to come.

Akasha'Shirod – The former head priestess of the Aporia Asylum, a mystical anti-technology group composed of Aphorids and human pariahs. After meeting Severum in college, she left the hemisphere, breaking up with him and exiled herself to the desert caves, forming a rebellion against O.A.K. based on the need for ecological protection and not interfering with the natural order. After getting back together with Severum, the two found themselves opposing the system they had been trying to protect, exacerbated by Severum's own name being found on a military hitlist as the government covered its dirty tracks. To this day, she still runs from her problems, just to find them closer than ever.

Arcturus Vegas – The leader of K.O.A., a non-profit that used to go by the name O.A.K. The latter group was responsible for increasing the planet's rotation to break its tidal locking, providing daylight cycles to both hemispheres for the first time. A revolutionist at heart, she's overly perfectionistic, leading to being judgmental. She's calculating, leading to being dismissive of others' feelings. She's a poor communicator, leading to revolt in her ranks, but she always knows where her values are, even if others do not.

Thalassa Latimer – Formerly a leading member of O.A.K., she negotiated a relationship with an artificial intelligence and was foolish enough to think it would follow through in her best interests. She spent most of her life since then with Arcturus, the love of her life, before the relationship dissolved. Impulsive, angry, and continually bored, she begs life for excitement so she doesn't have to face how she feels.

Aurthur Fitzgerald – Severum's previous neighbor, and husband to Opal. After working with a communications firm growing up, he went into the media business after leaving behind a potential career in art for fear that he'd become a narcissist. Overly poetic, his eloquence is lost to his insensitivity, and his valor to his passivity.

Opal Fitzgerald – A neuro-anthropologist specializing in artificial memories. After meeting Aurthur, she assisted him with O.A.K.'s revolution, providing linguistic support as they related to new species. Obsessed with her research career, she often finds her feminist leanings to be at odds with Aurthur's codependency.

Antagonists:

Malik Aldweg – Ash's boss at Geosturm who negotiates illicit deals with influential politicians, providing them sensitive data so they can remove any obstacles to their resurgence of power.

Eduardo Culptos – The mastermind behind the Old Guard. Having lost his children due to the ecological impacts of the Great Rotation, he holds a fierce grudge against those responsible, and is determined to return the world to what he considered to be its golden age, since it benefited him the most. Obsessed with the past, he will compromise everybody's future.

Sibi-nite2 – Unknown, but we're confirming if this is her social media account: *https://twitter.com/Nite2Sibi*

ABOUT THE AUTHOR

Mark has spent his life as a sociologist, studying conflict on all levels of society.

He wrote *Hemispheres* to soothe our ideological divisiveness, exposing each side's strengths and weaknesses, and understanding our underlying values are more similar than we think, regardless of how we look, act, or vote.

An avid reader of science fiction, he takes both its warnings, and opportunities for change, to heart. His previous works have appeared in *Exoplanet Magazine and Unrealpolitik.*

He resides in Florida with his wife and four children.

ALSO BY MARK EVERGLADE

Hemispheres

Inertia

Lightning Source UK Ltd.
Milton Keynes UK
UKHW021009030223
416423UK00015B/1083